MONGRELS

STEPHEN GRAHAM JONES

HARPER
Voyager

HarperCollins*Publishers*
1 London Bridge Street
London SE1 9GF

www.harpervoyagerbooks.co.uk

Published by Harper*Voyager*
An imprint of HarperCollins*Publishers* 2017
1

Book Design by Lisa Stokes

Illustrations by AldanNi/Shutterstock, Inc.

A catalogue record for this book is available from the British Library

ISBN: 978-0-00-818245-8

Set in Centaur MT

Printed and bound in Great Britain

MIX
Paper from
responsible sources
FSC™ C007454

FSC is a non-profit international organisation established
to promote the responsible management of the world's forests.
Products carrying the FSC label are independently certified
to assure consumers that they come from forests that are managed
to meet the social, economic and ecological needs
of present and future generations.

Find out more about HarperCollins and the environment at
www.harpercollins.co.uk/green

Stephen Graham Jones is the author of fifteen novels and six short story collections. He has received numerous awards including the NEA Literature Fellowship in fiction, the Texas Institute of Letters Jesse H. Jones Award for Best Work of Fiction, the Independent Publisher Book Award for Multicultural Fiction, and the This Is Horror Award, as well as making Bloody Disgusting's Top Ten Horror Novels of the Year. Stephen was raised in West Texas.

He now lives in Boulder, Colorado, with his wife and children.

stephengrahamjones.com
🐦 /stephengrahamjones
📘 @SGJ72

ALSO BY STEPHEN GRAHAM JONES

Thea Lucas

1914–1999

Thanks, Pop

Eventually I went to America.
There no one believes in werewolves.

—JAMES BLISH

CHAPTER I

The Moon Is a Harsh Mistress

My grandfather used to tell me he was a werewolf.

He'd rope my aunt Libby and uncle Darren in, try to get them to nod about him twenty years ago, halfway up a windmill, slashing at the rain with his claws. Him dropping down to all fours to race the train on the downhill out of Booneville, and beating it. Him running ahead of a countryside full of Arkansas villagers, a live chicken flapping between his jaws, his eyes wet with the thrill of it all. The moon was always full in his stories, and right behind him like a spotlight.

I could tell it made Libby kind of sick.

Darren, his rangy mouth would thin out in a kind of grin he didn't really want to give, especially when Grandpa would lurch across the living room, acting out how he used to deal with sheep when he got them bunched up against a fence. Sheep are the weakness of all werewolves, he'd say, and then he'd play both parts, growling like a wolf, his shoulders pulled up high, and turning around to bleat in wide-eyed fear, like a sheep.

Libby would usually leave before Grandpa tore into the flock, the sheep screaming, his mouth open wide and hungry as any wolf, his yellow teeth dull in the firelight.

Darren would just shake his head, work another strawberry wine cooler up from beside his chair.

Me, I was right at the edge of being eight years old, my mom dead since the day I was born, no dad anybody would talk about. Libby had been my mom's twin, once upon a time. She told me not to call her "Mom," but I did, in secret. Her job that fall was sewing fifty-pound bags of seed shut. After work the skin around her eyes would be clean from the goggles she wore but crusted white with sweat. Darren said she looked like a backward raccoon. She'd lift her top lip over her teeth at him in reply, and he'd keep to his side of the kitchen table.

Darren was the male version of my mom and Libby—they'd been triplets, a real litter, according to Grandpa. Darren had just found his way back to Arkansas that year. He was twenty-two, had been gone six magical years. Like Grandpa said happened with all guys in our family, Darren had gone lone wolf at sixteen, had the scars and blurry tattoos to prove it. He wore them like the badges they were. They meant he was a survivor.

I was more interested in the other part.

"Why sixteen?" I asked him, after Grandpa had nodded off in his chair by the hearth.

Because I knew sixteen was two of eight, and I was almost *to* eight, that meant I was nearly halfway to leaving. But I didn't want to have to leave like Darren had. Thinking about it left a hollow feeling in my stomach. All I'd ever known was Grandpa's house.

Darren tipped his bottle back about my question, looked over to the kitchen to see if Libby was listening, and said, "Right around sixteen, your teeth get too sharp for the teat, little man. Simple as that."

He was talking about how I clung to Libby's leg whenever things got loud. I had to, though. Because of Red. The reason Darren had come in off the road—driving truck mostly—was Libby's true-love ex-husband, Red. Grandpa was too old by then to stand between her and Red, but Darren, he was just the right age, had just the right smile.

The long white scar under his neck, he told me, leaning back to trace his middle finger down its smoothness, that was Red. And the one under his ribs on the left, that cut through his mermaid girlfriend? That had been Red too.

"Some people just aren't fit for human company," Darren said, letting his shirt go, reaching down to two-finger another bottle up by the neck.

"And some people just don't want it," Grandpa growled from his chair, a sharp smile of his own coming up one side of his mouth.

Darren hissed, hadn't known the old man was awake.

He twisted the cap off his wine cooler, snapped it perfectly across the living room, out the slit in the screen door that was always birthing flies and wasps.

"So we're talking scars?" Grandpa said, leaning up from his rocking chair, his good eye glittering.

"I don't want to go around and around the house with you, old man," Darren said. "Not today."

This was what Darren always said anytime Grandpa got wound up, started remembering out loud. But he *would* go around and around the house with Grandpa. Every time, he would.

Me too.

"This is when you're a werewolf," I said for Grandpa.

"Got your listening ears on there, little pup?" he said back, reaching down to pick me up by the nape, rub the side of my face against the white stubble on his jaw. I slithered and laughed.

"Werewolves never need razors," Grandpa said, setting me down. "Tell him why, son."

"Your story," Darren said back.

"It's because," Grandpa said, rubbing at his jaw, "it's because when you change back to like we are now, it's always like you just shaved. Even if you had a full-on mountain-man beard the day before." He made a show of taking in Darren's smooth jawline then, got me to look too. "Babyface. That's what you always call a werewolf who was out getting in six different kinds of trouble the night before. That's how you know what they've been doing. That's how you pick those ones out of a room."

Darren just stared at Grandpa about this.

Grandpa smiled like his point had been made, and I couldn't help it, had to ask: "But—but *you're* a werewolf, right?"

He rasped his fingers on his stubble, said, "Good ear, good ear. Get to be my age, though, wolfing out would be a death sentence now, wouldn't it?"

"Your age," Darren said.

It made Grandpa cut his eyes back to him again. But Darren was the first to look away.

"You want to talk about scars," Grandpa said down to me then, and peeled the left sleeve of his shirt up higher and higher, rolling it until it was strangling his skinny arm. "See it?" he said, turning his arm over.

I stood, leaned over to look.

"Touch it," he said.

I did. It was a smooth, pale little divot of skin as big around as the tip of my finger.

"You got shot?" I said, with my whole body.

Darren tried to hide his laugh but shook his head no, rolled his hand for Grandpa to go on.

"Your uncle's too hardheaded to remember," Grandpa said, to *me*. "Your aunt, though, she knows."

And my mom, I said inside, like always. Whatever went for Libby when she'd been a girl, it went for my mom.

It was how I kept her alive.

"It's not a bullet hole," Grandpa said, working the sleeve of his shirt down. "A bullet in the front leg's like a bee sting to a real werewolf. This, this was worse."

"Worse?" I said.

"Lyme disease?" Darren said.

Grandpa didn't even look across the room for this. "Diseases can't touch you when you're wolfed out either," he said down to me. "Your blood, it's too hot for the flu, the measles, smallpox, cancer."

"Lead poisoning?" Darren asked, in a leading-him-on voice.

"When you change back, the wolf squeezes all that lead back out," Grandpa said, no humor to it anymore. "Unless it's in the bone. Then it kind of works around it, like a pearl."

Darren shrugged a truce, settled back to listen.

"What, then?" I said, because somebody had to.

"A *tick*," Grandpa said, pinching his fingers out to show how small a tick is. How little it should matter.

"A tick?" I said.

"A tick," Darren said.

"It probably came from this fat doe I'd pulled down the night before," Grandpa said. "That tick jumped ship, went to where the beating heart was."

"And then when he shifted back," Libby said, standing all at once by the kitchen table, my faded blue backpack in her hand so she could drop me off at school on her way to work, "when he shifted back, when the *werewolf* hair went back into his skin to wrap around his bones or wherever it goes, it pulled the tick in with it, right?"

"You do remember," Grandpa said, leaning back.

"Like trying to climb a flagpole that's sinking," Darren said, probably reciting the story from last time Grandpa had told it. He did his bored hands up and up the idea of a flagpole to show, the bottle cocked in his fingers not even spilling.

"The word for it is 'impacted,'" Libby said right to me. "It's when something's most of the way into the skin. A splinter, a tooth in your mouth—"

"A tick," Grandpa cut in. "And I couldn't reach it. That was the thing. I couldn't even *see* it. And your grandma, she knew that the fat ones like that are full of babies. She said if she grabbed it with the needle-noses, popped it, the babies would all go in my blood, and then they'd be like watermelon seeds in my stomach."

"That's not how it works," Libby said to me.

"So you went to the doctor," Darren said over her. "In town."

"Doc, he heated up the end of a coat hanger with his lighter," Grandpa said to me, trying to be the one to tell the story right, "and he—" He acted it out, stabbing the burning-hot bent-out coat hanger down and working it around like stirring a tiny cauldron. "Why there's a scar there now, it's that I wouldn't let him dress it, or stitch it. You know why, don't you?"

I looked from Libby to Darren.

They each directed me back to Grandpa. It was his story, after all.

"Because you've got to be born to the blood to take it," Grandpa said, his voice nearly at a whisper. "If that doctor had got even one drop into a cuticle, he'd have turned into a moondog, sure as shooting."

My heart was thumping. This was better than any bullet hole.

Libby was making lifting motions with her hand for me to get up already, that she was going to be late, she was going to get fired again.

I stood from this dream, still watching Grandpa.

"Let him finish," Darren said to Libby.

"We don't have—"

"If you're bit, or if you get the blood in you," Grandpa said anyway, "then it burns you up fast, little pup, and it *hurts*. All you can do is feel sorry. Those ones, they just have these wolf heads, a man body. They never understand what's happening to them, just run around slobbering and biting, trying to escape their own skin, sometimes even chewing their own hands and feet off to stop them hurting."

He wasn't looking at me anymore, but out the window. The eye I could see on my side, it was his cloudy one.

I think it was the one he was looking with.

Neither Libby nor Darren said anything, but Libby did accidentally look out the window, like just for a peek. Just to be sure.

Then she set her mouth into a grim line, pulled her face back to the living room.

I was going to be late for school and it didn't matter.

"Come on," she said, taking my hand, and on the way past Grandpa I brushed my hand on the sleeve of his shirt, like to tell him it was okay, I think. That it was a good story. That I'd liked it. That he could keep telling me these stories forever, if he wanted. I would always listen. I would always believe.

He flinched away from my hand, looked around for where he was.

"Here, old man," Darren said, handing a strawberry wine cooler across to him, and I climbed into my side of Libby's El Camino, the one she had from finally breaking up with Red, and halfway to school I started crying, and I couldn't figure out why.

Libby switched hands on the wheel, pulled me over to her.

"Don't think about it," she said. "I don't even know how he really got that scar. It was before we were all born."

"Because Grandma was there," I said.

Just like my mom, Grandma had died the day she gave birth. It was like a curse in our family.

"Because Grandma was there," Libby said. "Next time he tells that stupid story, the tick won't even be on the back of his arm anymore. It'll have been that old cut up on his eyebrow, and the doctor heated his pocketknife up, not a coat hanger. One time when he told it to us it was that one scar that pulls beside his mouth."

This is the way werewolf stories go.

Never any proof. Just a story that keeps changing, like it's twisting back on itself, biting its own stomach to chew the poison out.

The next week we found Grandpa out in the pasture without any clothes. His knees were bloody, not scabbing over yet, and the heels of his hands were scraped raw, and his fingertips were chewed by the gravel and the thorns. He was staring at us but he wasn't seeing us, even with his good eye.

Darren and me got to him first. I was riding on Darren's back. He was running everywhere at once, and there were tears coming back on the side of his face.

He let me down slow when we saw Grandpa.

"He's not dead," I said, to make it true.

It worked.

Grandpa's back lifted and fell with his next wheezy breath.

Darren took two steps away and slung his bottle out as hard as he could, the pale pink liquid tracing drippy circles for the first few feet, then nothing. Just a smell on the air like medicine.

"How old you think he is?" Darren said to me.

I looked up to him, down to Grandpa.

"Fifty-five," Darren said. "This is what happens."

Libby heard his bottle break into whatever it broke into, and traced it back to us. She ran over, her hands in a steeple over her mouth.

"He thinks he's shifted," Darren told her, disgusted.

"Help me!" Libby said, falling to her knees by her dad, trying to get his head into her lap, her long black hair shrouded over both of them.

That was one day.

I quit going to school for that week, and promised myself to keep Grandpa alive.

The way I did it was with stories. By keeping him talking.

"Tell me about Grandma," I said one night after Darren had left, after Red had come and stood at the gate like a statue until Libby drifted out to him. She couldn't help it.

I was asking about Grandma because if he thought he was really shifting into a werewolf, then talking to him about it wasn't going to make him any better.

"'Grandma,'" he said in his new halfway slur, then shook his head no, said, "she never ever got to be called 'Momma,' did she?"

I wanted to take my question back. To start over.

Grandpa breathed a deep important breath in, then out. He said, "You know werewolves, they mate for life, right? Like swans and gophers."

He pretty much only sat in his chair now. Used to when he smiled one side of his mouth, it meant something good was coming. Now it meant something bad had happened, Libby said.

"Gophers?" I said.

"You can smell it on them," he said, snuffling his nose to show.

I'd never seen a gopher. Just the mounds.

"Grandma," Grandpa said then, clearer. "You know when she first figured me out, what I was, she thought it meant I was married to the moon, like. That that was the only time I would go out howling."

I narrowed my eyes and he caught it, added, "That's not how it works, little pup. Too short a leash. We'd starve like that. Anyway. I was married to *her*, wasn't I?"

A log in the fire popped sparks up the chimney. Darren called it an old-man fire. It was September.

"Another thing about werewolves," Grandpa said at last. "We age like dogs. You should know that too."

"Like dogs," I repeated.

"You can burn up your whole life early if you're not careful. If you spend too much time out in the trees, running your dinner down."

I nodded. As long as he was talking, he wasn't dead.

"Grandma," I said again, because that's where we'd been, before the werewolves.

Grandpa swallowed a lump, coughed it back up and spit it in his hand, rubbed it into the blanket on his lap.

"There used to be a secret," he said. "A way for them, for the wives, for them not to . . ."

Not to die, I knew. Since Grandpa'd started living mostly in the living room, he'd decided to solve the family curse. It was what all the stolen library books by the couch were for. So he could find the old way for a human woman to live with a werewolf and not die from giving birth.

His research was the big reason Libby stayed mostly in the kitchen. She said nothing he did was going to bring her mom back, was it? There wasn't any big werewolf secret. Grandma had just died, end of story.

Darren thought Grandpa's books were funny. They were all strange stories, amazing facts.

"We buried her in the church graveyard," Grandpa said then, on some different part of the Grandma-story running in his head. "And they—they dug her up, little pup. They dug her up and they—they—"

Instead of finishing, he lurched forward so I had to push back to keep him from spilling out of his chair. I didn't know if I could get him back into it.

By the time he looked up, he'd forgot what he'd been saying.

He'd told it to me before, though, when Libby wasn't around to stop him.

It was another werewolf story.

After Grandma had died giving birth, a rival pack had dug her up as a message to him. It was about territory.

Grandpa had taken the message back to them on the end of a shovel, and then used that shovel on them.

This had all been *his* territory back then, he usually said, to end that story out. His territory as far as he could see, as much as he could fight for. Some days he'd claim all of Arkansas as his, even, ever since the war had spit him up here.

But I wasn't stupid. I wasn't at school that month, but I was still learning. Libby had finally told me that the scar on Grandpa's arm, it was probably from a cigarette he'd rolled over on once. Or an old chickenpox. Or a piece of slag melting into his sleeve, burning down into his skin.

What I had to do to get to the truth of the story was build it up again from the same facts, but with different muscle.

Grandma had died and been buried. I knew that. Even Libby said it.

Probably what had happened—no, what *had* to have happened, the worst that *could* have happened—was that some town dogs had got into the cemetery the night after the funeral, when the dirt was still soft. And then Grandpa had gone after that pack with his rifle, or his truck, even if it had taken all month. And then used his shovel to bury them.

I preferred the werewolf version.

In that one, there's Grandpa as a young man, a werewolf in his prime. But he's also a grieving husband, a new and terrified father. And now he's ducking out the doorway of the house this other pack dens up at. And his arms, they're red and steaming up to the shoulders, with revenge.

If Libby grew up hearing that story, if he told it to her before she was old enough to see through it to the truth, then all she would remember would be the hero. This tall, violent, bloody man, his chest rising and falling, his eyes casting around for the next thing to tear into.

Ten years later, of course she falls for Red.

Everything makes sense if you look at it long enough.

Except Darren showing up at the house two or three hours later. He was naked, was breathing hard, covered in sweat, his eyes wild, leaves and sticks in his hair, one shoulder raw.

Slung over his shoulder was a black trash bag.

"Always use a black bag," he said to me, walking in, dropping the bag hard onto the table.

"Because white shows up at night," I said back to him, like the three other times he'd already come back naked and dirty.

He scruffed my hair, walked deeper into the house, for pants.

I peeled up the mouth of the bag, looked in.

It was all loose cash and strawberry wine coolers.

The last story Grandpa told me, it was about the dent in his shin.

Libby leaned back from the kitchen sink when she heard him starting in on it.

She was holding a big raw steak from the store to her face. It was because of Red, because of last night.

When she'd come in to get ready for work, she'd seen Darren's trash bag on the table, hauled it up without even looking inside. She strode right back to Darren's old bedroom. He was asleep on top of the covers, in his pants.

She threw the bag down onto him hard enough that two of the wine-cooler bottles broke, spilled down onto his back.

He came up spinning and spitting, his mouth open, teeth bared.

And then he saw his sister's face. Her eye.

"I'm going to fucking kill him this time," he said, stepping off the bed, his hands opening and closing where they hung by his legs, but Libby was already there, pushing him hard in the chest, her feet set.

When the screaming and the throwing things started, one of them slammed the door shut so I wouldn't have to see.

In the living room, Grandpa was coughing.

I went to him, propped him back up in his chair, and, because

Libby had said it would work, I asked him to tell me about the scar by his mouth, about how he got it.

His head when he finally looked up to me was loose on his neck, and his good eye was going cloudy.

"Grandpa, Grandpa," I said, shaking him.

My whole life I'd known him. He'd acted out a hundred werewolf stories for me there in the living room, had once even broke the coffee table when an evil Clydesdale horse reared up in front of him and he had to fall back, his eyes twice as wide as any eyes I'd ever seen.

In the back of the house something glass broke, something wood splintered, and there was a scream so loud I couldn't even tell if it was from Darren or Libby, or if it was even human.

"They love each other too much," Grandpa said. "Libby and her—and that—"

"Red," I said, trying to make it turn down at the end like when Darren said it.

"Red," Grandpa said back, like he'd been going to get there himself.

He thought it was Red and Libby back there. He didn't know what month it was anymore.

"He's not a bad wolf either," he went on, shaking his head side to side. "That's the thing. But a good wolf isn't always a good man. Remember that."

It made me wonder about the other way around, if a good man meant a bad wolf. And if that was better or worse.

"She doesn't know it," Grandpa said, "but she looks like her mother."

"Tell me," I said.

For once he did, or started to. But his descriptions of Grandma kept wandering away from her, would strand him talking about how her hands looked around a cigarette when she had to turn away from the wind. How some of her hair was always falling down by her face. A freckle on the top of her left collarbone.

Soon I realized Darren and Libby were there, listening.

It was my grandma, but it was their mom. The one they'd never seen. The one there weren't any pictures of.

Grandpa smiled for the audience, for his family being there, I think, and he went on about her pot roasts then, about how he would steal carrots and potatoes for her all over Logan County, carry them home in his mouth, shotguns always firing into the air behind him, the sky forever full of lead, always raining pellets so that when he shook on the porch after getting home, it sounded like a hailstorm.

Libby cracked the refrigerator open, pulled out a steak, held it under the water in the sink so it wouldn't stick to her face.

Darren eased into the living room, sat on his haunches on the floor past the chair he usually claimed, like he didn't want to break this spell, and Grandpa went on about Grandma, about the first time he saw her. She was in a parade right over in Boonesville, had a pale yellow umbrella over her shoulder. It didn't look like a huge daisy, he said. Just an umbrella, but in the clear *day*time.

Darren smiled.

His face on the left side had four deep scratches in it now, but he didn't care. He was like Grandpa, was going to have a thousand stories.

In the kitchen Libby finally turned the water off, pressed the steak up to her left eye. It wasn't swelled all the way shut yet. Her eyeball was shot red like it had popped.

I hated Red at least as much as Darren did.

"Go on," Darren said to Grandpa, and for two or three more

minutes we went around and around the house with him, after Grandma. Until Grandpa leaned forward to pull up the right leg of his pants. Except he was just wearing boxers. But his fingers still worked at the memory of pants.

"He wanted to hear about how this happened," he said, and tapped his finger into a deep dent on his shin I'd never noticed before.

This was when Libby pushed up from the sink.

Her lips were red now too, and part of me registered that it was from the steak. That she'd been chewing on it.

The rest of me was watching Grandpa's index finger tap into his shin. Because I'd asked about the scar by his mouth, not one on his leg. But I wasn't going to mess this up.

"Used to have this dog . . ." he said to me, just to me, and Libby dropped her steak splat onto the linoleum.

"Dad," she said, but Darren held his hand up hard to her. "He can't, not this——" she said, her voice getting shrieky, but Darren nodded yes, he could.

"You weren't *there*," she said to him, and when Darren looked over to her again she spun away with a grunt, crashed out the screen door, and I guess she just kept running out into the trees. The El Camino didn't fire up, anyway.

"What happened?" I said to Grandpa.

"We had this dog," Grandpa said, nodding like it was all coming back to him now, moving his fingers up by his eyes like the story was filaments in the air, and if he held his hand just right he could collect enough of them to make sense, "we had this dog and he——he got tangled up with something, got bit, got bit and I had to, well."

"Rabies," I filled in. I knew it from the kid in class who'd had to get the shots in his stomach.

"I didn't want to wake your sister," Grandpa said across to Darren. "So I—so I used a ball-peen hammer instead, right? A hammer's quiet enough. A hammer'll work. I dragged her out by the fence on that side, and—" He was laughing now, his wheezy old man's laugh, and fighting to stand, to act this out.

"Her?" I said, but he was already acting it out, was already holding that big rangy dog by the collar, and swiping down at it with the hammer, the dog spinning him around, his swings missing, one of them finally cracking deep into his own shin so he had to hop on one leg, the dog still pulling, trying to live.

He was laughing, or trying to.

Darren was leaning his head back, like trying to balance his eyes back in.

"I like, I like to—" Grandpa said, finding his chair again, collapsing into it, "once I hit her that first time, little pup, I like to have never got that next lick in," which was the punch line.

He was the only one laughing, though.

And it wasn't really laughing.

The next Monday Libby took me back to first grade, sat there at the curb until I'd stepped through the front doors.

It lasted two days.

When we came back from school and work Tuesday, Grandpa was half out the front door, his cloudy eyes open, flies and wasps buzzing in and out of his mouth.

"Don't—" Libby said, trying to snag my shirt, keep me in the El Camino.

I was too fast. I was running across the caliche. My face was already so hot.

And then I stopped, had to step back.

Grandpa wasn't just half in and half out of the door from the kitchen. He was also halfway between man and wolf.

From the waist up, for the part that had made it through the door, he was the same. But his legs, still on the kitchen linoleum, they were straggle-haired and shaped wrong, muscled different. The feet had stretched out twice as long, until the heel became the backward knee of a dog. The thigh was bulging forward.

He really was what he'd always said.

I didn't know how to hold my face.

"He was going for the trees," Libby said, looking there.

I did too.

When Darren walked up from wherever he'd been, he was still buttoning his shirt. It was so it wouldn't be sweaty when he got wherever he was going, he'd told me.

I'd believed him too.

Used to, I believed everything.

He stopped when he saw us sitting on the El Camino's tailgate.

We were splitting the lunch I hadn't eaten at school, since the teacher had sneaked me some pepperoni slices from a plastic baggie.

"No," Darren said, lifting his face to the wind. It wasn't for my half of the bologna sandwich. It was for Grandpa. *"No, no no no!"* he screamed now, because he was like me, he could insist, he could make it true if he was loud enough, if he meant it all the way.

Instead of coming any closer, he turned, his shirt floating to the ground behind him.

I stepped down to go after him but Libby had me by the shoulder.

Because we couldn't go inside—Grandpa was in the doorway—

we sat in the bed of the El Camino, Libby's fingernails picking at the edge of the white stripes that came up the tailgate. There was faded black underneath them, like the rest of the car. When night cooled the air down we retreated to the cab, rolled the windows up so that soon we were breathing in the taste of Red's cigarettes. I pushed the pad of my index finger into a burn on the dashboard, then traced a crack in the windshield until it cut me.

I was asleep by the time the ground shook underneath us.

I sat up, looked through the rear window. The trees were glowing.

Libby pulled my head close to her.

It was Darren. He'd stolen a front-end loader.

"Your uncle," Libby said, and we stepped out.

Darren pulled the front-end loader right up to the house, lowered the bucket to the doorway, and then he swung down, stepped around, lifted Grandpa into the bucket, Grandpa's mouth hanging open, his legs shaped more like they had been. His mouth was still trying to push forward, though. Into a muzzle.

"He was too old to shift," Libby said to me, shaking her head at the tragedy of it all.

"But what if he'd made it?" I said.

"You're not going to be stupid too, are you?" she said, and the way she tried to smile I knew I didn't have to answer.

Darren couldn't call to us because the front-end loader was too loud, but he stood on the first step, hung out from the grab bar, waved us over.

"I don't want to," Libby said to me.

"I don't want to either," I said.

We climbed up with Darren, sat on the swells to either side of his bouncy, ripped-up seat, the glass cold on my left arm.

Darren drove right out into the field and followed it until there was only trees, and then he pushed through the trees back to a creek. He lifted Grandpa out, cradled him down to the tall dry grass, and then he used the bucket to dig out the steep side of the bank.

He picked his dad up in his arms, looked across to Libby, then to me.

"Your grandpa," he said, holding him right there. "One thing I can say about his old ass. He always liked to run his dinner down instead of getting it at the store, didn't he?"

He was kind of crying when he said it, so I looked away.

Libby bit her lip, pulled at the hair on the right side of her face. Darren lowered Grandpa into the new hole, and then he used the front-end loader to drag all the dirt back down over him, and he piled more on, finally even digging up the creek and dripping that silt down, then crushing that mound down harder and deeper and madder and madder, breaking all Grandpa's bones, so it wouldn't matter if anyone dug them up.

This is the way it is with werewolves.

"What about me?" I said on the way back, in the cab of the front-end loader.

"What do you mean what about you?" Darren said, and when I looked over the moon had just broke over the top of the trees, was bright and round. It outlined him perfect, the way he leaned over that steering wheel like he'd been born to it.

Every boy who never had a dad, he comes to worship his uncle.

"He means what about *him*," Libby said, angling her words at Darren in a different way.

"Oh, oh," Darren said, throttling up now that we were out of the trees. "Your mom, she—"

"Not all kids born to a werewolf are a werewolf," Libby said. "Your mom, she didn't catch it from your grandpa."

"Some don't," Darren said.

"Some are lucky like that," Libby added.

The rest of the ride was quiet, and the rest of the night too, at least until Darren started sucking air through his teeth at the kitchen table, like he'd been thinking of something the whole time and finally couldn't keep it in his head even one minute more.

"Don't," Libby said to him.

I was sitting with her at the hearth, the fire banked high for as late as it was.

"Don't wait up," Darren said, his eyes looking away, and then walked out before Libby could stop him.

I don't think she would have, though.

The front-end loader fired up, dragged its lights across the kitchen window, and was rumbling back toward town, the bucket lifted high, to look under.

"Pack your things," Libby said to me.

I used a black trash bag.

When Darren came back in the morning I was standing at the El Camino's tailgate, looking for my math book.

Werewolves don't need math, though.

Darren was naked again.

Instead of loose cash and strawberry wine coolers, what he had over his shoulder was a wide black belt.

"Remember when you used to want to be a vampire?" he said down to me, watching the house the whole time.

His hands and chin were black with dried blood, and he smelled like diesel.

I nodded, kind of did remember wanting to be a vampire. It was from a sun-faded old comic book he'd let me read with him when he first got back.

"This is better," Darren said, his infectious smile ghosting at the corners of his mouth, and then Libby was there, her hands dusted white with flour, her sleeves pushed up past her elbows.

She stopped a few steps out, dabbed a line of white off her face, then looked down the road behind Darren and all the slow way back to him. To his hands. To his chin. To his eyes.

"You didn't," she said.

"Wasn't my fault," Darren said. "Wrong place, wrong time."

The creaky black belt hooked over his shoulder was a cop's. You could tell from all the pouches and pockets. The pearl-handled pistol was even still there in its molded holster, the dull white handle flapping against his side, flashing a silver star with each step.

"Bet we can get seventy-five for it at the truck stop," he said, hefting it out like to show what it was worth.

"Go inside," Libby said, pushing me toward the house.

She should have pushed harder.

"This is the end of the liquor stores," she said to Darren, her voice flat like the back edge of a sharp knife, one she could flip around to the blade in a flash.

"Bears and wolves aren't meant to get along . . ." Darren said. The cool way he looked to the left and touched a spot above his eyebrow when he said it, it sounded like a line he'd been saving, his whole long way home.

Libby shoved him hard in the chest.

Darren was ready, but still he had to give a bit.

He tried to sidestep past her, for the house, for clothes, for a wine cooler, but Libby hauled him back, and because I was close enough, I heard one of them growling way down in their chest. A serious growl.

It made me smaller in my own body.

But I couldn't look away.

Darren's skin was jumping on his chest now.

It was Grandpa, rising up in his son. What I was seeing was Grandpa as a young man, itching to roam, to fight, to run down his dinner night after night because his knees were going to last forever. Because his teeth would always be strong. Because his skin would never be wax paper. Because fifty-five years old was a lifetime away. Because werewolves, they live forever.

And then the smell came, the smell that's probably what birth smells like. Like a body turned inside out. A body *turning* inside out.

"Dad's *dead*, Lib," Darren said, and all his pain, his excuse for whatever had happened in town, it was right there in his voice, it was right there in the way his voice was starting to break over.

"And *he's* not," Libby said, flinging a hand down to me. Darren flashed his eyes over to me, came back to Libby. "We can't just do whatever we want anymore," she said, her teeth hardly parting from each other. "Not until—"

I balled my hand into a fist, ready to run, ready to hide. I knew where Grandpa's creek was.

"Until what?" Darren said.

"*Until,*" Libby said, saying the rest with her eyes, in some language I couldn't crack into yet.

Darren stared at her, stared into her, his jaw muscles clenching and flaring now, his pupils either fading to a more yellowy color or catching the morning sun just perfect. Except the sky was still cloudy. Right when he flashed those dangerous new eyes up at Libby, she slapped him hard enough to twist his head around to the side.

Her claws were out too, pushed out not from under her fingernails like I'd been thinking but from the knuckle just above that. I hadn't even seen it happen.

My eyes took snapshots of every single frame of that arc her hand traced.

A piece of Darren's lower lip strung off his mouth, clumped down onto his chest. The lower part of his nose sloughed a little lower, cut off from the top half.

His eyes never moved.

By his legs, his fingers stretched out as well, reaching for the wolf. *"No!"* Libby yelled, stepping forward, taking him by both shoulders, driving her knee up into his balls hard enough to stand him up on tiptoes.

Darren fell over frontward, curled up there naked and skin-jumpy on the caliche, and Libby stood over him breathing hard, still growling, the canine muscles under her skin writhing in the most beautiful way, her claws glistening black, and what she told him, her tone taking no questions, was that his liquor-store days, they were goddamn *over*, that he was a *truck* driver now, did he understand?

"For Jess," she said at the end of it all—my mother, Jessica, named for her mom—and then wiped at her eyes with the back of her hand, another dab of claw-shiny black showing on her inner forearm for the briefest instant, for not really long enough to matter.

Except it did. To me.

It made the world creak all around us, into a new shape. This moment we were standing in, it was a balloon, inflating.

Inside of ten minutes, we'd have the bed of the El Camino piled with cardboard boxes and trash bags, Grandpa's house burning down to the cement slab, the three of us stuffed into the cab of the El Camino, to put as much distance between us and this dead cop as we could in a single night.

Now, though.

In this moment where everything went one way, not the other.

Because of that dab of shiny black on my aunt's inner forearm, I was listening to my grandpa again.

This is one of the first stories he ever told me, right before Darren rolled back into town to keep Red off Libby. His left eye then, it was probably already pressuring up to burst back into his brain.

The story was about dewclaws.

And none of Grandpa's stories were ever lies. I know that now. They were just true in a different way.

He had been telling me secrets ever since I could sit still enough to listen.

On dogs, he told me, dewclaws, they're useless, just leftover. From when they were *wolves*, Grandpa insisted.

Dewclaws, they're about birthing, they're about being born.

Just like baby birds need a beak to poke through their shells, or like some baby snakes have a sharp nose to push through their eggshells, so do werewolf pups need dewclaws. It's because of their human half. Because, while a wolf's head is custom made for slipsliding down a birth canal, a human head—all pups shift back and forth the whole time they're being born—a human head is big and blocky by comparison. And the mom's lady parts, they aren't made for that. You can cut the pups out like they tried to do for Grandma, but you need somebody who knows what they're doing. When there's not a knife, or somebody to hold it, and when the mom's human, not wolf—*that's* the reason for the dewclaws. So the pup can reach through with its paw. So that one flick of sharpness high up on the inside of the forearm can snag, tear the opening a bit wider.

It's bloody and terrible, but it works. At least for the pup.

And now I understood, about Grandpa's tick. That smooth divot of scar tissue he'd shown me on the back of his arm.

It was so I would look at my own arms, someday.

On the inside of each of my forearms there are two pale slick scars that Libby'd told me were from the heating element of Grandpa's stove, when I'd reached in for toast when a piece of bread was still as big as my head.

Grandpa had been telling me the whole time, though: dogs?

I'd seen dogs through the window driving to school, but there'd never been a dog at Grandpa's place.

Dogs know better. Dogs know when they're outmatched.

"No," Libby said, looking across to me, looking at my inner forearms with new eyes, matching my two scars up with her dewclaws.

It wasn't a dog Grandpa had to drag out by the fence.

I can see it now the way he would have said it, if he could have said it the way it happened.

A fourteen-year-old girl starts to have a baby, a *human* girl starts to have a *human* baby, only, partway through it, that baby starts to shift, little needles of teeth poking through the gums months too early. It's not supposed to happen, it never happens like this, she was the one of the litter born with fingers, not paws, she's supposed to be safe, is supposed to throw *human* babies, but the wolf's in the blood, and it's fighting its way to the surface.

My mom, I didn't just tear her open, I infected her.

Werewolves that are born, they're in control of what they are, or they can come to be, at least. They have a chance.

If you're bit, though, then it runs wild through you.

"We're going to go far from here, so far from here," Libby was saying right into my ear, the rest of me pressed up against her, both of us trembling.

Her breath smelled like meat, like change.

Darren wasn't there the night it happened, when I was born. But she was.

The real story, the one she saw, the one Grandpa was trying to say out loud finally, it's that a father carries his oldest daughter out past the house, he carries her out and she's probably already changing for the first time, into an abomination, but he holds his own wolf back, isn't going to fight her like that.

This is a job for a man.

He raises the ball-peen hammer once—the rounded head is supposed to be kind—but he isn't decisive enough, can't commit to this act with his whole heart, but he has her by the scruff, and she's on all fours now, is snapping at him, her just-born son screaming on the porch, her twin sister biting those baby-sharp dewclaws off for him once and forever, and for the rest of that night, for the rest of his *life*, this husband and father and monster is swinging that little ball-peen hammer, trying to connect, his face wet with the effort, the two of them silhouettes against the pale grass, going around and around the house.

We're werewolves.

This is what we do, this is how we live.

If you want to call it that.

CHAPTER 2

The Heaven of Werewolves

I vant . . . to bite . . . your neck," the vampire says, tippy-toeing to see himself in the mirror again.

"No, no no *no*," the vampire's uncle says for the third time. "It's 'suck your blood.' That's what vampires do. They suck your blood."

"Then what do werewolves do?"

"They buy their sister a reasonable costume, for one," the vampire's aunt says, trying to get elbow room in the tight bathroom to adjust her habit.

She's a nun tonight, all in white.

The vampire's uncle is in a rubber werewolf mask, CANDY WOLF traced onto his bare hairless chest in blue marker.

This is Florida, where it's so wet that soft green fuzz grows on the guardrail posts. They only stopped driving away from Arkansas because of the ocean, not the El Camino. The El Camino would have kept going, probably. The vampire is eight, now. His uncle says that's the perfect age for Halloween, except for all the other ages too.

Halloween is the one night of the year werewolves go to church.

To get there, they have to drive through the edge of town. There's mummies and zombies and cowboys and pirates up and down the sidewalks.

"They going to church too?" the vampire asks from the back-seat.

"Different church," the vampire's uncle says.

The vampire's uncle is in the passenger seat in his mask, and about every third time a princess or a soldier looks over at this big long four-door'd Caprice creeping past, he lunges half out the window, growling and clawing.

"You're going to get us pulled over," the vampire's aunt says.

"Not this night, sister of the ragged bite," the vampire's uncle says back.

In the backseat the vampire wants to smile but he can feel the white makeup on his face like a shell of dried mud, and knows it'll crack.

And vampires bite necks, anyway. They don't go around smiling.

He falls asleep once town is gone, wakes in his uncle's hairy arms, doesn't realize they're long gloves until he remembers what night this is. They're not even walking on a trail through the trees, are just following where his aunt says, from the one time she was here years ago. Her white costume almost glows.

"Who showed you this place?" the vampire's uncle says.

The vampire's aunt doesn't answer this, just keeps walking.

Werewolves aren't afraid of the dark. Even ones dressed like ghost nuns.

Humans can be, though.

It's what the vampire still is, under his makeup. It's what his aunt says he'll be until he's twelve or thirteen—and maybe forever, if he never shifts. You never know.

The vampire chews on his plastic fangs and tries to look ahead. They're going uphill now. His face is cracking into pieces, he can tell.

He doesn't want to be a vampire anymore. This isn't like the comic book. He can hardly even remember the comic book anymore.

Ten or twenty or thirty minutes later the aunt stops, lifts her nose to the air. Right above him, the vampire's uncle does as well.

"Tell me that isn't who I think it is," the uncle says.

"You're just smelling things," the aunt says back. "He'd never leave Arkansas."

"He would for his El Camino," the uncle says, and wants to spit after saying it, the vampire can tell, but has the mask on.

The church is an outside church. They're not the first ones there. There's no fire, no light, not even a clearing, really. But there are shapes streaking past in the darkness. One of them brushes the vampire's uncle and the uncle starts to stand the vampire up on the ground like a big chess piece, but the aunt looks back, shakes her nun-head no.

"But—" the vampire's uncle starts, a whine rising in his voice.

The ghost nun stares at him with her faceless face and the uncle gathers the vampire back up.

"It's only Halloween . . ." the uncle says.

"It's Halloween when I say it's Halloween," the aunt says, and reaches back with her hand sideways like the coach at school says you do, to take a baton you're being handed. It's for them to follow her around the smelly pond, through the blown-over trees with their roots sideways in the air. To the center of the clearing that's not a clearing. To the nearly caved-in side of the trailer part of a trailer-tractor rig, like the vampire's uncle is learning to drive.

This one's old and rusted. Grown over with bushes and vines.

On the panel part of the side, where the picture goes when there's a picture—it's why they're here.

A wolf head in a circle of yellow.

This is a holy place.

The vampire rearranges himself in his uncle's arms to look around them, at all the motion in the darkness. It feels like whispers. It sounds like smiling. It smells like teeth.

This is the one night a call to the police about werewolves isn't going to get answered. The one night werewolves who don't usually see each other, see each other.

The vampire feels his uncle's arms go from normal to steel.

Nosing up to the vampire's aunt, on all fours but only about as tall as her ribs, is her ex-husband. The vampire can tell from his hair. And from his eyes.

"Perfect," the vampire's uncle says, standing the vampire up on his own two feet without any permission from the vampire's aunt.

The vampire finds his uncle's belt loop with his fingers.

"It's okay," the vampire's aunt says back to them.

Her ex-husband is touching his wet nose to her hand now. His whole body is rippling with tension. And it does look like a man in a suit, bent over onto his too-long arms. Only, this is the best suit ever. With the best mask. The most alive mask. The long snout that twitches. The same eyes.

"*Red*," the vampire's uncle says, like you say hello. But it's not that. It's a warning, the vampire can tell. Because you can't trust the ones that shift and never come back.

How long they live is ten or fifteen years if they're lucky, and have found a big enough place to run, to eat.

The vampire's aunt says it's selfish, it's stupid, it's *not* heaven being a wolf all the time, and some nights she cries from it, from all the ones dead on the interstate. From all of them running away with bullets in them like pearls made from lava. From all of them stopping at a fence line, a calico cat in their mouths, something about that yellow window in the house keeping them there. Some nights the aunt cries from all of those wolfed-out werewolves kicking in their dreams, strange scent-memories rising in their heads: barbecue sauce, pool-table chalk, hair spray.

Not dreams, nightmares. Of a past they can't recall. A person they don't know.

Her ex-husband can't say anything to her about it either, the vampire knows. Werewolf throats aren't made for human words. Human words would never fit. There would be too much to say.

They can lift their lips, though. They can growl.

"He knows, he remembers," the vampire's aunt says loud enough for the vampire's uncle to definitely hear.

"That car's long gone," the uncle says. "It wasn't that fast anyway."

"Shh, shh," the aunt says, "it'll be all right this time." The back of her hand is still to her husband's velvet muzzle. But when he snaps his teeth together a heartbeat later, her hand's already back to her chest, her lips drawn back from her own teeth.

"You idiot," the vampire's uncle says, stepping forward, and when the vampire looks up, his uncle is peeling the rubber mask off.

The wolf snout remains. And the ears.

The uncle doesn't even wait to finish shifting. He dives into the ex-husband and it's a frenzy, a tangle, a fight on this of all holy nights, snapping and snarling and long curls of blood slinging out, other churchgoers coming in to stand up on two legs, to watch, to wait—two of them are human, naked—and what's going to last forever for this vampire is the image of his aunt in a white nun costume. She's stepping away from the fight but she's reaching in, holding her other hand to her mouth.

"Now it's Halloween," the vampire whispers, just for himself.

After that it's all running. Faster than before. So much faster.

The vampire's aunt, she still has most of her billowy white nun costume on, but she's on all fours now, her sharp dangerous killer teeth clamped over the high collar behind the vampire's neck, and even though he's eight years old, they're going so fast through the trees that the vampire's face is cracking into a hundred pieces, into a thousand.

It doesn't matter to the aunt once she shifts back, reties her nun-suit back on, turning her face into a shadow, into a face at the end of a long tunnel.

Coming back through town, she stops all at once in front of the last house with the porch lights on, explains to the vampire what he's supposed to do here, then fishes a burger sack up from the floorboard, dumps the trash. She shakes the sack open, makes him take it.

"Just knock," she tells him, waving him up the sidewalk with the back of her hand.

Halfway to the house the vampire hears her crying in the car behind him, but he doesn't turn around.

"Oh no, cover your neck," the unsteady woman who answers the door says in a too-high voice.

The vampire holds his paper sack out and waits for whatever the next part is.

CHAPTER 3

American Ninja

We were in Portales, New Mexico, just long enough for me to wear a dog path between the back door of our trailer and the burn barrels. That's what Darren called it when he came through, and then he'd punch me in the shoulder and get down in a fighting stance, his shoulders curled around his chest like he was a boxer, not a biter. Sometimes it would turn into a wrestling match in the living room, at least until a lamp got broke or Libby's coffee got spilled—I was twelve and tall by then, needed a yard to wrestle in, not a living room—and other times I'd just hike another half-full trash bag over my shoulder, slope out the back door again.

Because night was falling. Because night's always falling, when you're a werewolf.

There were eighty-nine steps to the burn barrels.

And it wasn't a dog path.

That was just Darren funning me about not having shifted yet.

It was probably supposed to be him reminding me not to worry, that I was like him, I was like Libby, I was like Grandpa.

It didn't feel that way.

I didn't mind the trash runs, though.

You can always tell who might be a werewolf by if they're careful like we are, to take the trash out each night, even if it's just a little bit full. Even if it's just wasting a trash bag. But I wouldn't waste them. I'd upend the day's leavings into the flaky black drums, tuck the white bag into my pocket, use it again the next day.

What I was doing was making deals. With the world.

I'll take care of you, you take care of me, cool?

Darren had told me that the first time he shifted it was three years early, and that had triggered Libby to shift, and my mom, she hadn't even flinched, had just stood and pulled the kitchen door shut so they couldn't get out, and then cornered Darren and Libby with the business end of a small broom until Grandpa got home.

Three years early would put Darren and Libby at about ten.

I was coming in late, it looked like.

If ever.

Libby never said it out loud, but I could tell she was pulling for "never." She didn't want her and Darren's life for me—moving every few months, driving cars until they threw a rod then walking away from them to the next car. She wanted me to be the one who sneaked through without getting that taste for raw meat. She wanted me to be the one who got to have a normal life, in town.

We're werewolves, though.

Each night at dusk one of us leans out the door to burn the trash, just because we all know what can happen if that trash is left in the kitchen: Somebody'll go wolf in the night, and because shifting burns up every last bit of fat reserves you have and even leaves you in the hole for more, the first thing you think once you're wolf—the *only* thing you can think, if you're just starting out—is food.

It's not a choice, it's just survival. You eat whatever's there, and fast, be it the people sleeping around you at the rest stop or, if you've got a trailer rented for four months, the kitchen trash.

It sounds stupid, but it's true.

When we first open our eyes as werewolves, the trash is so fragrant, so perfect, so right there.

Except.

There's things in there you can't digest, I don't care how bad you are.

Ever wake up with the ragged lid of a tin can in your gut? Darren says it's like a circle-saw blade, in first gear. But it's only because you're so delicate in the morning, so human. Even a twist tie can stab through the lining of your stomach.

The wolf doesn't know any better, just knows to eat it all, and fast, and *now*.

Come daylight, though—so many werewolves die this way, Libby had told me once. So many die with a broke-tined fork stabbing them open from the inside. With a discarded but whole beef rib pushing through their spleen, their pancreas. She said she'd even heard of somebody dying from a house dog that had had its pelvis put together with a metal rod. That metal rod, it went down the wolf's throat fine, along with the crunchy domestic bones, but in the morning, for the man, it was a spear.

Libby had stopped meaningfully on *spear*, settled me in her stare to make sure I was paying the right kind of attention.

I had been. Sort of.

Because I was sure I was going to shift just any night now, was going to pad on all fours down the long hall from my bedroom at any moment, sniff at the coffee table then turn my attention to the much richer scent of the kitchen—because that was definitely going to happen, I always lugged the trash out. Never mind that Libby'd always been careful to not leave steel wool or bleach containers in there. Never mind that we kept a jug of black pepper right there on the counter, to sprinkle onto the trash as it built through the day.

I'd be able to smell through that, I knew.

I was going to be that kind of werewolf. In spite of Libby's prayers.

The life she wanted for me, it was the life my mom should have had, the life that, her not being a werewolf, should have been mine by birthright. But something had gone haywire. Just once, or just waiting, though? That was the part her and Darren couldn't figure. I had the blood, but was that blood ever going to rise again, or had it been a onetime thing? With Grandpa five years gone, there weren't even any old-timers to ask. Had this happened before? Had there ever been somebody like me?

There had to have been.

Werewolves have always been here. Every variation of us, it has to have happened at some point.

Just, it's the remembering that's tricky.

Until we knew for sure one way or the other, Libby was packing my head with facts, like trying to scare me back across the line.

Driving here from East Texas, the big Delta 88 eating up the miles, the trunk empty because all our stuff had burned a move or two ago, she'd evened her voice out to sound like a safety pamphlet and recounted all the ways we usually die. It was the werewolf version of The Talk. Just, with more dead bodies.

It took nearly the whole ten hours, no radio, no books, nothing. I stared a hole into the dashboard, not wanting to let her see how perfect all this was. How much I was loving every single wonderful fact.

She'd already told me about the trash.

The rest, though—being a werewolf, it's a game of Russian roulette, Darren would say. It's waking up every morning with that gun to your temple. And then he'd snap his teeth over the end of that sentence and give a yip or two, and I'd have to look away so Libby wouldn't see me smiling, I wanted to be him so bad.

What he was doing those four months we were in New Mexico—the farthest west we'd ever been since splitting east out of Arkansas once and forever—was dragging trailer homes between Portales and Raton, up in Colorado. And if the p-traps of those kitchens and bathrooms were packed with baggies of anything, then he didn't know about it, anyway.

His logbooks were meticulous, his plates screwed on top and bottom, and his license wasn't even expired, for once. It wasn't his name on that license, but, other than that, he was completely legal, right down to the depth of the tread on his tires.

His bosses insisted.

Libby didn't approve, but you do what you can.

And, up in his truck, the only werewolf death he really had to worry about was that old one of going wolf up in the cab, behind the wheel.

According to Libby, that's the main way most werewolves cash out. Not always in cab-over rigs on a six-percent grade, the jake brake screaming, but on the road at highway speed, anyway. Usually it's just making a run to the gas station for ketchup packets. Somebody cuts you off and you wrap your fingers extra tight around the steering wheel, until the tendons in the backs of your fingers start popping into their canine shape. At which point you reach up for the rearview to check yourself, to see if this is really and truly happening. Only, the rearview, it comes off in what's now your long-fingered paw. And, if the glue's good, then maybe a piece of the windshield craters out with the mirror, and you *know* how goddamn much *that's* going to cost, and thinking cusswords in your head, that's no way to hold back the transformation.

Give it a mile, you tell yourself. Just another mile to reel things back in. No, there's no way to unsplit your favorite shirt, to save the tatters your pants already are. But you're not going to wreck another motherf—

But you are, you just did. Scraping the passenger side along a guardrail, for the simple reason that steering wheels aren't designed for monsters that aren't supposed to exist. You can hardly grip on to it, much less the gear stick, and the shoe your foot's burst through now, *great*, it's wrapped in the gas pedal in some way you couldn't make happen again in a thousand tries.

This is the time that matters, though. Heading down the road at eighty, now ninety, not really in control, having to hang your new head out the window like a joke, just to *see*, because the windshield's all shattered white from you punching it, and, though you run out of gas every time you go anywhere, *now* the tank's sloshing full, of course.

It's only a matter of miles until the semi crests at the other end of the road. The one with your name engraved on the bumper you know is your headstone. Or maybe it'll be a long drop off the road, into some culvert you'll never walk up from, werewolf or not. Even just a telephone pole.

Werewolves, we're tough, yeah, we're made for fighting, made for hunting, can kill all night long and then some. But cars, cars are four thousand pounds of jagged metal, and, pushing a hundred miles per hour now, the world a blur of regret—there's only one result, really.

And, if a bad-luck cop sees you slide past the billboard he's hiding behind, well, then it's on, right? If he stops you, you're going to chew through him in two bites, which, instead of making the problem go away, will just multiply it, on the radio.

So you run.

It's the main thing werewolves are made for. It's what we do best of all.

Every time I see a chase like that happening on the news, I always say a little prayer inside.

It's just that one word: *run*.

And then I turn around, leave that part of the store because I want that chase to go on forever. I don't want to have to know how it ends.

Another one of us dead.

Another mangled body in a tangle of metal and glass. Just a man, a woman, two legs two arms, because in death the body relaxes back to human bit by bit. In death, the wolf hides.

But cars and highways aren't the only ways we go. The modern world, it's custom-designed to kill werewolves.

There's french fries, for one.

The idea, Libby said, switching hands on the Delta 88's thin steering wheel and staring straight ahead, boring holes into the night with her eyes, the *idea* is werewolves think they'll burn all those calories up the next time they shift. And they're not wrong. You burn up your french-fry calories and more. But calories aren't the dangerous part of the french fry. The dangerous part of the french fry is that once you have a taste for them, then, running around in a pasture one night, chasing wild boar or digging up rabbits or whatever—all honest work—you'll catch that salty scent on the air. If you still had your human mind, you'd know not to chase that scent down. You'd know better.

You're not thinking like that, though.

You run like smoke through the trees, over the fences, and, when you find those french fries, they're usually on a picnic table in some deserted place. Which is the dream, right?

Except for the couple sitting on opposite sides of that picnic table. They can be young and broke, having had to dig into couches for enough change for this weekly basket of fries to split out at their favorite place, or they can be the fifty-year-anniversary set, indulging themselves on exactly the kind of greasy fat they're under strict orders to stay away from.

What they should really stay away from, it turns out, it's eating those french fries out in the open.

They don't know they live in a world with werewolves. And by the time they do know, it's too late.

Blind with hunger, you barrel up onto that table and snatch the fries in a single motion, have eaten them bag and all by the time that picnic table's two leaping bounds behind you. At which point you register that distinct flavor of salt on this couple's fingertips as well. Around their lips.

Your paws skid in the gravel, the dust under that gravel rising in a plume you're about to rip open, explode back through.

The newspaper the next day won't show crime-scene photos of the remains, or the blood-splashed picnic table.

You won't need them. You'll have those photographs in your head already, in those kind of visual flashes Darren says you get in the daytime, like half-remembered dreams.

And you'll think *french fries*.

And the next time you follow that salty scent in from the pasture, an honest rabbit dangling limp from either side of your jaws, that two-lane highway you have to cross to get to that tanginess, maybe this time there'll be a semi hurtling down the near lane, its grille guard thick and purposeful. Or there'll be men on the roof of the cinderblock bathroom, their scoped rifles waiting, obituaries folded in their tall leather wallets.

They'll shoot you like they always do, and you'll run off like werewolves always have, but, like with wrecks at a hundred miles per hour, there's only so much the wolf can do to knit itself back together. At least when you're made mostly of french fries.

Maybe your human body turns up two years later in a drainage ditch, mushroomed lead slugs pushed out all around it, but the rest of that body will have been starved down to the bone—coming back from gunshots takes a lot of calories, and you can't hunt when you're laid up like that—or maybe the buzzards got there first, for the eyes, the soft parts, until you turn up as another drifter, another vagrant, another tragedy. Unlabeled remains.

Werewolves, we didn't come up eating french fries through the ages.

It's taking some time to adapt.

Maybe more time than we've got, even.

We're not stupid, though.

We know to stay mostly to the south and the east. I mean, we're made for snow, you can tell just by looking at us, we're more at home in the snow and the mountains than anywhere, but in snow you leave tracks, and those tracks always lead back to your front door, and that only ever ends with the villagers mobbing up with their pitchforks and torches.

That's one of Darren's favorite ways to say it: *pitchforks and torches.*

Like what we're in here, it's a Frankenstein movie.

Frankenstein didn't have to worry about Lycra, though. Or spandex.

Stretch pants are just as dangerous to werewolves as highways.

Libby's always careful to wear denim, and Darren wouldn't be caught dead in anything but jeans.

Me either.

The good thing about jeans, it's that they rip away. Not at the seams like you'd think—that yellow thread there is tough like fishing line—but in the center of the denim, where it's worn the thinnest. It sucks always having to buy new jeans, or finding ones at the salvage store with long enough legs, but that's just part of being a werewolf.

A pair of tights, though, man.

Panty hose are murder.

Libby'd only heard about this, never seen it, but supposedly what can happen is you've wriggled into a pair of hose or tights— except for color, I really don't understand the difference between the two—and then, over the course of the day, they're such a constant annoyance that you kind of forget them altogether.

Enter night, then.

Begin the transformation.

Where pants will tear away, split over the thigh and calf, burst at the waist no matter how double-riveted they are, your fancy panty hose, your stretch pants, they wolf out *with* you. I'd imagine you look kind of stupid, with your legs all sheer and shiny, but anybody who laughs, you just rip their throat out, feast on their heart. Problem solved.

At least until morning, when you shift back.

Just like that tick that impacted itself into Grandpa's skin, a pair of panty hose, they'll retract *with* your legs. Except, instead of one tick embedding itself in your skin, flaring into some infection, this time *every* hair is pulling something back in with it.

What happens is your skin, your human skin, it's part panty

hose now. Like the hose have melted onto you, but deeper than deep. And, because you just used all your calories shifting back— it's not easy like on television—and because you're hurt, now, you probably can't go back to wolf yet, can't get tough enough to sustain this kind of all-over injury.

Worse, this isn't an immediate death.

You linger through the day.

If your family—your *werewolf* family—if they really love you, they'll end it for you. If you're alone, then it's hours of trying to pull those panty hose up from your bloody skin. It's fine, slippery threads of that hose ducking into your veins and getting pumped higher, into your body.

If you're lucky, one of those clumps makes its way to your brain.

If you're not lucky, then you end up trying to use your human teeth to peel up all the skin from the top of your thigh, the back of your calf. Wherever you can reach.

It doesn't help.

I don't know what the coroner calls these kind of deaths. Probably drug psychosis. Obvious enough to him that a blood test isn't even necessary. Look at this trailer, this living room, how they were living. Look at how she was picking at her skin. Bag her up, team. And drop a match on your way out.

But there's another way to die too.

The oldest way, maybe.

Darren had been gone five weeks without checking in, long enough that Libby'd started calling the DPS, asking about wrecks, when his rig rumbled up, shaking every window in the trailer.

She ran out in her apron and hugged him hard around the neck almost before he'd even stepped down from the truck, hugged him hard enough that her feet weren't even on the ground. Hard enough that I remembered that they'd been pups together. That they're all that's left of their litter. Of their family.

Except for me.

It's why Libby was trying so hard to save me, I think. Like, if I never went wolf, she'd be keeping some promise to my mom. Like she'd have saved one of us.

I'm not sure I wanted to be saved.

I stood there in the doorway, too grown-up for hugs, too young not to have been drawn to the sound of a big rig, and Darren lifted his chin to me, pulled me out into the driveway with him. He had a box of frozen steaks in the sleeper. We were going to eat like *kings*, he said, messing my hair up and pushing me away at the same time.

All those movies, where the werewolves eat their meat raw? Libby at least seared our steaks on the outside. I didn't have a taste for it yet, but I could pretend. Darren cued into how long I was having to chew and planted a bottle of ketchup right by my plate, and nobody said anything.

Each veiny, raw bite swelled and swelled in my mouth, but I swallowed them down hard. Because I'm a werewolf. Because I'm part of this family.

After dinner, after Libby'd gone in to work the counter at the truck stop, Darren pulled out the next way to die but, before showing it to me, made me promise I wasn't a cop, a narc, or a reporter.

"I tell you if I was?" I said to him.

"You report back to Lib about this, it's both our asses," he said, then added, "But mostly yours."

I flipped him off at close range.

He guided my arm to the side, opened the fingers of his other hand one by one and dramatic.

On his palm was a throwing star, like I'd seen at ten thousand flea markets.

Only this one, Darren said, it was *silver*.

That's a word werewolves kind of hiss out, like the worst secret.

Every time he spun it up in the air, reaching in to pinch it on both sides and stop its spinning, it was in slow motion for me.

Not just the points were sharp either. Somebody'd ground the edges down, then used a small, patient whetstone on them. Just the weight of this star, it was enough to pull those razor edges down the middle of Libby's magazine pages. We'd taken turns doing it, just to prove that something so small could be so dangerous, so deadly, so wrong.

When we were done Darren passed it to me reverently, holding it sideways. With a knife, you usually hold the blade yourself, offer the handle like's polite. There was no safe part of this throwing star, though.

Even the slightest nick and our blood would be boiling.

Darren being careful with it when he handed it across, watching my eyes to make sure I understood what we were playing with here—my heart swelled, my throat lumped up, and I wondered if this is what it feels like, changing.

He was only telling me to be careful because this was dangerous to me as well.

I was part of this family. I was in this blood.

So he wouldn't see the change happening to my eyes, I tilted my head back, gathered up the trash, and walked the eighty-nine steps to the burn barrels.

The trash was all bloody cardboard from the steaks and fluttering pages from Libby's magazines we'd cut all to hell.

When I heard the *thunk* from inside, I knew what was happening. Darren thought he was a ninja. He always had. The first of the new breed, deadlier than either a werewolf *or* a ninja. He was diving across the living room, falling in slow motion through the movie playing in his head. Diving and, midfall, flinging his throwing star at the paneling of the walls.

With a throwing star, you can't miss. It's all edges.

I scratched a flame from my book of my matches, held it to the celebrity gossip magazines Libby would never admit to, and stood there in the first tendrils of smoke, watching my uncle's blurry silhouette against the curtains.

I watched him finally stop, jerk the index finger of his right hand to his mouth, to suck on it.

I turned back to the fire and held my palms out, waiting for the heat, and I remembered what I saw on a nature show once: that dogs' eyes can water, sure, but they can't cry. They're not built for it.

Neither are werewolves.

CHAPTER 4

The Truth About Werewolves

But this is for *class*."

The reporter doesn't start with this. This is where the reporter finally *gets* to.

The reporter's second-grade teacher said interviewing a family member would be easy.

Teachers don't know everything.

The reporter's uncle has been awake, he says, for sixty-two hours now. To prove it he holds his hand out to show how it's trembling, at least until he wraps it around the top of a make-believe steering wheel.

This is right before the move back to a different part of Florida in the nighttime. This is Georgia homework.

"Just do it already," the reporter's aunt says to her brother. She's in the kitchen rehabbing the stove, trying to coax Christmas from it.

The reporter's uncle drags the weak headlights of his eyes in from the road he can still see, settles on the blue spiral notebook the reporter's holding.

"You really want an A?" the uncle says. "An A-*plus*, even?"

In the kitchen the aunt clears her throat with meaning for the uncle. The reporter's already up past his bedtime for this assignment.

So far she's pulled two melted Hot Wheels from the oven. They don't roll anymore.

"If he doesn't pass school—" she starts, her voice as big as the inside of the oven, but cuts herself off when her fingertips lose whatever it is they've latched on to. Another Hot Wheels?

"I remember school . . ." the reporter's uncle says, his voice dreamy and half asleep. Like it's dragging out across the years. "You know the ladies love our kind, don't you?" he says, talking low so his sister won't have anything to add.

"*I'm* supposed to ask *you* the questions," the reporter says, his lips firm.

Because he lost his sheet of interview questions, he's made up his own.

"Shoot," the reporter's uncle says, yawning so wide his jaw sounds like it's breaking open at the hinge.

"Why do you always pee right before?" the reporter asks, no eye contact, just a ready-set-go pencil, green except for the tooth marks. It's from the box of free ones the teacher keeps on the corner of her desk.

"Pee?" the uncle says, interested at last. He looks past the reporter to the kitchen, probably with the idea that the reporter's aunt is going to prairie-dog her head up about werewolf talk.

No such aunt tonight.

The reporter's uncle shrugs one shoulder, leans in so the reporter has to lean in as well, to hear. "You mean before the change, right?" he says.

Right.

"Easy," the uncle says. "Say—say you've got a pet goldfish. Like, one you're all attached to, one you'd never eat even if you were starving and there was ketchup already on it. But you have to move, like to another *state*, get it? 'State'? You don't put the whole fishbowl all sloshing with water up on the dashboard for that, now do you?"

"You put it in a bag," the reporter says.

"Smallest bag you can," the uncle says. "Makes the trip easier, doesn't it? Shit doesn't get spilled everywhere. And the fish might even make it to that other state alive, yeah?"

In his notebook, angled up where his uncle can't see, the reporter spells out *fish*.

"But, know what else?" the reporter's uncle says, even quieter. "Wolves, *were*wolves like us, we've got bigger teeth to eat with, better eyes to see with, sharper claws to claw with. Bigger everything, even stomachs, because we eat more, don't know when the next meal's coming."

In the reporter's notebook: four careful lines that might be claw scratches.

"Bigger everything but *bladders*," the uncle says, importantly. "Know why dogs always end up peeing on the rug? It's because a dog can't hold it. Because they're not made to be inside. They're made to be *out*side, always peeing all over everything. They never had to grow big bladders, because there's no lines to wait in to get to pee on a tree. You just go to a different tree. Or you just pee where you're already standing."

"But werewolves aren't dogs," the reporter says.

"Damn straight," the uncle says, pushing back into the couch in satisfaction, like he was just testing the reporter here. "But we maybe share certain features. Like how a Corvette and a Pinto both have gas tanks."

A Pinto is a horse. A Mustang is a car.

In the notebook: nothing.

"So what I'm saying," the uncle says, narrowing his eyes down to gunfighter slits to show he's serious here, that this really is A-plus information, "it's that, if you shift across with like six beers in you, or six cokes, six beers or cokes you already needed to be peeing out in the first place, then you're going to be trying to fit those six cokes into a two-beer fish bag, get it?"

The reporter is trying to remember what the next question was.

"We got any of those balloons left?" the reporter's uncle calls into the kitchen, for the demonstration part of this lesson.

Balloons? the reporter writes in the notebook in his head.

His aunt answers with a rattle on the linoleum: Hot Wheels number *three*. This one rolls into a chair leg, is the best of the lot, the real survivor.

"Corvette," the reporter's uncle says, nodding at that little car like it's making his case for him.

Before the reporter can remember his next question, the aunt comes slipping around the half-wall counter between the kitchen and the living room. Her hand is on the top of the half-wall counter for her to swing around, and her bare feet are skating, rocking the chairs under the table, two red plastic cups that were on the table knocked into the air and, for the moment, just staying there.

In this slowed-down time, the reporter looks from them all the way across to his aunt. Her face is smudged black with a thousand pieces of burnt toast, and there's a look in her eyes that the reporter can't quite identify. If it were on a test, the kind where you have to put some answer to get partial credit, what he might write down is "reaching." Her eyes, they're *reaching*.

Her feet, though.

That's what the reporter can't look away from.

They're not slipping anymore now, just only one step later. They're *gripping*. With sharp black claws.

Before he can be sure, time catches up with itself and she's flying across the coffee table, her whole entire body level with the floor, her arms collecting the reporter to her chest and then crashing them both into the reporter's uncle, who only has time to make his mouth into the first part of the letter *O*, which is just a lowercase *O*.

The three of them are halfway over the back of the couch when the spark the reporter's aunt must have seen in the blackness of the oven does its evil thing and the whole kitchen turns into a fireball that blows all the windows in the trailer out, that kills all the lights at once, that leaves the three of them deaf against a wall, feeling each other's faces to be sure they're all right, and if there are any real answers about werewolves, then it's a picture of them right there doing that, a picture of them right there trying to find each other.

CHAPTER 5

Billy the Kid

Everybody goes to jail at some point.

Werewolves especially.

And even just one night in the tank, that can be a straight-up death sentence. For all the other drunks locked up, who don't know any better than to push you, who think they can steal your blanket *and* keep their throat, sure, a death sentence for them, but for you as well, once you're the only one standing knee-deep in the blood and the gore, your chest rising and falling with the rush of it all. And, that deep into the night, it doesn't matter if you're standing on four feet or two. Either way the cops on duty'll line up into a firing squad, give you that twenty-one-gun send-off.

That's a warning *Darren* gave me. Not Libby. Her jobs were always aboveboard, with set hours, sometimes even a uniform or apron.

Darren, he always got paid in cash.

Thirteen years old, I would sit at the table with him, help

straighten out his tens and twenties, get them rubber-banded into coffee tins and tucked behind baseboards. On a flush night there might even be a tip involved. Kind of just sneaked across the table after it was all said and done, Darren's eyes telling me not to say anything—that, by sharing this with me, he was including me in the danger.

Libby knew, I think, could probably hear that giveaway scrape of cotton-paper from the living room, but you pick your fights.

What she didn't know was that Darren was teaching me to flex the ropy muscles of my wrists out like a puffer fish. What she wasn't home to see was Darren with those dummy cuffs from the dollar rack, me pushed up against the wall of the living room, hands behind my back to see if I could slip a middle finger up under that plastic silver jaw. It was an old Billy the Kid trick, according to Darren. Billy the Kid was the first werewolf. He was probably even the one who figured out you could bite your own thumb off if you absolutely had to and then go wolf around that next corner, pray that the transformation won't be counting fingers this time.

It was gospel. I lapped it up.

We were in the alien part of Texas then, north of Dallas, west of Denton. The Buick we'd had in New Mexico hadn't been able to take us any farther. Bridgeport looked like another planet, especially with the ice storm. All the long branches the trees had been growing for forty years had snapped off from the weight, shattered over the broken-down fences, breaking them down even more. Dallas was more than an hour away, and a dogleg at that, and too bright besides. Decatur was closer and a straighter shot, and it had cheaper groceries. Because the junkyard three miles down the road from us had fired Libby for not coming into the job knowing which wheel would fit what year of truck, she was pushing a mop at a two-story office building on the north side of Decatur. What she was driving back and forth was a rehabbed Datsun minitruck from the yard. It had been spray-painted bright blue ten or fifteen years before, and had the number 14 carefully paintbrushed onto the driver door, "41" on the passenger side.

Some mysteries you never solve.

Darren wasn't working then. It was because of his right hand. It was still infected from that throwing star—and it had been *months,* long enough for me to have a birthday. Watching game shows in the daytime, he would lick the side of his index finger constantly, like a huge fleshy blow-pop that swelled up instead of ever going down.

"It's what werewolves do," he told me when I was staring.

"What is a tank?" I told him.

The question on the game show was about panzers.

"Ding ding ding!" he chimed, not a hint of a smile at the corners of his mouth.

Where I could read, and did, Darren just listened to talk shows on the radio. It made sense: You don't drive truck with a paperback open on your thigh.

Or with a hand that can't work a shifter, as it turned out. He'd tried wrong-handing it—right on the wheel, left crossed over his body for the stick—but it had ended in a jackknife, with Darren just walking away from it, his hand up by his shoulder like a throbbing lantern that could light his way home.

We'd got to town a couple of weeks earlier, running on stolen gas, the Buick's temperature gauge hovering deep in the red, but instead of checking me into school like usual, to keep me on the straight and narrow path to a sophomore year, Libby was giving me January off. I was angling for February too. Then I might just make it all the way to summer.

I liked reading enough, but what was I supposed to do with a diploma? Getting a degree would be like I was deciding to trade in my heritage, my blood. And if I started making those kinds of gestures, then that was the same as asking to never change, to just stay like this forever, not need all Darren's advice.

Later that night we were sitting at the table with Libby. For her it was breakfast, but for us it was dinner. Except we didn't have any.

"You'll run something down for him?" Libby said to Darren, her runny eggs balanced on her fork.

They were the last three eggs.

"Say *what?*" Darren said, scrunching his face up.

I'd understood Libby, but it had taken some effort: She was talking like her mouth was hurt. Like she had a big wad of chewing gum.

She said it again, pointing her words harder.

"Oh," Darren said, biting his lower lip in, staring right at her. "Already, sis?"

Libby shoved her plate across the table at him and didn't say another word.

Darren lifted her plate with his good hand and slurped her eggs off, smiling the whole time.

"What?" I said when she stomped back to her bedroom for her hairnet. It was so she wouldn't wax any more of her black hairs into the lobby floor. There'd been complaints.

"When you change," Darren said, wiping the yellow from his lips with his bandaged hand, "your tongue's the first thing to go."

He hung his tongue out the side of his mouth and panted, to show.

"That's because the human tongue has more muscles—" I started, but he looked to the side like checking if I was for real, came back with: "You think we're talking *human* tongues, here?"

"But she's not even—" I started, meaning to say she wasn't shifting. She was maybe changing her shirt or something, but she was coming back up the hall on two feet, not four. Before I could get into all that, Darren made his eyes big to keep me quiet.

Libby's footsteps.

"Not that they don't taste good when they're fresh," he said like she was catching us midconversation, just another discussion about tongues. But the way he smiled behind it, I didn't know if he was funning me or if that's what you're supposed to do with a kill: muzzle into its mouth, clamp on to the tongue, stretch it back out until that white tendon down the underside snaps.

It made me gag a little.

Darren shh'd his swollen finger across his lips and, like always, I kept his secret.

"And don't bring back anything sick this time," Libby said right to him. To punctuate it she threw down a dollar and a half on the table, most of it in change.

The change was for me, for the ketchup I would definitely need for whatever Darren ran down in an hour or two. For the first few weeks in Texas, she'd been just swiping packets from the condiment tray at the gas station that fronted the junkyard, but now she couldn't go back in there anymore, and they'd learned to keep an eye on me as well.

The change she threw on the table, I was pretty sure it was from the office building. It had to be. From the ashtrays and drawers and drains of people who knew how to tie a tie, even without a mirror. I cupped my hand over the quarters and dimes and pennies. They were still wet. She'd just washed them in the bathroom. Because werewolves who aren't werewolves yet, they can still die from normal human sicknesses.

"So . . ." Darren said, like figuring this out as he went, "so you mean I'm only to get a raccoon with a clean bill of health like *tied* to its neck? They still make those? Good thing you told me, I was probably just going to get the first thing I saw down at the animal hospital."

Libby stared at him.

This was the tenth or fifteenth week of him being around too much. Of her bringing home half the money that was supposed to go twice as far.

It didn't help at all that Darren was shifting every night, to try to get his hand to forget it was infected. What that meant for us was that he was spending his days mummied up on the couch. And werewolf sleep, that's caterpillar-in-a-cocoon deep, about as close to coma as you can get and not flatline.

Another way we always die? House fires. Come in from a night of blood and carnage, burn most of those calories shifting back to human, then dive headfirst into your pillow, go deeper down than dreams, down so far that, when the smoke starts building from the stove or the cigarette or the villagers' torches, well, that's that. Barbecued wolf, babydoll.

That was one of Darren's words since we'd hit Texas: *babydoll.*

It made Libby's top lip snarl up in a way Darren couldn't get enough of.

He usually woke right around *Wheel of Fortune,* and, even though he'd yell the solutions to make them right, none of them ever were.

It didn't help Libby sleep.

We weren't going to be in Texas for much longer, I could tell. Texas was bad for werewolves. We'd been there not long ago already, coming back from Florida, so should have learned. But Texas was so big. That was the thing. If we wanted to get back into Louisiana and Alabama and all those places without ice and snow, we had to drive across Texas, hope none of the cowboys were watching.

Just, werewolf cars aren't made to go that far in a single push. The LeSabre back by the propane tank was proof of that. There was grass growing up all around it already, and probably coming up through the holes in the floorboard, like Texas was doing everything it could to keep us here.

Not because it wanted us to find work, to make lives. It was because it wanted to eat us.

And it was working.

After Libby was gone, that little Datsun's four-cylinder screaming in pain, Darren hung his tongue out again, panted in imitation of her in the most profane way, somehow getting his head involved.

"Maybe a deer," I told him, because Libby wasn't here to defend herself.

"Bambi's mom again," he said, looking out the window like considering this.

So far he'd brought back two skinny does, but they'd each been roadkill. I could tell, but didn't say anything. If I did, then we'd both have to see him darting between headlights, just another dog, a big rangy one, trying to drag this bounty off the highway. Instead of running it down like we're meant to.

Three paws aren't fast enough, though. You can't corner hard, just flop over onto your chin instead.

"Up for some good old USDA beef?" Darren said.

"Libby says no," I told him.

"'Libby says no,'" he repeated, mocking her thick tongue again.

If we even stole a *calf* away from the pastures all around us, not even a whole cow, still, ranchers would come asking, and we'd be the new tenants, the hungry tenants, the ones with big thick bones stashed in the crawlspace.

Not that a calf wouldn't taste exactly like heaven.

Darren stood up, started peeling out of his clothes. It's what you do when your sister can't steal enough nickels and dimes for new pants. He kicked the back door open, arced a splattery line of pee out into the night.

"How old do you have to get for it to stop hurting?" I asked, pretending to watch the news on television. Pretending this was no big deal. Just casual conversation.

Darren rolled his head away from his right shoulder, something in there creaking and popping unnaturally loud.

Inside, he was already shifting.

"It's worth it," he said, then pulled the door shut so he could part the see-through curtain, make sure there was nobody hiding behind the LeSabre. Before he stepped out he looked back to me, said, "Lock that door?"

Because I didn't have sharp teeth, or good ears. Because I couldn't protect myself.

And then he was gone.

I rushed to the back window like every time, to try to see him halfway between man and wolf, but all I caught was a shadow slipping across the pitted dull silver of the propane tank.

Instead of ketchup, I bought a whole hot dog off the little Ferris wheel on the counter at the gas station. I pointed out which one I wanted. The old man working the register looked up to me, asked was I sure?

It's what he did every night, like he was trying to direct me away from what was probably the oldest hot dog in the case.

I told him a different one, then a different one, and by the end of it I didn't know if I had the oldest worst hot dog or the one that had just cycled in.

I wasn't supposed to go out on my own, not without telling Darren or at least leaving a note—he could read that much—but there weren't going to be any truant officers here. Libby was a werewolf, wasn't she? Not a mother hen.

I'd thought of that one myself.

I sat on the far side of the ice machine and savored that hot dog. I'd put every condiment on it the gas station had, except mustard, and even doubled up on some, just because the old man couldn't say anything about it. With Darren or Libby around, I'd pretend not to like this bland human food, would make a big production of wanting something with blood, something for *wolves*.

The hot dog was so good, though.

I scooped some relish off my pants, onto my finger, into my mouth again.

When I looked up, three kids from my grade were watching me.

"Animal boy," the one in the red hat said, showing his own teeth.

"Don't mess with him," the girl of them said.

"Might catch something," John Deere Hat agreed.

"He Mexican?" the third of them said, a boy with yellow hair. If I stood, we'd have been the exact same height.

"Still wet," John Deere Hat said—"piso mojado, right?"— then pulled the girl along with him, heading into the gas station. Yellow Hair stood watching me.

"Piso mojado?" I said to him.

"What are you really?" he said back.

I held my hot dog out to him, not quite straightening my elbow out all the way. When he reached for it I growled like I'd heard Darren growl and lunged forward, snapping my teeth.

Yellow Hair fell back into the Nissan parked in the first slot and crabbed back onto the hood, denting it in perfectly, in a way he was definitely going to have to answer for.

I stood the rest of the way, tore another bite off my hot dog and threw the rest down, pushed past the torn-up pay phone, into the night.

Walking the fence back to our little white rent house, I kept looking behind me. Like I was hearing something. Like I was listening. Like my ears were already that good. Trick is, if somebody's really sneaking up on you, then you've already made them, you know they're there, but if you're all alone, then spinning around every few steps, staring into the darkness, nobody'll ever know.

Except Darren.

"Spook much, spooky?" he said from right beside me, naked as the day he was last naked. I wasn't sure if that's how all werewolves were, or if it was just Darren.

I didn't even look over, just kept walking.

"I smell horseradish?" he said, crinkling his nose up.

I looked down at the commotion by his thigh. It was a big horned owl, probably three feet tall, with a wingspan twice that. A real grandfather of a bird, like from the dinosaur days of birds. It was flapping slow. Darren had bitten the feet off, it looked like, was just holding it by the bloody stumps.

Because I needed to learn, Darren let me crack the owl's neck over when we got back to the house. It took three tries. Owls' necks aren't like other birds'. There's more muscle, and they're made to turn farther anyway. And they don't blink the whole time you're killing them. And the skull of a big one like that, it's as big as your palm, like you've got a kid in your lap, clamped between your knees.

We sat back on the propane tank to pull the feathers out. They drifted around us, stuck in our hair, in the dead grass. It looked like a whole flock of birds had just exploded, flying over. Like they'd suicided into the propeller of a plane. Air chili.

"Owls taste any good?" I asked.

"Thought you were hungry like the wolf?" Darren said, throwing a clump of feathers at me.

Because the oven didn't work, we cut the breast meat into long thin strips for frying. Because Darren was trying to be polite, instead of sucking them down raw like he probably would have if I wasn't there, he breaded them up with crushed crackers, dropped them in a pan of butter. He said we could save some this way. Maybe make owl jerky with the leftovers. It would be the only owl jerky in all of Texas, probably. We could open a stand, get rich overnight.

His finger was seeping again, I could see. And he wasn't holding the fork with that hand.

"It's not going to heal, is it?" I said.

He didn't answer.

Libby'd told him he knew what the cure for a silver cut was, but he'd come back that he needed *both* hands to drive, thanks.

The owl tasted like a thousand dead mice.

Thirty minutes after eating it, we both started throwing up fast enough that we barely made the back door in time.

"Poison," Darren got out.

The owl had got dusted out in some field. It had eaten some house rat, its brain fizzing green with bait. It had seen Darren coming, and taken a secret-agent suicide pill.

"I'm telling—telling Libby," I said, having to cough it out, and

Darren flashed his eyes up hot at me, said some criminal I was turning out to be, then he smiled, pushed me away. I had to fall farther than he pushed to avoid my own puke. He laughed so hard it made him throw up again, and, watching him throw up, I had to throw up some more. When I could I picked up a vomited-on rock, rolled it weakly at him. He pretended to be a bowling pin, fell flat over into the grass with his eyes open like a cartoon character then rose wiping his mouth with his unbandaged hand, reached his other hand down for me just to start it all over again, and, it's stupid, I know, but if I'd died right then from the poison, died without ever even changing, died with owl feathers stuck all over me, that would have been pretty all right.

I was up with the television on by lunch, my stomach as empty as it had ever been. That's what being thirteen's about, Libby had told me. It didn't mean I was changing, it meant I was normal.

She didn't know everything, though.

Darren was dead to the world on the other couch, his mouth open, one skinny leg hooked over a scratchy pillow. The big bad werewolf in his natural state.

I could have drawn any number of mustaches and eyebrows on his face, and since the light bulb in the bathroom was dead, he wouldn't even know for a day or two, if Libby could keep from cracking up. To commemorate my right guess on *Wheel*— "Where's the Beef Pudding"—I arced a line of pee out the back door, imagined I was telling all the other dogs to stay the hell away. That they didn't want any of this.

When we'd moved in, there'd been a bobcat living under the kitchen, raccoons in the pump house, coyotes yipping out in the scrub.

Once they got a good whiff of who'd moved in, they all found better dens. Even mice and rats know better than to hang around us, and forget horses. Dogs'll do their back-hair-snarling-and-barking number, ringing the alarm for their humans, but horses, they just watch with their big eyes. Track your every step. And if there's no place for them to slink off to, then they come in hard, front hooves slashing.

We're in their blood, I guess. Or, we've *been* in their blood, anyway.

Go ahead, horse. Run away.

Catch you later.

To keep Libby from Darren's throat, I pulled my pants on and policed the backyard for feathers. The owl's leftover beak was neat, all black and shiny. I puppeted my fingers behind it, pretended it was an octopus, snapped at the air with it.

Like I'd ever seen an octopus except on a nature show.

The way werewolves won't go up a tree, even though we've got the reach, got the claws, we also won't go in the ocean. Evidently Darren had tried once our first time living in Florida, while he wasn't even wolfed out, but he'd lost it, had to splash back, halfway hyperventilating. How far he'd made it was his knees. Among werewolves, making it even that far meant you had nerve to spare.

Leave the water to the fish, the trees to the cats.

Everything between, it's ours.

Waiting for *Jeopardy!*, I scoured the kitchen for a sandwich, finally had to make do with store-brand peanut butter on a plastic spoon, sugar sprinkled on top after every lick, the licks shallower and shallower.

Darren just slept, and slept deeper.

I licked my peanut butter and watched him. His index finger was shiny. Not from the stretched-out swollen-up skin so much as from the antibiotic cream he'd finally slathered on, because wolf saliva wasn't cutting it.

Jeopardy! was a repeat. I knew all the answers, said them in my head to prove it.

An hour later I was in the bathroom with a lighter, stretching my tongue out in the medicine-cabinet mirror.

Was it blacker than usual? Flattening out just a little? A dark stripe down the middle? Were my words getting thicker?

By three, Darren still wasn't awake.

I turned the second *Wheel of Fortune* up louder, so that every tick of that big wheel filled the living room like a roller coaster coasting to a stop.

Nothing. No response.

Not even from the back bedroom. And Libby kept a mop handle by her bed special for banging on the wall.

On ghost feet I crossed to the front window.

No number 14 Datsun pointed east. No number 41 Datsun ready to watch the sun set.

I looked down the hall to Libby's bedroom, flared my nostrils like I'd been training.

She wasn't going to be there, I knew.

Just like I'd been right at the game shows all day, I was right about this as well. It made my heart hammer in my chest, made my mouth dry out even more.

All her ways to die were flashing through my head faster and faster, until I was sure she'd been scalped for bounty, netted for a sideshow, kidnapped for science, and the hair that had been left behind from her last desperate fight, it was waxed under in the lobby of her office building now.

I paced from the kitchen to the front door twenty times, fifty times, practicing what I was going to tell Darren. Practicing what wasn't going to make me sound like a scared baby. Finally I just sat down on the sun-bleached cable spool we called a coffee table, shook him by the shoulder.

It didn't change his breathing, didn't make him roll over.

I shook him harder, pulled the couch cushion out from under his head, even cupped a handful of water over from the kitchen sink, let it dribble down onto him, then splash all at once.

He didn't wipe it away.

Had he eaten more of the meat than I had, was that what it was? More of the poison?

I shook my head no, no, that this wasn't happening. That any other time, sure, hibernate away, go deep and fall asleep, hide inside yourself, dream your Red Riding Hood dreams. But not now.

I screamed at him, right in his face, my slobber misting his cheek, and finally pulled the couch forward enough to tump it over backward, him riding it back into the wall.

Nothing. The ragged, snuffling end of a snore.

I slapped the wall hard above him, then got our two pans from the sink and clanged them together, then opened the door to go out to the Datsun, honk the horn, but there was no Datsun.

Libby was gone. She was really gone.

I sat down on the cable spool, my face in my hands.

I would have cried, except I'm a werewolf.

It left me with just one option.

I stood again, stepped over the upended couch, planted down right over Darren, my knees on either side of his scrawny chest.

"Don't kill me," I told him, and lifted his sick finger up, slipped it into my mouth, and bit down as hard as I could.

The pus filled my mouth, warm and tangy and medicinal, and probably infectious if I wasn't already blood, and the next thing I knew I was on my back and Darren was over me, his mouth full of new teeth, a growl coming from his throat that made me into every rabbit that had ever died.

"*No no no!*" I yelled, trying to cross my hands in front of my face, and rolled out from under him. Only because he let me.

He stood breathing deep, his nose tasting everything in the room all at once, I knew. The peanut butter. The owl feathers smoldering out in the burn barrels. The circuits in the television heated up from all the useless vowels people had been buying all afternoon.

"She's not here," I said, my voice breaking up like a kid.

Darren turned his head sideways to listen down the hall, and then crossed to the front window like I had, parted the curtains just as they lit up with real and actual headlights.

"It her?" I said, stepping across, ready to run out and meet her, but Darren held his hand up, keeping me in place.

"Sheriff's deputy," he said, and looked around the living room for anything illegal, and for the first time I saw the grey shot all through his buzz cut. It was from shifting every night for so long, now. He was using up his man-years.

Used to, he'd been the runt of the litter, the one lifted out last. The little brother. Maybe he still was. Except he was probably four years older than Libby now. As clean-shaven as the day he was born.

"Did she call?" he asked, the curtains behind him still glowing yellow, then blue-and-red, blue-and-red.

"We don't have a phone, Darren."

Darren looked over to the counter where I guess the phone would have been for a better family, and he hissed through his teeth. Nothing was working. I could have told him that.

And now the cops were here.

"She doesn't live here anymore," he said, staring at me so it would stick.

I nodded once.

Two seconds later, the butt of a nightstick knocked hard on the top of the door, over to the side. Because that's where the sheriff's deputy was standing, out of the way of the shotgun we didn't have.

What had Libby done?

Darren rubbed his eyes red, leaned one arm up on the paneling above the door, and creaked the door out, wincing from the sheriff's deputy's flashlight, raising his lip about the K-9 the backup deputy was holding on a leash. The dog filled the night with its species panic, with what-all it was screaming to the law, about us.

"Some of that chicken," he said back to me, his breath frosting with the cold.

I stood there trying to process this, and then went to the refrigerator to see if Santa'd delivered us a bucket of mixed.

"Problem?" Darren said to the sheriff's deputy, still blocking the door with his scrawny, shirtless self.

Mumble-mumble. A light hot on Darren's chest.

"Oh, yeah, her," Darren said, massaging his smooth chin in memory. "What'd she do this time, Officer?"

I popped the knuckle of each of my middle fingers.

It's what Billy the Kid would have done.

I couldn't make out what the sheriff's deputy was saying about Libby, but the way Darren looked away as if trying to make this make sense, I had an idea.

"Shit, she left—what was it?" Darren said back to me.

At which point the sheriff's deputy backed around off the steps, to shine his light in on me.

I was holding the plastic bowl of breaded owl I'd forgotten to burn.

"Three weeks?" I said.

"Maybe even a month," Darren said. "You know what she drives, right? Little Datsun *racing* truck." He had to laugh about this. "Or maybe it's a pace car with a bed, I don't know. She's always been into El Caminos, El Rancheros. Even had a *Brat* once. But, come on in, you want. Nothing to hide."

From outside, hesitation.

From the small of Darren's back, two secret fingers, hooking me over.

I drifted to him, my feet numb, my face numb, my heart slamming.

He took the bowl from me, peeled up a cold soggy strip, bit into it and chewed, chewed.

"Some?" he said, offering his bit-off piece to the sheriff's deputy.

The sheriff's deputy didn't answer, was studying me, now.

"I bet *he's* hungry," Darren said, and, neat as anything, arced that stringy piece of meat past the sheriff's deputy, right into the dog's face. The dog caught it more out of reflex than hunger, but, when it was what it was, it slurped the big bite down.

"He likes it," Darren said around the mouthful he had, fingering another piece up from the bowl.

"Sir," the sheriff's deputy said, his elbow cocked back, hand to his gun, and Darren, being the good citizen he was, flung his hands up, dropping the bowl in the process. With some guidance from his knee—pure accident, just bad luck, Officer—the bowl tumbled down to the lower step and slingshot the rest of the meat at the sheriff's deputy's pants legs. The sheriff's deputy stepped out of the way like he'd been trained, his gun fully drawn.

Behind him, where he couldn't look now, the dog was feasting, and growling while he did it, his eyes never leaving Darren.

"What do you feed him?" Darren said, leaning over to spit his own poisoned bite out, his hands still up. "Donuts?"

The LeSabre wasn't close to street legal anymore, and still had wrong plates on it—the front was from an Audi at a rest stop, the rear from a farm truck at a diner—and the water pump probably hadn't fixed its *own* self, but it got us into Decatur, Texas, by nightfall.

Because the sheriff's deputy hadn't had anything to charge Darren with, after searching the house, actually smelling Libby's bedsheets like that would tell him when she'd last been in them, he left, with instructions for us to call if she showed.

"Phone's right on the counter," Darren had said, daring the sheriff's deputy to look back in, be sure he hadn't seen what he was pretty sure he hadn't seen.

His K-9 unit was surely dead by now, or wishing it was. Circled back on itself to chew its own intestines out, and go deeper, try to get its teeth all the way around the pain, the spasms.

We pulled into a single-story motel to siphon gas from some sad-sack station wagon. Darren was as casual about it as could be, studying the fresh end of his toothpick like he was just getting water from a public well, here.

"So she lose it?" I asked. "Libby?"

"More like she found it," Darren said, staring hard at the manager's office, "only, it was four or five inches inside somebody else's throat. Serious as that cop was, I'm guessing it was one of his little brothers."

"His little—?"

"Security guard," Darren said, pulling his siphon hose from the car and holding it up to drain the last of the gas across. "It's good news," he added.

"How?"

"If they're still looking for her, then that means they don't have her, right?"

We eased away from the motel parking lot, found a high place for Darren to kill the car.

He stood from his seat, one foot on the rocker panel, turning his head this way and that. Listening to the city.

I did too.

"There," he said, nodding into a warren of what looked like condemned buildings. "Dogs."

When you're a werewolf, the way you say "dogs," it's the same as spitting out a hard bite of macaroni.

I looked at Darren, wanting to ask, but we were already moving.

He'd never put a shirt on. Werewolves aren't into shirts, even in January in North Texas.

"They're all looking for her back at her work," Darren said, cruising slow through the narrow streets. "But she ran flat out of there, right? On all fours, if I know her."

I studied ahead of us, and beside us, and in my mirror.

"What's wrong with her?" I said, then had to squint from the headlights filling my mirror.

Animal Control, with the low, flat light bar above the cab cycling. No sound, but still.

Darren let the van pass, then crept in behind it.

"Thirty minutes or less, right?" he said, clicking the LeSabre's headlights off.

It took me a moment to get it: The dogcatcher, he was delivering him*self*. To the commotion Libby was causing, but, really, to Libby.

She was going to be hungry.

We walked the last two blocks.

"You going to . . . you know?" I asked. I was ready to keep up with his pants when he shifted. They were his only pair.

"This is town," he said like an answer.

"For her too," I told him.

The first dog we walked onto was dying. Its guts were trailing behind it for maybe three feet.

"Worth it?" Darren said to the dog, and shook his head, impressed.

I looked back to the dog, its tongue hanging out on the concrete. There were already ants crawling in and out its mouth. I'd thought they only came out in the daytime. But maybe there are night ants. Maybe it's that nobody ever sees them.

The next dog was a St. Bernard. Its head was in the gutter, its body on somebody's stoop.

"They're rescue dogs, aren't they?" Darren said, squatting down to stare into the dog's face. He picked it up to look into it better. "Rescue thyself," he said, walking on, his fingers curled in the top hair of the St. Bernard's head. He looked like a kid going trick-or-treating, his spooky Halloween bag swinging by his leg.

He lobbed the shaggy head up onto a roof thirty yards down. The house's porch light came on. We didn't step around it to hide from whoever'd turned it on, just walked right through it, daring them to say something.

"She's right, you know," Darren said. "About my hand."

He held up his index finger like it was glowing with silver.

"That you can't keep it?" I asked.

"Her—remember Red, from back when? He used to melt silverware, pour it onto his skin just to watch the smoke."

"Red," I said up. It was the first time I'd said his name in years.

"Good riddance," Darren said.

"Grandpa said werewolves mate for life," I said.

"May be," Darren said. "Doesn't mean they have to like it, though. This is better for her anyway, probably."

"This?" I said.

We were walking into the outer edge of a milling crowd.

Because people are sheep and know it, they parted, let us approach the barrier.

It wasn't one dogcatcher, it was all of them—including Denton, going by the jackets.

In the middle, in swirling flashes of fur, was what had to be some kind of dire wolf, to them, except with longer front legs, and taller ears, worse eyes, less hair. Fingers where there should have been toes. I couldn't see her all at once, though. Too many dogcatchers. Too many dead dogs.

If she would just be still, just stop spinning, stop snapping at the giant of a mastiff-Rott behind her, trying to climb over her. No, not just behind her, *hooked* to her. Hooked *into* her.

"She's in heat," I said, just out loud.

"Big-ass *man* of a dog," Darren said, and flinched away just as water sprayed our whole part of the crowd.

Somebody'd spun the cap off a fire hydrant. To throw a bucket onto these two lovers.

It barely got them but was hitting us full force, knocking us all back, letting me see even less of Libby, who was always shy about being wolfed out, always tried to hide it—the same way

Darren had triggered her to change when they were ten, maybe she thought seeing her would trigger me.

It made me lean in farther, fight for a line of sight.

Two of the dogcatchers used the distraction of the gouting water to slip their metal nooses around Libby's neck, and pull opposite directions.

She came alive in a new way, curling around farther than her spine should have allowed. Just for a flash I tried to take a mental snapshot of, I saw her through the mist, biting behind her, her black lips pulled back from her flashing white teeth, her eyes burning a hole through that massive Rott.

This time she hooked a mouthful of his right foreleg, and then the water closed over them again.

A few moments later, that right leg and its shoulder and half of the rib cage came clumping out.

Five seconds later, the Rott's limp body flung the other way, taking a kid out at the stomach.

"No!" Darren yelled, stepping forward, wiping the stinging water from his eyes, but it was too late: One of the dogcatchers had a hot shot, was holding it like a stubby spear, even though underhand is the way to use them, because everything's belly skin is thinner, more conductive.

He applied it to Libby somewhere in that rush of water and she screamed, snapped at him, pulling her two noose-bearers to their knees before they even realized they needed to set their feet.

Then a town cop parted the crowd, stepped into the ring with a pistol. Not standard-issue either, but a full-on Dirty Harry hand cannon.

I was diving for his legs before I even realized I'd jumped. My right shoulder caught him perfect at the back of the knees and we rolled in the water and the grime of the street, and the pistol clattered away. I tracked its slide. I tracked it right into the square toe of Darren's truck-stop boot.

He squatted, picked the gun up, looked to the cop wrenching my arm around behind my back, my feet leaving the ground for it.

The world slowed down, was hardly moving.

Now Libby was lunging forward out of the water, for the cop. To protect me. To keep Darren from having to do it, like she had to know he was about to, damn the manhunt that would follow. The *wolf* hunt. She was going to make it too. She was going to chew through that cop, the dogcatchers, the bystanders, and not stop until all of Texas was in bloody clumps behind her.

At which point Darren did the last thing I would have guessed in ten thousand lifetimes.

He angled the pistol over to Libby, shot her.

Three hours later we walked away from the burbling flood the street was—*walked*, not ran. We weren't in handcuffs anymore.

Darren had explained that that overgrown Rott had been mine. Clint Eastwood was his name. I had been mad with grief. I knew better than to ever tackle the law.

And—and he was sorry for having discharged the weapon. But somebody had to.

It was a different Darren than I'd ever known.

We were sitting in the LeSabre before I said it: "You killed her."

"I wish," he said, twisting the ignition. "Pissed as she's going to be. Takes more than one slug to keep one of us down, man. Takes a *wall* of lead, serious. I've seen it. And sometimes even that's not enough. You can always get one more bite in. Remember that."

I stared at him.

"You shot her," I said.

"I saved her," he said. "Same as you were doing."

I was breathing deep now, the whole scene catching up with me.

We were supposed to report to the precinct in the morning. Because, bare-chested like we were, we were obviously just up from bed, didn't have our identification. They were going to officially commend Darren, they said.

It was so obviously a trap that we didn't even have to talk about it.

By dawn, we needed to be in Georgia, or South Carolina.

At the gas station on the corner we filled the LeSabre's radiator, then filled all four milk jugs in the trunk as well. And then we waited for what Darren knew was coming: a certain Animal Control van. We followed it in, gave them an hour to unload, decompress, tell their war stories. Tell themselves the war was over.

Because the LeSabre had more change in it than we thought we'd left from the last dig-through, we split a hot dog. It was one of the three best hot dogs ever eaten in the whole history of Texas. Because two of the quarters turned out being early sixties, still silver—Darren's infected hand was like silver radar, now—he'd let me carry them in, trade them for a hot dog.

I'd rubbed them hard between my thumb and finger, to see if they'd burn.

At five, dawn just starting to lighten the bottom edge of the sky, Darren stood from the car, looked back to me once, licked his lips and stepped forward, no shirt, no identification, no nothing.

I wasn't supposed to, but I followed.

We knocked until a tech came out, unlocked the door.

Darren explained how we were moving, how we were driving out *right now*, but we'd gotten a call about my black Lab mix, that we just needed to pick her up. It was now or never. By saying no, the tech was going to be serving that imaginary black Lab mix a death sentence. Was that what she wanted? To give it the pink juice like all the other rejects?

"Who called?" she said.

"Thought it was you," Darren said back.

She led us in, not liking it.

Because we were what we were, the dogs all exploded in their kennels, turned instantly into the living barking definition of bat-shit.

"I'm good with animals," Darren said to the tech.

Down at the end of a run, in the back corner, the one probably reserved for exotics, was Libby.

She'd shifted back since they'd deposited her here to die. She was naked, had pushed herself back into the corner, was trying to hide behind her hair. There was blood seeping from her left side, electric burns on her shoulders, and her eyes were haunted and mad and sorry and crying and, mostly, they were trying to look far enough away from this kennel that they could maybe take her with them.

"Yeah," Darren said. "That's her, right there."

"Ma'am, *ma'am*," the tech was saying, fumbling with her keys, "how did you get in there, what did—"

Darren guided the shaking key into the lock for her.

"You okay?" he said to Libby.

She stood, steadying herself on the wall.

"I don't want to be here," she said, and then the tech was there, acting as a crutch so Libby wouldn't fall over.

Together they walked through the short door, Libby having to duck.

When her eyes caught mine, she pursed her lips, had to look away.

"Here," Darren said, stepping in to support Libby.

"Your hair's going grey," Libby told him.

"Don't you dare tell me I look like him," Darren said.

"What do you think?" she said to me, and I nodded yes, yes yes yes, couldn't speak around the lump in my throat.

The tech beat us to the front desk, was trying to tell somebody on the phone what was happening.

Because mine was the free hand, I guided her handset back to its cradle, held it there.

"But, but—" the tech was saying, and in answer Darren held his swollen index finger up for her like a magic trick, inserted it all the way into his mouth, his teeth chocked as close to the knuckle as they'd go, then he widened his eyes out and slammed his chin with the heel of his hand.

He spit the still-curling finger out onto the counter.

"For your trouble," he said, winking a truly scary wink, and Libby pulled his new stump to her mouth to stop the bleeding, or for strength, and like that we left, me driving a car for the first time in my thirteen years, going the exact other way from the little white rent house, the lights of Texas falling away behind us.

"I'm sorry," Libby said, somewhere in all of it.

"Shoot, babydo—baby*face*," Darren said back to Libby. "Everybody goes to jail at some point, don't they?"

In the rearview mirror Libby blinked once to me, thank you.

I pushed the gas pedal of the LeSabre hard, stabbed us deeper into the night.

CHAPTER 6

Werewolves on the Moon

Call me 'Mom,'" the criminal's aunt tells him just before walking up the wide stairs, into his elementary school.

This is second grade for the second time, even though he's already nine. It's because Alabama needed school records to prove third grade, and Georgia knew the criminal by a different name.

"And we're not werewolves," she says back to him at the double doors, "we're not *anything*," and heats her eyes up so he knows this is important. Then she takes his hand in hers.

Mrs. Luc-Casey's classroom is all the way at the end of the hall. His aunt's heels click on the concrete floor. The janitor stops mopping for them to pass. His name is James Kent. He lives in a rhyme but doesn't know it. The criminal does. He sings it in his head as they pass by.

The reason he's a criminal is that he told the truth.

Mrs. Luc-Casey is waiting for them behind her desk.

She looks up when she gets to the bottom of a page, straightens her current stack of papers in that way she has like she's making a decision, then stands, meets the criminal's aunt halfway across the classroom.

"Mrs. Baden," she says.

It's the name for Alabama.

"Ms.," the criminal's aunt corrects, gently.

"Of course," Mrs. Luc-Casey says, and leads the three of them to the front row of the classroom.

The desks are too small for her and the criminal's aunt. They slide them out before sitting, so they can face each other.

"Sit," the criminal's aunt says to the criminal.

"Thank you for coming in," Mrs. Luc-Casey says, studying the criminal like the criminal he is.

"I always like to meet his teachers," the criminal's aunt says.

She hadn't prepared the criminal for this particular lie, but a good criminal knows when to keep quiet. When to just shuffle his sneakers, look anywhere else.

"Would he rather use the playground?" Mrs. Luc-Casey says to the criminal's aunt. "It's not quite dark yet, is it?"

"He needs to hear this as well," the criminal's aunt says.

"It's not uncommon," Mrs. Luc-Casey starts in. "Perhaps it's even commendable, or indicative of . . . of better things to come."

"Better things?" the criminal's aunt says.

"Imagination shouldn't be a handicap," Mrs. Luc-Casey says.

"Of course, of course," the criminal's aunt says.

"So long as there's clear division between the imaginary and— and where we all have to live, right?"

"Right?" the criminal's aunt passes on to the criminal.

He looks from face to face, being sure what they want to hear, then nods.

"So . . ." Mrs. Luc-Casey says, like her voice is shifting gears, "the assignment was two pages, front and back. 'What I want to be when I grow up.'"

"You know he's supposed to be in third grade?" the aunt asks. "We're just waiting for the paperwork to catch up to us."

"If I hold this to third-grade standards—" Mrs. Luc-Casey says, then cuts herself off: "No, if he's in second grade, I have to consider him a second grader. It's only fair. And I haven't seen anything to suggest—"

"I'm just saying if he messed up on the assignment, maybe it was because—"

"The assignment was to draw *pictures*," Mrs. Luc-Casey says.

The aunt looks to the criminal about this. "This is about not following instructions, then," she says.

The criminal tries to make himself smaller. More invisible.

"Not exactly," Mrs. Luc-Casey says. "It's . . . well. Most boys will default to their father's profession, see."

"That's not an issue for us," the criminal's aunt says.

"Which is of course where the imagination comes into play," Mrs. Luc-Casey says. "He had to make that profession up, as it were. I'm starting to understand."

"Surely he wasn't the only astronaut, was he?" the criminal's aunt asks, leaning her elbows onto her small desk. "You had firemen and policemen as well, didn't you?"

"He was the only one who went into such . . . *detail*," Mrs. Luc-Casey says, and slides the guilty piece of paper from her yellow folder.

The criminal's aunt looks over to him and takes the evidence into her own lap.

She studies it for nearly as long as it had taken to draw them, and then flips it over for the rest of the story.

The front side is the criminal on the surface of the moon. You can tell it's the moon because it has craters, and because of the stars all around, and it's because it's only a quarter full, a sliver of itself leaned back in the sky. The criminal's rocket is parked in the background.

What's happening is one of the other astronauts is running up the steep top of the bowl, trying to reach the point so he can climb over, jump back to Earth.

Chasing behind him is the criminal, being what he's going to be when he grows up.

On the back side of the page, the one he'd had to hurry to finish, so had just red-crayoned over everything because blood floats in space, he's *caught* that other astronaut in his long jaws, is ripping at his stomach and somehow howling at the same time. The howl is letters filling the sky. Mostly the letter *O*, in a kind of kite-tail ribbon.

At first, when Mrs. Luc-Casey had sent the note home, the criminal thought the mistake was that he'd drawn another moon above, to howl at. It's hard to remember every single thing.

"Well," his aunt says, and folds the drawings into her purse before Mrs. Luc-Casey can get them back. "I can assure you this won't be happening again."

"Does he—did his father hunt?" Mrs. Luc-Casey asks. "Sometimes children who come from that culture will—"

"His father is out of the picture," the criminal's aunt says for the *third* time, her lips tighter.

"And it's not that I don't appreciate the *humor* of it," Mrs. Luc-Casey says, sitting back but keeping the aunt in her teacher-stare. "If werewolves were real, then of course putting one on the moon would have disastrous effects."

The criminal and his aunt are walking across the room by now.

The aunt stops them, has to close her eyes.

Only the criminal sees this.

It makes him hold on to her hand harder.

"I'm sorry," he says.

His aunt looks down to him, her eyes starting to fade to yellow, and she gives his hand a squeeze, then turns back to Mrs. Luc-Casey, her face so pleasant, so ready. So public.

"If werewolves *were* real, Mrs. Luc-Casey," the criminal's aunt says, giving her words teeth, "then they would know better than to go to the moon, don't you think? They wouldn't have lived this long otherwise, would they have?"

It's exactly what the criminal's real mom would have said.

"If they were real . . ." Mrs. Luc-Casey repeats, studying the criminal's aunt for the first time, it seems. How much taller she is than a fourth-grade teacher. How empty the school is at this hour. And were her eyes like that before?

"Thank you," the criminal's aunt says, and ushers the criminal out the door.

The clicking of her heels fills the hall.

It's dark outside, now. It's always getting dark in werewolf stories.

And the floor is still wet in the exact same place.

Stepping through it, the criminal's aunt stops, her nostrils flared, and looks over with just her eyes to the janitor, watching her as well without quite looking up.

He's wearing a scented paper pine tree from his neck like he's a car.

But he isn't a car.

He's more.

The criminal's aunt nods once to him and the janitor takes that nod like the best gift ever, looks back to his mopping.

Two miles down the road the criminal clicks his seat belt off,

lets it reel up, then pulls it across his chest again, pushes it shut
without pinching his hand like usually happens.

"Was he——?" he asks, afraid to say it because they're still so
close to school. "Was he a——?"

In reply his aunt looks up into the rearview mirror, like the
criminal is supposed to look there too.

He unclicks his seat belt again, turns around to look behind
them.

Pacing them on the other side of the fence is a shadow. It's running on all fours, going faster and faster, having to pump its head
with the effort of keeping up.

The speed limit here is fifty-five.

"Faster," the criminal whispers, and his aunt does it for him
like a secret, smiling, both hands on the wheel.

When the shadow on the other side of the fence jumps a dry
creek, something from that shadow's neck floats up into the air
above him and hangs for a snapshot of an instant.

A pine tree.

Because gravity isn't the same for astronauts.

Nothing is.

CHAPTER 7

The Lone Ranger

The only fight I ever saw Darren lose was in the daytime in Hattiesburg, Mississippi, by an ice cooler at the gas station. The ice cooler had a polar bear on it. I was thirteen.

I was holding my hot dog and, now, Darren's six-pack of strawberry wine coolers. The wine coolers weren't why the fight was happening. The wine coolers were all still in their cardboard carrier, for one. For two, the guy Darren was fighting never even saw them, and probably wouldn't have said anything about them if he had.

This fight was all Darren's doing.

Or, it was his werewolf blood's doing, anyway.

Part of being deathly allergic to silver is a deep-seated hatred of the Lone Ranger. According to Darren, he was the first werewolf hunter. It's how he made his name. "But, see how he always wears *gloves*?" Darren would say, pleading his case.

"Sure?" I said the first time he took me through it.

"It's because he can't touch his own bullets!" Darren said. "And you never see him at night, do you? Why is that, do you think?"

I shook my head no, that this was too far, too much.

Darren nodded his head yes. Yes yes yes.

You never saw him at night for the obvious reason that he was out running through campfires, because he was out barking at the moon.

For that last gasp of the Old West, when trains and horses were both there at once, and hand-crank movie cameras too, the Lone Ranger was a werewolf, and the worst kind: a self-hating one. A werewolf who hunted down other werewolves. A werewolf too weak to just start with himself.

So when Darren saw the linebacker walking into the gas station he was just walking out of, and that linebacker had a shiny-black domino mask *painted* on his face for some football game, Darren tried to pretend this hadn't just happened.

That lasted for about three steps. Three of my hot-dog-chewing steps, anyway.

Darren was standing still, I think. Telling himself not to.

But then he did.

He slapped the wine coolers into my chest like a newspaper he was done with and reached back to catch this big Lone Ranger by the shoulder, spin him around, make him answer for his many and serious crimes.

"Watch this," he said, smiling what I know he thought of as his wolf smile, and I did watch. All of it.

This Lone Ranger might have been a linebacker, but he was a scrapper too, and maybe some breed of cage fighter as well.

Darren tagged him with the first punch out of nowhere, but that was just hello, as it turned out.

Over and over, this Lone Ranger finished the conversation.

The problem was, Darren had gone up against black bear boars and momma cougars and bull alligators and wild hogs, just to prove he could, and he'd tore his way through cops and were-wolves and ex-husbands because he had to, but that was all when he had sharp teeth, and claws.

On all fours, you couldn't take Darren down without a truck rolling at seventy, and even then he'd crawl up out of the tall grass of the ditch for round two.

In town, though, in the *city*, on the front stoop of a gas station in the daytime, it was a different story. A worse story.

His balled-up fists weren't as hard as fists are in the movies. There wasn't that same two-by-four *crack* when they landed. Even when this Lone Ranger was sitting across Darren's chest, pummel-ing his face, it sounded more like meat slapping meat than it did a movie punch.

"Enough?" this linebacker Lone Ranger said to Darren after a couple minutes of it, and Darren—I could see him do this, I could see it happening—he looked up through the blood and the haze and saw that oily black domino mask looking back at him across history, looking down at him from the sky, where it had been mounted.

Darren shook his head no, tried to spit through his torn lips, and then there were more meat sounds. Less tender meat sounds.

Afterward I dragged Darren around the corner of the gas sta-tion and stole one of the ten-pound bags of ice for him. He was propped against the cinderblock wall in exactly the same ragdoll pose as the polar bear on the side of the ice cooler.

I twisted the cap off one of his wine coolers, folded his fingers around it, guided his hand to his mouth. His effort to drink bloomed a swallow of deeper red back into the bottle, and then he drank that too. It was like the tank part of a hypodermic getting plunged, flushed, injected.

"Your—your hot dog," he said when he could, because it was gone.

"I ate it."

Of all the lies I've told, this is the one I always come back to, to listen to again. To watch. It's the only one that's ever really been perfect, the only one I didn't have to hesitate before saying.

From where we were sitting the rest of the afternoon, we could hear the crowd at the football game, their cheers swelling and falling, cresting and crashing.

"Hope they lose," Darren said, and toasted his wine cooler that direction.

"Me too," I said, and arranged the blanket I'd found over his legs, so he'd stop shivering.

Because my smell was still normal, wouldn't cause a panic, Darren and Libby sent me into the pet store for the rabbit.

It was supposed to be a juicy one. A fat one with floppy ears, a soft throat.

It wasn't for them.

Darren said he would have got it himself, damn the racket, but his face still looked like Frankenstein, and the stump finger of his right hand was a terror to little kids.

Libby tried to fake like she was amused.

What she wasn't saying was that, if her or Darren stepped one foot inside that pet store, it would be a riot. The cats would bite the dogs, the dogs thrash through the fish tanks, and the birds would end up flapping all around everywhere, screaming about the end of the world.

Because animals know the smell.

The reason I was the one going in was that I didn't have it yet.

Libby'd humored me, leaning in, her nose snuffling right at my throat in a way that made me feel weird.

I stood fast from the car, fourteen dollars in singles wadded in my hand.

"Just one?" I said.

"One's enough," she said.

Mississippi wasn't the bull's-eye we were aiming for, slipping east out of Texas in the nighttime—the plan was to push until the Bonneville we'd picked up in Louisiana cried mercy, then look for work—but Hattiesburg was the home of an old friend of Libby's.

The way she said "old friend," I could tell there was a different, better term hiding under there. One she didn't have to say aloud to Darren.

I knew she didn't have any friends, anyway.

The rabbit was a gift, she said. An offering.

I pushed the door of the pet store open, sure at least one of the dogs in their cages would know me for what I was.

Instead, the pet-store clerk did.

The same way animals and cops know werewolves, so do security guards and salespeople and clerks. If you asked them why, they might not say "werewolves," would probably just shrug, say there's something shady about us, isn't there? Something that says keep this one on camera, keep this one in the mirror. Don't let him go into the dressing room without offering to count his items first. Tell him the bathroom's out of order. Watch that bag he's carrying. Keep an eye on the bulge of his pockets.

What it made me want to do was stuff iguanas and hamsters and canaries down the front of my pants, try to wriggle and bluff my way out the front door.

With this particular clerk, there was an immediate sadness to his eyes. It was that I was wearing a shirt, and shoes. That he was going to have to go to the effort of manufacturing some excuse to usher me out.

I did what I'd seen Darren do: flashed my fold of bills, assuring the clerk I was here for a cash transaction.

He still watched me.

Werewolves can feel that kind of constant attention. It's a special radar we're born with, that gets more and more sensitive every year.

"You old enough to buy one of those?" the clerk asked, suddenly close enough to look over my shoulder into the rabbit bin, far enough to not have to touch my back with his chest.

"How old do you have to be?" I said back.

He didn't answer.

There were all-size rabbits in the bin. All kinds and ages mixed together, like a survival test, a proving ground.

I reached down, pushed one hand flat onto the straw bedding so I could lift the fattest rabbit up by the ears. It was like unplanting a carrot.

The rabbit pedaled at the air sluggishly with its snowshoe feet.

The clerk looked at me about this one.

"You probably want a younger one," he said. "If you're looking to breed."

"A her or a him?" I asked, trying to see between the furry legs.

"He's a buck," the clerk said.

"I just want a pet," I told him, unprompted. "Not a dad."

"Do you have supplies?" the clerk said.

This was how he'd been taught to separate the dinner-plate crowd from the animal lovers.

Werewolves are both, of course.

"My last one just died," I said, or heard myself saying. "His name was Tolbert."

"Tolbert," the clerk said, collecting the rabbit from me. Cupping it under the front legs, supporting it by the rump.

"It's an elf from a book I used to read," I lied.

"Tolbert the Elf," the clerk said, making his way back to the counter, the rabbit held up to the hollow of his chest, so its nose would be right at the side of his neck.

That's not how you carry a rabbit.

They've got teeth too.

I followed him to the register, running my hand along the top shelf, finger-jumping the price-tag holders.

I straightened my fourteen dollars out on the counter.

It was just enough, the way the clerk rung it up. In spite of the thirty-dollar price tag on the rabbit bin.

He wanted me out of his store, and was willing to pay half a rabbit to get it done.

I didn't thank him.

"Do you want to know his name?" he asked, pushing the rabbit across the counter.

"Tolbert," I said, picking the rabbit up the same way he had, under the front legs. "They're all Tolbert."

"Lawrence," the clerk said, his voice flat with disappointment, and I left.

Libby passed a paper sack up from the window of the car for the rabbit, because it was already screaming and thrashing. It knew where it was going.

I finally had to just put it in the cavernous trunk of the Bonneville, under a winter coat. Then I settled into the backseat.

"So?" Darren asked, looking at me in his vanity mirror.

Because his face would attract cops, Libby was driving.

What he was asking was what did I steal. It's what he always asked. Because, if that's what the clerks are expecting, that's what the clerks'll get.

I passed the baby rabbit ahead to him.

It had been so easy, such an obvious grab with my off-hand, the one I was using to push against, to haul the distraction of the *big* rabbit up.

If the baby rabbit had been a mouse, which it practically was, it would have crawled out of my pocket, sky-dived for the floor, scurried away to lick its broken foot and be cat food.

The baby rabbit was too young to fight my pocket, though. Too young to know.

Darren took it, held it in his hand like half a burrito, and looked it in the eye.

"What do you call baby ones?" I said.

Not kit, not cub, not joey or pup or fawn.

"Tasty," Darren said, and bit in.

Libby knew the way to a motel that took cash.

"Been eight years," Darren said. "Think it's still there?"

"It'll be there," Libby said.

"Who is it?" I said from the backseat. "Some cousin I don't know?"

Darren sneaked a look over to Libby, like saying he could get this but checking if that was all right.

"*Kind* of a cousin," he said, and wiped the bright red blood from his lips, caught the way Libby had speared him with her eyes. "More just a . . . an old acquaintance."

I couldn't tell if the blood was the baby rabbit's or if his face was seeping again, from the Lone Ranger.

I'd never seen someone cry red before.

His pee was no better.

Libby hauled our wounded Bonneville around a corner. It was wounded and cockeyed because, when Darren had been driving us out of Alabama two nights ago, he'd eased over onto the shoulder, tagged a calf just enough to shatter its pelvis, leave it pulling itself around in slower and slower circles in our taillights.

You could do that between places, sometimes. All the rancher would find would be a coyote-scavenged calfsicle in the ditch if it was winter, a pile of bird-coated red smear if it was summer.

Libby hadn't eaten.

It was because of this, because of coming to Hattiesburg. She'd been quiet ever since she announced we were stopping here if it worked out. Now she was starving herself too.

It was why Darren and me had left her at the motel, gone to the gas station alone. She needed room to think, Darren had told me. Someday I'd understand. "Hopefully not, I mean," he added, but then shrugged like I would, someday, have to understand.

"Just tell me already," I told him.

Darren stretched his arms back, popping his chest like he could, like what he had for a sternum was a bone zipper, and did his gunfighter eyes across all the vacant islands of the gas station.

Then he came back to me, like gauging was I old enough.

"You remember that story your grandpa used to tell," he said, "about having to go into Little Rock that time?"

It was a war story.

Darren had just been a pup then, too young to make the trip. Too young to carry a rifle, anyway.

This had been a job for men, the way my grandfather told it. Not wolves.

What had happened was a werewolf had tore into somebody,

and then not finished it. Grandpa spat after he said it, just thinking of the idea of doing that.

It wasn't about mercy or sportsmanship, like it is with deer hunters. It's about self-preservation. It's about protecting the species.

You put an arrow through a deer's gut and it runs off into the twilight, all that happens is that deer probably dies alone out there, panting its last breaths into the leaf litter, the coyotes already tying their bibs on.

Or, if the territory's right, one of us will be circling downwind for a good pull of air, to be sure.

Hunter-shot deer tastes just as good as anything you run down yourself.

You bite some punk, though, tear away a bite of meat and keep on running down the road, then there's a chance that punk's caught the blood, is going to start experiencing strange urges, going to start growing hair he's not expecting, is going to start staying out later and later. It's like a second puberty, only, the adult that comes out of this one has teeth, and is a bitch to put down.

I've never seen one, but these man-wolves, these moondogs, they're what the movies are based on. They can't go the full distance, can't transform like you can if you were born into it, but they can get half the way there, anyway. The claws, too much hair, the ears and the snout. The teeth. Their body, it's trying to fight the blood, to keep it down. But the moon, it sings that blood up to the surface like a tide.

Since they're not born into it, the transformation, it's like being killed for hours. It's like they're trying to shift between granny gear and second, but are getting ground up between the whole time. Chewed up from the inside. So then they try to chew the world up, the same way a dog with rabies bites just because it feels good, because the world is pain. Might as well spread it around.

Darren can shift in the time it takes a spilled can of coke to empty all the way out, and come out with most of himself still locked between those new ears. It hurts enough to leave him with a definite edge, and there's the smell, there's a thousand instant tastes and smells and sounds to try to corral, and there's the hunger to deal with, the mouthful of saliva to help ease the new teeth into place, but it's all doable. Or, it's all worth it, anyway.

These half wolves, though, the man-wolves of the movies, the shift takes them hours, and the searing, dragged-out pain of it, all their bones breaking and re-forming, trying the whole time to stay human, the hundreds of hairs forcing their way out, pores or not, the sharp teeth stabbing through a mouth not fitted for them, the bone structure of their skull creaking and cracking, pressing their brain into flashes and seizures, tapping open memories buried for a reason, it erases who they used to be completely, so that only the animal remains. They're lumbering around on two feet, now, but they're all wolf.

Worse, shifting for hours, it leaves them even more blind with hunger than a real werewolf is after the change.

All they know is eating. If they don't, they keel over, they die.

It's easy to see this is where the legends come from.

They're monsters, sure. But you feel sorry for them at the same time. They don't know any better. And they didn't ask for this.

All they want is to live, and to live they have to eat, and because they've probably gone wolf in their own bedroom, the first meat they go after is their own family.

So, killing your kill all the way, it's not about mercy, no. It's about responsibility.

Grandpa's war story, it's that some twenty years ago in Little

Rock, Arkansas, some werewolf had forgotten his or her duty. Either that or some werewolf had fallen hard for a human—happens all the time, Darren said, had happened with Grandpa and Grandma—so was trying to bring her or him over to the blood instead of just throwing some pups with her then walking away.

It's never worked even once, though, bringing somebody over to the werewolf side of things. With a werewolf, loving and killing, they're the same act.

That's the curse part of this life. It's why Darren was never going to settle down, he said. Because it's murder, basically.

"What if you marry one like you?" I'd asked him once.

"I'm one of a kind," he'd said back, tipping his wine cooler like toasting himself.

"A werewolf, I mean. It's got to happen, doesn't it?"

"Too much blood," Libby cut in. Darren shrugged it true.

The way they explained it, tag-teaming because the facts were so ugly, the wolf blood was strong enough that, if every grown werewolf is *half* full of it—half man, half wolf—and they throw pups with some human, then that kid should just be a quarter wolf, right? Wrong. Because the wolf blood, it's hungry. Even a quarter is enough to really be half. That's just the way it is. But if a werewolf and a werewolf try to start a family, well. The pups live, but they never shift up to two legs. Being born half full of wolf blood, it's like being nearly all the way wolf. There's not enough man in there to rise.

"So we're parasites?" I'd said. "We can only breed in hosts of a different species?"

"Look who's a scientist now," Darren said back.

It had been his favorite dig lately, making fun of the classes I was taking, the books I was reading—"Like werewolves need algebra to know which way the wind's blowing?"

I just took it.

Getting called a bookwolf, it meant I wasn't a worm, anyway.

The gist of their explanation, though, the place where Grandpa's Little Rock war story started, it was that anybody stupid enough to try to bring someone across, into the blood, that would have to be some lone wolf, operating on his or her own. To be that blind. That in love.

Not that how it happened changed *what* was happening.

There was one of these man-wolves ravaging its way through the suburbs of Little Rock, making the tabloids, but, instead of chewing through all the dogs, it was impregnating them.

It can happen.

Libby and Darren didn't like to talk about it, but we're enough like a dog for it to happen. And so are the man-wolves. Only, the little hybrids that wake up in that momma dog's belly, they grow too fast, they chew their way out in two weeks.

The ones that live through that, they're seriously dangerous, are faster than us, even. According to Darren, they're kind of like starved-down, wrong-shaped coyotes. Bald coyotes. Burn-victim coyotes. Tails-tucked-under coyotes. Darren said that Grandpa's name for them was Sad Eyes, but I'd always thought he heard wrong. They're supposed to have these human-looking eyes, but "Sad Eyes" feels like a corruption of something Arabic. Like they've known these animals over there as well. If they even are animals. Thing is, they're too smart. They're not rabid-in-the-head like their fathers, anyway. They're distinct, they're their own thing, they can throw litters and everything. And if you don't wipe them all out down to the last hidden baby, then they'll infest a whole county, leave the nighttime flashing with teeth.

Grandpa's war story is of him and a buddy cruising the streets of Little Rock, Arkansas, each of them with rifles they're so careful not to angle down even at their own feet, because it's not about where you get shot with silver, it's *that* you get shot.

The man-wolf was easy to find, of course. Moondogs always are. They don't know to hide.

Grandpa pops him the first night, then drags him to a culvert until the thing's snout can lower back down into its face, and when the wolf doesn't leave it all the way human, they use a cinderblock to hide the evidence.

The babies are another matter.

My grandfather and his buddy are gone for five weeks, the way he told it. Setting bait and popping Sad Eyes after Sad Eyes between the ears. Just with normal bullets. Silver doesn't matter with them. That's how removed they are from us.

According to Darren, to show him and Libby and my mom, to teach them a lesson they needed to learn, he'd brought a just-born one back in a cardboard box.

Its eyes hadn't even been open yet, and its skull had been pinched together like you do when you kick into a litter of them. It gave Libby and Darren and my mom nightmares for months.

"I should have known better than to look," Darren said, settling in behind the wheel of the Bonneville, the tank sloshing with regular because the alcohol in unleaded would vapor-lock the carburetor.

"How many toes did it have?" I asked.

Darren looked over to me, said like he was just now figuring it out all over again, "You *are* a scientist, aren't you?"

"Dogs have four," I said, and then held up my own hand, fingers spread, to show we had five.

"Really?" he said, and held up his right hand, complete with the finger stump that hadn't grown over right.

The whole way back to the motel to get Libby, he kept himself leaned over onto the wheel, as if he were driving us into a storm.

I think he was.

It wasn't a cousin Libby was going to visit.

It was someone she'd bit.

Darren was just like Grandpa, telling me one story, meaning another.

Libby'd left a moondog behind. She'd been coming to Mississippi to see it for years.

When she stepped out the hotel door, her hair was blowing across her face. She slung the mass of it away to clear her eyes, thread her sunglasses on, and I wish I hadn't been watching her so close.

"Remember when you used to think werewolves couldn't cry?" Darren said.

"I never thought that," I said.

In that half second before her sunglasses were in place, we'd both seen her eyes. How she wasn't crying. Not anymore. Now her lips were firm, just a straight line. And now her eyes were hidden.

I didn't want to go with her anymore.

Not for this.

We were all three so nervous about going into the huge hospital that we forgot the rabbit.

In the lobby waiting for the elevator, I said it aloud, what had to be true: "It wasn't just any—*any* werewolf in Little Rock that time, was it?"

Because all of my grandfather's stories were apologies.

I hadn't forgotten this.

"Everybody makes mistakes," Darren said.

Meaning that man-wolf, it hadn't been some lone wolf's failed romance. It had been *Grandpa's* partial kill. He'd been cleaning his *own* mess up, not playing hero for a whole species. Meaning that that Sad Eyes he lugged home in the cardboard box, its skull pinched together, its front paws tucked under its stubby muzzle, that had been, by blood anyway, Libby and Darren and my mom's baby brother or baby sister.

This is what it means to be a werewolf.

"There didn't used to be that desk there," Libby said, studying the information counter, then she turned to Darren: "You get it?"

Darren patted his pockets like for a pack of cigarettes, then made a show of looking out to the parking lot, to the idea of the rabbit.

"Seventh floor," she said, lobbing him the Bonneville key.

"We're splitting up," I narrated to Libby in the elevator.

"So?" she said.

"Nothing," I told her. Because the answer would have been movies, and I wasn't supposed to be watching them.

The seventh floor on the east side was the coma ward.

"You," a nurse behind the desk said.

"Me," Libby said, and signed her name on a clipboard. "My brother's coming up too. He looks just like me."

"He'll have to sign himself," the nurse said.

I signed my name—the last name that matched the one Libby had used—and followed her down the antiseptic hall, planted in a waiting room chair beside her.

The television was on like they always are, so you can have somewhere else to look. Something to lose yourself in.

Because we were the only ones there, we could hear it for once. It was an unsolved-mysteries episode. We caught the spooky-voiced end of a tornado segment about a kidnapped girl, then, after the commercial, it was the firsthand account of how Bigfoot had robbed a liquor store in Arkansas eight or nine years ago. The spooky voice had some joke to it, now, like this was an intermission, after the seriousness of the missing girl. Like this was the joke part of the program.

The woman recounting the story of the robbery was dragging on a cigarette every three words, and was careful to keep to the side, so the front of her liquor store was over her shoulder. There was a carved wooden Bigfoot by the front door, the wood still raw. It was holding the carved shape of a pistol, pointing it into the stomach of anybody standing in front of it.

According to the spooky, amused voice, the case was still open, pending evidence. Pending explanation. If anybody had information concerning these daring heists, there was a toll-free number to call. Then they flashed the dates.

They matched the year Grandpa died. The year Darren had come home to stand between Red and Libby. They matched a black plastic trash bag on the kitchen table, stuffed with loose cash and strawberry wine coolers.

I wanted to see that Bigfoot statue one more time. Most werewolves don't get statues.

The segment ended with a photograph of a state trooper who had been killed trying to stop a liquor-store robbery he'd stumbled onto. Whether it was related or not was uncertain.

"Wrong place, wrong time," I said.

"Don't tell him," Libby said, reading my mind, and jerked her head over when the elevator down the hall dinged. "It wouldn't make us do anything different. Not one single thing. Except he'd think he was famous. He'd think they wanted him to keep doing that."

"He is famous," I said.

She just stared at me until I nodded okay, sure.

After the theatrics necessary for Darren to both smuggle a large domestic rabbit into a coma ward *and* lean over to sign a name on a clipboard, we led him down to room 77, on the seventh floor.

"My burger, it's alive!" Darren playacted, holding the paper bag up. The rabbit was kicking in there. I don't know how he'd made its mouth be quiet. Tape, I would guess. Or staples, the stapler borrowed from the information desk downstairs. He'd have had to have gone into the bathroom with that stapler, though. It would have been complicated.

"Ready?" Libby said to him.

"Ready," Darren said, then, to me: "You can wait out here, you want. I won't think less of you. I mean, I don't see how I *could*, but—"

"He should see," Libby said, and pushed the door open. "He's old enough."

She was trying to inoculate me, I knew. She was trying to teach me to always kill my kills all the way. If I ever even got teeth.

It was making me forget how to breathe normal.

"Party of three," Darren said, the brown paper bag hugged to his chest, "seating now . . ."

Once we were all in, Libby pointed to the door for me.

I wedged a chair under the knob, locked us in there.

His name was Morris Wexler. There were some wilted flowers on his nightstand. The nurses were probably supposed to keep them watered. They were busy enough keeping the patients watered, I supposed. And, in this ward, the families came less and less, I'd imagine.

The front of Morris Wexler's throat was a mass of scar tissue.

It made me look at Libby's mouth in a different way.

"I thought he was dead," she said, in explanation.

"He *was* dead, Lib," Darren said.

"Who was he?" I said.

"It was right after Red, the first time," Libby said. "I wasn't—wasn't thinking right."

She was standing at the window. Looking away from Morris Wexler. And crying again, I was pretty sure. Not her usual kind. Quieter. Like the sadness was just leaking from her face.

"Shhh," Darren said into the top of the bag.

In return, a rabbit foot kicked through the side.

Darren cupped it. He only had two hands, though.

"Better make it fast," he said to Libby.

"We dated," Libby said to me. *For* me. "Nothing serious."

When she said it, I saw her then. And seeing her at eighteen was seeing my mom, getting to have done that: dated.

But she must have.

Here I was, right?

"Tell the rest," Darren said, more serious now.

"He was—it wasn't his fault," Libby said.

"He beat her up," Darren said, staring straight at Morris Wexler. "He used her as a punching bag just like Red always did, so she paid him a certain kind of visit. Right, Lib?"

At the window, Libby snuffled.

"He was dead when I left that room," she said.

"The paramedics brought him back," I said, figuring it out.

She raised the back of her hand to her nose.

One thing werewolves had never been anticipating, it was CPR.

There's all the stories about taking the head off a werewolf to finally kill it. Which would work, sure. If you could catch it. If it didn't kill you first, ten times over.

Whose head should really be pulled off, it's the werewolf's *victims'*. Just to be sure.

But not this time.

Ten years ago, some hero paramedic had got Morris Wexler's heart going again. Had sewn his throat shut. Had stuffed his intestines back inside his gut.

"Here," Libby said then, and bustled across the hospital room like she'd aged twenty years since walking in.

Darren lifted the rabbit from the bag.

It had had its snout forced into a bent-open, emptied-out Bonneville Brougham factory key ring. Doing that had broken some of the thin bones there, which was making its eyes bleed. But it was still alive. Alive enough. Libby threaded the key ring back out.

"Don't watch," she said when the rabbit's mouth was free, but I did.

She held the rabbit's hairless belly up to her mouth and ripped. With her flat *human* teeth.

They worked.

She let the blood sprinkle onto Morris Wexler's lips.

And then some more.

"What——?" I said.

Darren planted his hand in my chest, held me back.

Now I saw. Now I could see. Morris Wexler, he was shifting. Bit by bit, his snout was lengthening. He was going wolf.

The man was in a coma, but the wolf was locked in there too.

That's who Libby was here for.

When the mouth was big enough, Libby dropped the rabbit

onto Morris's chest. So fast that I flinched, his clawed hands were on it, forcing it up to his mouth. The rabbit was gone, bones and all, in under a minute.

The wolf, though, he remained. Just dead eyes staring straight up.

"I'm sorry," Libby said, openly crying now.

Darren moved over, hooked an arm around her.

I was still staring at Morris Wexler.

I kept swallowing, the sound loud in my ears.

Eventually Libby reached out, pulled me to them, and after a few more minutes, Morris Wexler was Morris Wexler again.

Libby cleaned him as best she could. Because his gown was a lost cause, she changed him, using one from his cabinet. That's probably why the nurse down the hall had remembered Libby: Seeing her meant one missing gown. When Libby didn't bother shutting the cabinet back, I caught the door, looked inside. On the top shelf by the folded sheets were all the pictures Morris Wexler's family probably left out for him. All the pictures the nurses didn't like having to dust, so just stored.

One was, I would guess, from ten years ago.

It was him with a certain dark-haired girl. Libby. She was standing beside him, her hand to his chest, neither of her eyes swollen up right then. She was just happy.

My face heated up, looking at her, seeing an aunt I'd never known, a Libby who smiled without having to think about it, and it made me have to run to the door, scrabble the chair away, fall out into the hall and run and run and run.

Where Darren finally found me was out by the pond. Ducks were having panic attacks all around us. Ducks know.

"Think we're ready to split, if you are," he said. Both his hands were in his pants pockets. It made his shoulders more innocent.

That's just another way of saying still guilty, though.

I wasn't even crying. Not on the outside.

"She looked just like her, didn't she?" I said. "In that picture. She looked like my mom. Like she would have."

I looked up to Darren and his mouth opened like to say something, but he lost it.

"I'm the exact same age she was when I killed her," I said, having to stretch my throat out to keep from crying hard like my whole body wanted to.

Darren mistook that, though.

"Let me see your tongue," he said, stepping in, leading with his dry, pushy fingers at my lips. "It might be happening."

I pushed him away as hard as I could, hard enough that his back foot planted in the edge of the pond and sank in.

Behind him all the ducks made their racket, whirred their wings, exploded up into the sky.

"These are my good boots," he said, trying to extract his leg before the water sloshed over the top.

"They're your only boots," I said, my voice mean and hard and as unforgiving as I could get it.

"Exactly," he said, and when he took the hand I was offering, instead of using me as anchor, he jerked, left me teetering.

It was either plant my hands in his chest and push, or go in myself.

I pushed.

Darren had to step back farther, both his feet in the muck now.

"Perfect," he said.

"Tell me," I said.

He looked up to me like checking was I serious. I was.

"They're twins," he said. "What do you think? Of course they looked the same."

It made my breath hitch in my chest.

My mom, smiling like that. Her hair blowing all around her face. Her open hand on her boyfriend's chest. On my father's chest.

Darren stepped up from the pond as easy as anything. He didn't care about his boots. No werewolf's ever cared about a stupid pair of boots.

"I miss her too, man," he said.

"I never even *knew* her!" I said, pulling my shoulder away from him.

"Every time I look at you, man," he said. "The way you do your eyes—"

"Just shut up," I told him, aiming away from him now.

He kept pace, his footsteps squelching with water, his hands in his pockets again.

I just wanted to be alone. So I said the worst thing I could come up with: "I know why you hate the Lone Ranger."

"What?" he said, some real hesitation in his voice for once. And on his face.

"Because *Grandpa* was the Lone Ranger," I said. "In Little Rock that time. With the silver bullets. Shooting all his other kids. It made you think he might shoot you someday."

He didn't say yes and he didn't say no. But he did fall a step behind.

I kicked ahead without him. But then I slowed, looked back.

He was just standing there, his shoulders rounder than usual. It made me realize that he wasn't a giant. I was almost as tall as him already.

And, the way I did my eyes—it didn't have anything to do with my mom. I'd modeled it on him. Practiced in the mirror and everything.

But I appreciated the lie.

"Still parked in the same place?" I said, like agreeing I'd forget I'd said that about Grandpa if he would.

He looked past me to the parking lot, to the idea of the Bonneville.

We went there, more space between us than usual.

"It's like walking through goldfish," he said, his steps sloshy.

"It's not like walking through goldfish," I said back, halfway smiling.

"Like you know?"

"That guy at the gas station," I said. "He was lucky."

Darren looked over to the stadium. To the idea of the stadium.

"You should have killed him," I said, my lip trembling again in that way I hated, my tongue flattening out in my mouth.

I was changing.

I didn't know into what.

CHAPTER 8

How to Recognize a Werewolf

Are there any ones with yellow fur?" the biologist asks in the grocery store, exactly two minutes before the hurricane's all the way there.

Florida has an actual *season* for hurricanes. The biologist's uncle says this "panhandle" they're in is really the bottom of Alabama, somebody just drew the lines wrong, but it would cost too much to reprint all the maps and books, and change all the road signs.

The biologist is nine already. He's not sure about this.

"Why do you ask?" the biologist's aunt says, also looking down the cereal aisle, at the biologist's uncle's new girlfriend.

The biologist has to hold his lips together not to smile.

"Anyway, we don't have *fur*," the biologist's aunt says. "We have *hair*. See?"

She pulls her own out to the side to show.

It's black like it's always been.

The new girlfriend's secret name is Sister Golden Hair.

"And you're supposed to say 'blond,' anyway," the biologist's aunt adds.

"Blond," the biologist says, then, quieter, "are there any *blond* werewolves?"

His aunt looks ahead to the new girlfriend, teetering up on her high heels, her leotard legs radiation green, her purple leg warmers bunched at her ankles.

Her name has something to do with a mountain. The biologist can never remember it. She's taking a box of cereal from the biologist's uncle's basket and trading it for another, even though most of the cereal boxes are already gone since it's the end of the world outside.

"How do you know she's not one already?" the biologist's aunt says, now that the biologist's uncle and the uncle's girlfriend are kissing again.

"She's not," the biologist says. "She wouldn't wear that much perfume."

"Good, good," the biologist's aunt says. "Because it would hurt her nose. If she had a real nose. That could smell."

"And her legs are too bright," the biologist says.

"Werewolves like the shadows," his aunt says. "And?" she prompts.

It's summer, but he's still in class.

It's always summer in Florida.

"And her breath would smell better," the biologist says at last, proud to have remembered.

Werewolves are paranoid about having dog breath, are always brushing their teeth and chewing mints.

"And her palms aren't hairy," he adds, "and she's not a seventh son and she wasn't born on Christmas and her ring finger isn't longer and she doesn't eat raw——"

"You've been watching movies while I'm at work," the biologist's aunt says.

Her tone isn't pleased.

The biologist studies the wires of their basket. How they weave over and under the whole way across.

"Pentagram too?" the biologist's aunt says, flashing her palm up to show what she means.

The biologist doesn't answer.

"Yes, her breath *would* smell better," the biologist's aunt says, nodding the biologist forward. "And she wouldn't wear those leggings, but not just because they're that color."

The biologist's uncle and the new girlfriend are at the meat department, now.

"I don't think there ever *has* been a blond one," the biologist's aunt says, one hand on the basket, to keep the biologist from flat-tiring the mom and her baby just ahead. "Maybe out in the desert? But—"

"It would be hard to hunt at night," the biologist says, trying to make up for the werewolf movies.

"*Impossible* to hunt," his aunt says. "And you'd be target practice too. The only place you could hide would be a wheat field, I guess. Or a stack of gold." This is funny to her. Hilarious. Werewolves never get the treasure.

"What about when you get old like Grandpa was?" the biologist asks.

"Old and grey," his aunt says, following where he's saying.

"Silverback," the biologist says. It's from the nature shows.

"It's better than being yellow on top," the biologist's aunt says, and they're close enough that this time the biologist's uncle *does* hear.

He raises his lip on one side just for an instant.

The biologist's aunt picks up a bottle of cranberry juice from his and his girlfriend's basket and inspects it. "Didn't know you were drinking this," she says, an innocent lilt to her voice.

"Oh, it's good for him," the girlfriend says with her eyes and with her mouth both, taking the cranberry juice away with the very tips of her fingers. Setting it back in its place in the basket.

"That's funny," the biologist's aunt says. "He's usually more into meat." To show, she plucks a juicy roast from the clearance bin and weighs it against her bicep.

"Red meat's more of a *luxury*," the girlfriend explains.

"A *luxury*," the biologist's aunt repeats, and is studying the roast now. "So . . ." she says, "then I guess doing *this* would be just sinful, wouldn't it?"

What she's talking about is biting into the top of the roast, right through the clear plastic.

She pulls away with her neck.

The way a human does it is with their hand, with their arm.

These are things all biologists know.

The aunt chews, chews some more, the girlfriend stepping back, her hands covering her mouth like trying to muffle a shriek that's going to come up anyway, once she can actually breathe in again.

The biologist's aunt teases the chewed-up plastic from the corner of her mouth, wipes it on her pants leg with a smear of blood. She swallows the meat in a big obvious gulp, doesn't even have to close her eyes to get it down.

"It doesn't have to be this way, Lib," the biologist's uncle says.

"You're right," the biologist's aunt says, picking the cranberry juice from the basket, twisting the golden cap off. "Here. You like it, right?"

The biologist's uncle is staring twin holes through his sister.

He knocks the cranberry juice away with the back of his hand. The mom with the baby gets splashed purple on her white pants, looks up to the biologist's uncle about this.

"I still like meat," the biologist's uncle says. "I'll *always* like meat."

"Dare, what's she—" the girlfriend says, but Darren raises his hand palm out, shuts her up.

"Dare?" the biologist's aunt says, liking it, and the biologist's uncle shakes his head like he's sick of this, he really is.

When she offers the roast, says it like a joke, *"Dare* you," he slaps that away too.

"I said I like *meat,*" the biologist's uncle says, and steps neatly past the biologist's aunt, snatches the baby from the mom with the white pants. The baby's already screaming. It's because babies always know a werewolf. They're even faster about it than dogs, than horses. "This is what you *want,* right?" the biologist's uncle says, holding the baby higher than the white-pants mom can reach, stiff-arming his new girlfriend away with his other hand so he can fake-lower the baby to his waiting mouth. Trained for just this sort of situation, the biologist pushes his basket around the corner, slips down the next aisle.

It's what the hurricane's left of the cokes, the chips, the peanuts.

Moving slow and deliberate, the biologist ignores the screaming behind him, ignores the end of the world pouring through the shattered windows at the end of the aisle. He simply picks this jar, not that jar. This bottle, not that bottle. He can take his time because he's famous, now. He's the one who finally figured out the real way to recognize a werewolf.

They're the ones who never grow up.

CHAPTER 9

Layla

You can't run away when you're a werewolf.

No, I'm not saying that right.

You can't run away when your *aunt's* a werewolf.

I'd tried once in Louisiana, and again the next year, in Texas, and that second time, in Texas, Libby even let it go on for three whole days.

In Louisiana, because she couldn't be late for her shift again, she'd just run me down, tracked me from the bus stop to this place back in the trees, half around the smelly lake. The lake hadn't cut my scent like I wanted. Or, it didn't cut it enough.

My plan—I didn't have a plan. I'd just got off the bus, kept walking.

Texas was different.

I could get away, I knew it. This state, it was big enough to hide in, wasn't it? To disappear in.

The first night I ate all three cans of beans I'd smuggled from the trailer. They were cold. The fire I'd meant to light wouldn't catch. It didn't matter. I was out there. I was doing it. The Texas sky was huge and empty, could swallow me whole if I'd only close my eyes, let it.

The second day I hung around the pay phone in front of a grocery store until somebody left their station wagon unlocked, and then I stole the half a can of Dr Pepper they'd left in the cup holder. That was it for that day. The Dr Pepper was warm.

The third night, when I finally hugged my knees and started crying, that kind where you can't control your stupid lips, Libby stood up from where she'd been ever since the first night: not forty feet away.

When she came in, stepping over my fire that would only make smoke, no flame, I pushed her away and even tried to hit her to keep her from hugging me.

This was fifth grade.

Everybody's stupid when they're eleven.

By Georgia I was fourteen, and had found a different way to escape: high school.

Instead of going home, I signed up for everything, came in early for study, stayed late for track.

It made me feel like Darren, like when I did finally come back to the duplex we were renting out in the trees—the other half was empty, and the rest of them had burned—when I came back it was like I was a ghost, just moving through a place I used to know. A place I should know.

I would touch this glass ashtray, that bunch of plastic orchids. The spoon that still had the scorch marks from jumping a solenoid. The screwdriver Darren had used to open a can of chili.

Libby was working nights, so I just saw her to say hey. But the truant officer never knocked, and the principal wasn't sending home notes that needed signatures, and two times in a row my report card came in passing.

If it'd been all A's, Libby would have known that Darren and me had forged it somehow, putting more effort into the process than it probably would have taken just to learn some Georgia state history.

I was okay with a C average, though.

Nobody expects anything different from a werewolf.

That we show up is enough of a surprise, I mean.

I did. For everything.

At least until Brittany started watching me.

Because I hadn't asked, Darren had already told me all about girl-friends. Not girls, girl*friends*. According to him, girl*friends* were a completely different breed. And any girl could suddenly turn into one. He told me I was going to count them for a while, and then I would stop counting. He said I would think I was getting better at it, being a boyfriend, but that I was going to have to learn not to listen to that kind of bullshit from myself. Just when I thought I'd figured out what made a girlfriend happy, what would make one stay, I would do something wrong again and that would be that.

"Something wrong, like, I don't know, like *eating their pet goat?*" Libby'd said, without looking over from the game show glowing all our faces light blue.

"It could have been anything ate that goat," Darren cut back, pulling his lips from his teeth like he couldn't help it.

"Anything," Libby said, and the way she moved her eyebrow on the right side—she knew exactly how to get Darren so pissed he'd have to stand up from the couch, pace to get his words straight.

"It was just a *goat*," he said. "One goat out of ten thousand goats."

"Did she have nine thousand nine hundred and ninety-nine others?"

Darren just stared at the window. At the curtains over the windows.

"I'm guessing this is the argument you used with her?" Libby went on. "What was her name? Sissy, Cecilia, Sicily . . ."

"Nobody named Sicily has ever owned a goat in the whole history of the world," Darren said.

"Sierra," Libby said, like she'd just answered the big question on the game show.

Darren spun away, clattered around in the kitchen with the ice tray until it snapped in half. He threw it into the sink and half walked, half dove out the back door, disappearing into the night, his clothes spread all across the knee-high grass so that, for probably thirty seconds after he was gone, his pants and shirt were still rocking back and forth, slower and slower.

Then it started to drizzle. On the only pair of pants he had left.

I watched them darken.

It rained all the time in Georgia.

Maybe because we were there, I don't know.

"He'll come back with a goat," Libby said, stretching out on the couch she had all to herself now. "I like goat."

I bored my eyes into the game show, not learning anything from it, shaking my head no to myself once, that I wasn't going to have a phone book of girlfriends like Darren. That just saying an old girlfriend's name wasn't going to drive me out into the wet night, so that when I came back I would smell like wet dog.

Again, I was wrong.

———

Brittany was the one who always wore the same black jeans every day. They fit her like the pants were fitting all the girls that year.

The rest of the girls were wearing half shirts or big sweaters or their boyfriends' jackets. Brittany wore black T-shirts with the sleeves cut off in a way that made me think of robots. And her boots were black and combat, never laced up all the way, but each of them not laced up the same as the other, the tongues always pulled up hard, so they could flop forward. And it must have taken her hours to raccoon her eyes up with black makeup. And when she could get out of the house with it, she had some kind of black lipstick too.

I'd been watching her too, yeah.

At the back of the class, or the group, or at assembly, it was always me and her. We were the two main members of the same-pants-every-day crowd.

I would nod to her here and there, like acknowledging our position, our status, and maybe even suggesting some vague notion about how little we cared about it, but, unlike Darren, I had no idea what words to ever say to a real live girl.

Hey, you don't know me, and I'll be gone in a few weeks. I remember my uncle eating roadkill off the actual road once. My aunt can open cans with her teeth, but she'll only do it when she thinks nobody's listening. We buried my grandpa with a tractor my uncle stole. I still remember how the diesel smelled on the night air. My aunt pulled her own hair to keep from crying, but then did anyway.

As it turned out, Brittany talked to me first.

Or, not talked. But she gave me something. Like a test. I could tell it was a test because her eyes were tracking my whole face all at once when she handed it to me, like if a muscle in my cheek twinged the slightest bit, she would know something. She would know everything.

What she handed me could have gotten us both expelled.

It was a bullet.

Brass at the shoulder, dull silver for a rounded-off point.

My guess is that I must have flinched. That a muscle on my cheek jumped. That the corner of my mouth jerked the slightest, most imperceptible bit.

Brittany bit her lower lip in. This counted as a smile with her.

"I knew it," she said, trying to take the bullet back, her breath hot she was so close to me.

I didn't let her have the bullet.

The silver didn't burn my palm. But then neither did the old quarters and dimes that always made Darren and Libby hiss.

I looked down the hall to geography or whatever I had next—I had no idea, couldn't have even said what state we were in this month—and said it, my first words to Brittany Caine Andrews: "You knew what?"

"That you're a werewolf," she said.

I held her eyes for a few steps, backing away, then turned, lowered my head to push my way through the bodies to geography.

If I smiled, then at least she didn't see it.

I don't think.

Three days later she sat down across from me in the cafeteria.

"I need it back," Brittany said. "He's going to miss it."

"What?" I said.

My vocabulary this close to her, it wasn't much.

"You know what," she said.

I slid my hand across the table, palm down, and the scraping sound told her I had the bullet.

"I'm not what you said," I told her.

"Yeah," she said, putting her hand over mine. "Prove it, then."

I shrugged.

She looked around for a teacher, a white apron, then turned my hand over. "Put it in your mouth," she said, exactly like the dare it was.

The silver bullet.

I hadn't shown it to Libby. Not because she wasn't there at dinner, but because she would have confiscated it.

Darren had just held it up, rolled it in his fingers.

"Quality work," he said. "Where from?"

"Found it," I told him.

Darren tongued his lower lip out, let that pass.

"Your grandpa," he said then, watching my eyes just as close as Brittany had, "he used to, when we were kids, he said he used to know a guy. He got him to make some of these for him once."

I took a bite of my hot dog. Hot dogs are quiet. You can chew them and not miss anything your uncle's about to tell you.

"Where'd you say you got this?" he said again, trying to push his thumbnail into the silver part.

It didn't leave a line.

Silver is about a six on the hardness scale. I'd learned it in science. It can't be scratched by a fingernail.

If it scratches you, though.

Darren sat the bullet down like a little rocket on the kitchen table.

"Got it from a girl," I said.

"A girl," he said, smiling around my word.

"Grandpa's friend," I said then, because I knew how this barter session was working.

"Not *friend*," Darren said, holding my eyes. "He just knew *of* him. Old wolf, even back then. He used to make these. Your grandpa had to buy some once, for—"

"For that time in Little Rock," I filled in. Because I was a good student.

"Old wolf's probably dead and buried by now," Darren said. "Mounted over somebody's fireplace."

I wanted to shake my head no, that this wasn't possible. That no werewolf would—

"Didn't live around these parts," Darren said, still watching me. "But we didn't used to either, did we?"

I didn't answer, was still trying to track this stupid, made-up legend. Trying to see an ancient old werewolf, melting down silver in one state, pouring it into molds fifty miles down the highway, pressing it into empty brass weeks later, the sounds of a different city all around.

Why, though?

"What's this girl's name?" Darren said then, taking the bullet between his thumb and index finger, tapping it onto the tabletop like seeing if it would fire.

Tap, tap, tap.

"Sicily," I said, and snatched the bullet before he could pocket it, kept on moving down the hall, to my precious home-work. None of which I'd done for the last two nights. Because I'd been mentally prepping for this specific possibility in the cafeteria—for Brittany, talking to me. Brittany, sitting right across from me.

"You want me to put it in my mouth," I repeated to her, to be sure I was hearing what she was saying.

"Unless it'll burn you . . ." she said back.

What she was doing now was cleaning the bullet with a bright white napkin, so I wouldn't have germs to argue about.

When she handed it across I took it, held it by the brass, studied it.

"You're stalling," she said.

"If what you say—if you're right," I said. "How did you know?"

"He told me."

"He?"

She nodded down to the bullet.

"The one who made this," I filled in.

Yes.

"He told me what to watch for," she said.

I smiled what I was pretty sure was my cool smile, leaned back in my chair, the bullet still in my hand.

I wasn't stupid, I mean.

As soon as I put that silver in my mouth and didn't exhale the smoke of scorched gums, Brittany was going to be gone, on to the next hopeful.

If Darren had known her name, he'd have nodded his serious nod, said that was good, she was at the front of the alphabet—of *my* alphabet. Now I just had to work through all the other letters, and then back around again.

What he didn't know, it was that you can stop at *B*, if you want.

I wanted.

After school, when I was supposed to be running forties for off-season football—like I was going to be in Georgia next fall—Brittany led me to a place behind the gym between the industrial-air-conditioner unit and a temporary classroom shed-on-wheels.

We sat with our backs against the dusty green metal of the air conditioner, its deep thrumming making our chests shake, and she smoked a cigarette like a poker player and told me she knew I was a werewolf because of algebra.

"Maybe I'm just bad at math," I told her.

She ashed by tapping the spine of the cigarette with the pad of her index finger—I'd never seen anything so perfect, so deliberate—and shook her head no.

"Algebra's at the other end of the building from this," she said, patting the air conditioner.

I shrugged that this was common knowledge. That all the other classrooms had first dibs on the cool air coming through the ductwork, so that there wasn't any left over by the end of the line, where algebra happened seventh period, the sun staring hard at Georgia, like accusing it.

"You do this," she said, holding her cigarette away from her mouth so she could nudge the flat of her tongue forward a bit and pant over it lightly, her lungs taking the shallowest gulps.

It made me close my lips tight.

She rubbed her cigarette out on the concrete.

"Wolves' sweat glands are in the pads of their feet, and—" at which point she somehow reached into my actual mouth, touched my tongue "—their tongues."

I could taste her, now.

Not with special werewolf taste buds. With fourteen-year-old taste buds. My whole body was suddenly coated in them.

I swallowed, wiped my lips, and told her I didn't do that, I'd never pant like a dog.

"Whatever," she said. "He told me that werewolves can hide—"

"He?" I interrupted.

"My *grandfather*," she said, watching the football off-seasoners huddling up for some reason. "He says that werewolves can hide all of it except that. It's like a habit. Something they forget to think about, it's so natural."

I promised myself to never breathe like that again. Maybe to never breathe again in public at all.

"What else did he tell you?"

"Silver," she said, like about to tick off a big list. "And that the moon, that's all made up for the movies. And that this"—she flashed her palm, a pentagram drawn there—"is junk too."

"Why do you do it then?" I asked, taking the excuse to hold her hand in mine, study that faded blue star.

She took her hand back, used it to pull up a second cigarette.

"Because I'm going to be one," she said one hundred percent matter-of-fact, looking across the flame of her lighter at me.

"A werewolf?" I said.

"And you're going to help me."

The next time she breathed out, she was looking away from me again. The thin grey smoke drifted back around her, to me.

Already breaking my promise, I opened my mouth to taste it.

I waited until Darren was gone for the night to ask Libby.

I had to accidentally wake up early to catch her just getting in, her hair down because leaving it in a ponytail all night gave her a headache, made it hard for her to fall asleep.

"Stranger stranger," she said about me, guiding her hair out of her eyes, trying to act like she still had enough energy to carry on a conversation.

Outside, our Ambassador wagon was still coughing. It was so stupid that you could turn the car off and it would keep trying to run for two or three minutes. Darren said it was this sea-level oxygen, the plankton and krill he always said were microscopic in the air, in the Gulf states. Libby said it was that AMCs were cursed.

I believed Libby. It was why I was coming to her for this, not Darren.

"Is the wolf kiss real?" I said, just all at once and as absolutely casual and offhand as possible.

Instead of answering at first, she broke two eggs carefully into the pan and shook it by the handle to keep the whites from sticking.

"Wolf kiss," she said.

Brittany had told me about it.

"It's where you, like," I said, not sure how to say it right without her looking at me, for me to act it out, "you put your mouth on somebody's skin, and then you, you know. *Change*. So the teeth—"

"So your teeth push right in, like a bite," she said. "Only it's a different kind of bite. A kiss, but with teeth."

"It's supposed to be a safe way," I said. "A work-around. A fluke. Like, that first saliva, it's special, to protect human gums from getting infected. Like colostrum."

She shook her pan again.

"Colostrum," she repeated, hunting the word down.

"First milk," I said, straight from Life Science. "Full of vita-mins and antibiotics and enzymes and all that."

She nodded, kept nodding.

From what Darren had told me, newborns that have the blood, that are born into this life, something about our chemistry or hormones makes us lactose intolerant for the first few months. It'd be bad news for a, you know, *mammal*, except raw meat can be chewed down to gruel, spit into a newborn's mouth.

He'd told me this over a bowl of vanilla ice cream we were sup-posed to be splitting, though, so I don't know.

Werewolf stories, they always have a reason. His was right in front of him, melting in the bowl. Or, it was in me, wanting so bad to be lactose intolerant.

"Enzymes," Libby repeated now.

"Is it real?" I asked again. "The wolf kiss?"

Libby shook her eggs again, said, "Darren told me about the bullet."

I touched my pocket when she said it, only realized just then that my pocket was empty.

Libby held the bullet up beside her shoulder.

"Maybe this girl isn't someone you should listen to so much," she said. "I'm just—"

The reason I didn't hear the rest was that I was already gone from the kitchen.

Not to my room either, like usual.

I'd taken the back door, like Darren.

Until it sounded like Libby was asleep, I sat in the empty half of the duplex, throwing lit matches at the wall, watching them smolder on the carpet. Stepping on the ones that needed stepping on. On the ones that needed stepping on that I could *reach* without having to get up. If the others caught, well, then they caught.

None of them did.

"How does your grandfather know so much?"

We were sitting high up in the old gym. It was lunch. You only hauled your tray all the way down to the old gym if you didn't want to eat. The old gym was for making out. Most of the lights had been knocked dim with twenty years of dodgeballs, and the one that was left on the side with bleachers had become a target for chewed gum. The wads that made it to the hot bulb melted back off, strung down to the light's metal cage, hung down like a giant dying kaleidoscope.

It was perfect.

Brittany snapped a carrot between her teeth and didn't answer my question about her grandfather. Instead she said that she'd tried everything else. Rolling in the sand under the light of a full moon. Drinking from a wolf's paw print—she wasn't sure it was a wolf, she guessed. She maybe could have turned into a Weimaraner. She'd tried drinking downstream from a wolf too, but the rules weren't clear on how *far* downstream still counted.

The water had made her sick for two days. She'd refused to go to the doctor, was sure she was transforming.

"But now there's you," she said.

"Wouldn't he use one of those bullets on you if you . . . you know?" I said.

She just stared down at the shiny floor of the gym, considering this.

"My grandpa's dead," I said. "Arkansas."

"That a disease?"

I smiled until she looked up, saw it.

"*He* wouldn't shoot me," she said. "He doesn't even have any guns. He just sells the bullets to collectors. He's the only one who makes them in all the sizes."

"All the calibers," I corrected.

"*Calibers,*" she said, making the word stupid and obvious the way she regurgitated it.

How close I was sitting to her was maybe four inches. I told myself I could feel her body heat.

Up in the corner behind us, Tim Lawson and Gina Ross were going at it.

Brittany stood up all at once, held her hand out sideways for me to take. It was a gesture I'd only ever seen in the movies on television.

"Want to show you something," she said.

I followed where she led, her hand soft and rough and hot and perfect. Where she took me was around beside the wooden bleachers, *under* the bleachers, all the galvanized metal of the scaffolding holding the wooden slats up.

We ducked under and, about halfway across the length of them, like crouching through a secret cave, she held her lighter out in front of us, sparked it.

The flame caught on the first scratchy roll and I looked around us.

At first I thought it was pep-rally trash, streamers and ribbons.

It was panties. They'd slipped through from above.

Brittany was still holding my hand.

"Wolf kiss," I heard myself saying.

She let the lighter go dark.

Two days later the silver bullet showed back up.

It was in the refrigerator, on a cracked saucer beside the ketchup. It had a coat of frost on it. Meaning it had been there for hours. Since Libby'd left. I could almost see her leaned over to balance it there. Setting it down then nudging it over to the exact center of the saucer. Going slow enough not to tip it over.

Darren was sitting behind me, eating his cereal without milk. Meaning he hadn't been in the refrigerator. This was for me.

I kept the door open, studied the bullet.

Its tip had been snipped off.

I reached in like for ketchup or leftovers, palmed the bullet. The way it frost-welded to my palm, I thought with a thrill that it was burning me.

It was only the cold.

"Leave it open," Darren said, about my time in the refrigerator. "Feels like Alaska."

"Like you've been to Alaska," I said to him from behind the door.

"I've been everywhere, man," he sung back, and then crunched another handful of cereal into his mouth, having to work it in in stages it sounded like.

I rolled the bullet in my hand, breaking the frost free. I looked at it from the top, where it had been snipped.

Inside the silver point, the metal changed, went dark and normal. Just lead, like from a car battery. Probably *from* a car battery. Meaning the silver on the outside, it was probably melted aluminum cans, or chrome trim from a truck, hammered to paste.

This wasn't a silver bullet.

I pocketed it, stood, let the door magnet shut.

Darren was sitting tall like a prairie dog, trying to see the television in the living room. It was the commercial he liked, with the guy falling backward into a series of swimming pools.

"You shouldn't hang your tongue out like that," I said.

He looked over to me, his mouth still open.

"Like what?" he said.

In the living room the car salesman fell into another pool and Darren laughed like every time, then stood, his chair scraping away, and held his Jesus arms out to the side, tried to get that same blank look on his face the salesman always had, falling back.

"Classic," Darren said, wrist-deep in the cereal again, the duplex already heating up for the day like the fire had never gone all the way out.

I ran away to school.

———

Brittany had a quiz for me from one of her mom's magazines. She wouldn't let me see it, would just read the questions aloud then look down to me with her teacher eyes all heated up and serious.

"Does your guy disappear each month for two or three days at a time?"

We were skipping English II, were up on the roof. For once it wasn't raining. Still, this was Georgia. You could about drink the air.

"Werewolves don't have gills," I said.

"That wasn't the question," she said, the magazine already rolled up to bop me on the top of the head.

I was lying down on the gravel roof, my head on the right thigh of her black jeans. My head on Brittany Andrews's leg. With her middle name, "Caine," she was ABC all at once. All the ABCs I'd ever need.

When I stood later the tar the gravel was swimming in would have ruined my shirt.

I was already planning not to care.

Somewhere below us a classroom of freshmen was reading *Romeo and Juliet* aloud, up and down the rows of desks, Shakespeare snaking from the window to the door, to escape like we had.

"Does your guy disappear each month for two or three days at a *time*?" she said again, with more push.

"That's the movies," I said. "The moon. Your grandpa already told you the moon is stupid."

"A thousand truck-stop T-shirts can't be wrong."

"Those are just wolf-wolves."

Because I hadn't put the silver bullet in my mouth, I could just be pretending to be a werewolf, I was telling myself. Meaning this was pretend too. Meaning I was making it all up.

If it was the right answers, that didn't matter. I wasn't betraying anything. I was just lucky.

It was the first time I'd ever felt like that.

"When your guy gives you jewelry, is it gems and gold, or is it silver?"

Far above some bird was circling slow. Just looking around.

"Werewolf jewelry is usually from those quarter machines," I told her. "Sometimes it's candy."

She pushed my head with her elbow.

No.

In the most tender way *possible,* she pushed my head with her elbow.

"Do dogs react unfavorably to your guy?"

"We can test," I said. "Do you have a dog?"

She shook her head no and narrowed her eyes, like having a dog was a thing that had never really occurred to her.

"Do y'all?" she asked.

"We have cousins," I said, trying not to smile all the way.

"You're not doing this right," she said.

"If this was a real test . . ." I said back. Then: "Next."

"Does your guy like his hamburgers rare?"

"I like ketchup," I told her. "On my *hot dogs.*"

She hissed through her teeth and shook her head, made like she was skipping down to the *hard* questions.

"Here. Do your guy's eyebrows meet in the middle?"

I made a V out of mine, trying to look up to them.

"Is that something?" I said.

"They don't," she said, disappointed. "How about fingers. Your ring one's supposed to be longer."

I held my hands out.

"What would it help to have a long ring finger?" I asked. "It take longer to get married, that way?"

"It's just a thing," she said, scanning for a question I could *pass.*

The sun turned up a few degrees. It was like some giant invisible kid had squatted down over us with a magnifying glass.

"Do you have a balcony at your house?" I asked.

She looked down at me, said, "You knew we were skipping class today. You didn't have to read."

I shrugged.

"Arise, fair sun, and kill the envious moon," I recited up through the magnifying glass, the fingertips of my right hand to my chest to show how earnest and dramatic a real werewolf could be.

She swatted me with the magazine again, then stopped, smiled her mischievous smile.

"Ay, me," she said, having to dig deep in her head for Juliet's words: "It's not hand or foot, not arm or face, not any part belonging to man."

"To wolf," I said. It was where she was going.

"I take thee at thy word," she said, threading her fingers into my hair.

"That's my line," I said up to her.

Next was that I knew not how to tell her who I was.

Instead I laid my head into her lap, let her use her black pen to connect my eyebrows.

"Stop sweating," she said, her lips so close to mine, the tips of her bangs brushing my face on both sides.

I tried.

After school—or, after what would have been school if we hadn't been on the roof the whole time, her skin red everywhere from it now—we went to the gas station like all the kids did. Just a herd of high schoolers, the glass doors never closed enough to have to open again.

Because we'd skipped lunch, Brittany had seventy-nine cents for a fountain drink.

We put two candy bars in the cup before hiding them with ice, drowning them in syrup. If you just barely pushed the paddle of the fountain in, you could fill the whole cup with syrup.

She was taking me to meet her grandfather.

Except, suddenly, Darren was in front of us in line.

"Children," he said to us, like he was so grown-up.

"This is my uncle," I said to Brittany. "He's a—a *mechanic*."

"A mechanic," Darren said, like saying it out loud so he could be sure to remember it. "Just a mechanic."

"Same as your nephew," Brittany said, her lips pursed tight because otherwise she'd be smiling big enough to give us all away.

"Big family of mechanics, yeah," Darren said.

"Nice buckle," Brittany said, in that meaningful way she'd been using with me, and Darren looked down at his belt buckle, smiled one side of his mouth out, showing off how many teeth he had.

The buckle was twice as big as it needed to be. The wolf on it was turquoise and running left to right, and the moon behind it was that yellowy resin that, with a belt buckle, usually has a scorpion in it. Darren had it to back up his "Wolf Man in the Sky" CB handle, like it could somehow serve as proof to all the other truckers that this was really him.

But this chance encounter, it wasn't supposed to be about him, I could tell.

"Here," he said, taking the coke from me, to pay for it, an ability I didn't know he had. Then he hefted it a couple of times, looked up to us like we were smarter than he'd thought.

Out front, he asked if we needed a ride.

I looked around for his truck, idling in the ditch or parked at the edge of the parking lot, or staring us down from the white clapboard church. It wasn't any of those places.

"Oh yeah," Darren said, looking around like he hadn't even considered how he'd got here. When there was no easy fix for giving us a ride with a truck that wasn't here, he just lifted his own coke in farewell, walked backward a few steps then turned, didn't look back.

"He leaves just like you do," Brittany said, taking the coke from me, finding the straw with her mouth.

Then she handed it back.

I let the straw find my mouth as well.

"Canteen kiss," she said, skipping ahead a step.

A block later we pincered our fingers into the ice for the candy bars. It was the only flaw in this kind of stealing: You had to be a certain distance from the gas station before lifting the lid, but by that time you've usually drank all your drink, and *now* you eat the candy bar, and you won't have anything to wash it down with.

"Sure he's there?" I said, about wherever her house was.

"He's always home," she said. "What was your uncle doing in town?"

I hadn't considered that. I did know to look behind us, though.

There was nothing, no one.

But there wouldn't have been.

If Darren had been in Brittany's kitchen to meet her grandfather with us, he would have whistled about how old the guy was. The same way you whistle when you see a custom bike parked across a curb in front of a grocery store.

In some book I'd read on my own, not for class, this old guy down on the Texas border had been described as having decades of sun folded into his face. That's how Brittany's grandfather was. Touching his face—I couldn't imagine what it would feel like.

His hair was a white bird nest. It had been in some version of a ponytail a week ago, I'd guess, but he'd slept since then. A few times.

"Granddad," she said, stepping aside to present me.

He looked up from the cast-iron torture machine bolted to the counter.

It was for pressing bullets into shells.

The ceiling above him had three ragged holes in it.

He followed my eyes up there, then came back down to me. "It's why you don't want to live in a two-story job," he said.

"Or ever get a deposit back," Brittany added.

Her grandfather smiled, never taking his eyes from me.

"So this is the young werewolf," he said, studying me from a slightly different angle now.

My face heated up.

It's exactly how it would heat up if I was lying, I told myself. If I was just saying I was a werewolf so this man's granddaughter wouldn't start sitting at some other table at lunch.

"You make the bullets," I said.

It was the only thing I could think of.

He waggled his eyebrows like a clown, shrugged. "Cartridges," he corrected, gently, as if it hardly mattered. "Or shells. The bullet is the little part at the end, that the gunpowder shoots through the barrel."

"At *werewolves*," Brittany said, with a thrill.

"'Silver cartridge' doesn't sound the same, though," her grandfather said, chuckling.

"Where do you get the silver?" I said, tipping the last block of the syrupy ice into my mouth.

"Customer brings it," he said, and like that I got the scam: pocket the silver, paint the lead up pretty, and be on down the road next month.

"So you two are like enemies . . ." Brittany said, about me and her grandfather. We looked at each other.

"If werewolves were real," he said at last. "Present company excluded, of course."

I lifted my cup in some stupid gesture and stepped over to the trash, dropped it into the new bag.

"He mostly makes them for collectors," Brittany said. "Rich guys who want to play make-believe."

"Make-believe is important," he said, nodding his head up to me, like I could chime in here if I wanted.

"Rich guys can do what they want," I said. It's a standard line. All werewolves know it.

"Hey," Brittany said, taking my hand again, "this is what I really wanted to show you."

I let her pull me but kept looking back to her grandfather, and his not-silver bullets. He was looking at me too.

"Door open!" Brittany's mom called from somewhere in the house, and Brittany sighed a whole-body sigh, pulled me into her room.

It was all wolves. Every wall a poster. Posters on top of posters. Every flat place an action figure, a statuette salvaged from a thrift store, or ordered from a catalog.

"My real family," she said, holding her arms out to spin in the middle of the room.

"Yours isn't so bad," I said, meaning her grandfather. Meaning the voice of her mom, trying to keep her safe from young wolves like me.

Brittany kept spinning, her eyes shut.

Darren couldn't stop laughing about my new eyebrow, the one Brittany had inked in. Even Libby was having a hard time swallowing her smile.

I stood at the sink until the water was as close to hot as it got and rubbed the bridge of my nose raw.

If only high school had night classes.

When I came back Darren held his hand up like to cup the back of my head, said, "Aw, here. Let me wolf-kiss it better . . ."

I pushed his hand away, was ready to fight.

He was trying so hard not to laugh that he was crying.

Libby looked over to him, her eyes hot, her hand open by her chair and cutting once, back, like this stops now.

It did, kind of.

I ate my beans and rice with a hot dog cut up into it and glared at the game show. Used to I'd wondered why werewolves loved game shows on television so much. But then I got it. We never go to college, hardly ever even finish high school. A good game show, though, if you listen right, you can get an education for free.

It's stealing back what you had stole from you in the first place.

Not that I would ever tell Darren or Libby this. Just one more thing for them to make fun about.

Reading *Romeo and Juliet* the night before, I'd made sure my door was closed all the way, and that I was tuned one hundred percent in to the floorboards in the hall. If Darren ever opened the door and found me with an open rabbit on my bed, my hands and mouth bloody, then he'd just nod good, probably. A book, though. Every time he caught me with one of those, he'd always ask what that book could tell me that he didn't already know?

Before either of them could, I answered the final question on the game show out loud—"Eli Whitney"; cotton was big in Georgia state history—left before the host could come back from the station break, confirm my win.

In my room I read *Romeo and Juliet* again. It was supposed to feel like revenge, but I forget that a scene or two in.

It was about love.

It was about me.

The reason I didn't want Darren opening the door, it was my eyes.

The wolf kiss was three days away. A Friday, so Brittany could hide away for the weekend, for whenever her transformation came.

I rubbed my tongue along my teeth. My flat, flat teeth.

I was already counting the days until she was going to hate me forever.

It didn't matter. This was worth it.

And I'd never hate her back, no matter what she said, no matter if she told the whole school I thought I was a werewolf.

I touched the raw space between my eyes, held my finger there and closed my eyes.

When I opened them, it was because of my window.

Scratching. Fingernails on wet glass.

My head fell back to the balcony scene and my heart swelled, but then the pane in the middle cracked, shattered, the night's humid breath sighing in.

I fell off the other side of the bed, tangled in my blanket, and now Brittany Andrews's grandfather was stepping through the window.

Darren had been right. Grandpa *had* known about an ancient old werewolf who forged silver bullets.

I should have known by the trash can in their kitchen. It had been empty at four in the afternoon—*after* breakfast, *after* lunch, with two people in the house all day. And there'd been three eaters there in the morning.

When you don't have the right nose yet, you've got to sniff our kind out by other telltales.

If I hadn't been standing next to Brittney, I might have.

If I hadn't been so blind, what was happening now might not be happening at all. But it was.

There was a dirty white werewolf standing half in, half out of my window, his hand shaking on the sill, his eyes rheumy, his nose still thick with the scent I must have been wearing when I walked into his kitchen, his white hair still pulled into the remnants of a ponytail.

He was here to save his granddaughter.

He hadn't got his other leg all the way in before Darren crashed in. Not through the door—with the way time was slowed down, I would have heard the floorboards creaking with his heavy steps—but *through* the thin wall between my room and the kitchen.

He must have started shifting when the sound of breaking glass pulled him from whatever movie he had on.

By the time his feet hit the curled linoleum of the kitchen, the soles were already going leathery.

And then he dove straight over the range. Because his nephew—because that sound, it was coming from his only nephew's room.

Darren had never taken one single hour of geometry in his

whole stupid life, but he knew about the shortest distance between two points. He knew where I was.

He landed half wolfed out, blind from the change, splinters in his face and hair, and never stopped for a second, even when I reached with one arm to stop him, to explain that this was all stupid, this was all a mistake, that Brittany's grandfather, he was *saving* us, he was putting dummy rounds in rifles. And that he was too *old* to have shifted. That this, it was already killing him. That there was no way he could go back.

A man would have caught Brittany's grandfather with his shoulder in the midsection.

Werewolves don't come from football, though.

Darren led with his claws, with his mouth, with his scream that was already becoming a roar, big dollops of saliva and blood slinging back from the corners of his blackening lips.

The two of them exploded through the window, out the side of the duplex, into the soft rain.

I vaulted out after them as best I could, a leftover shard of the window spearing my hand.

I looked to the front door for Libby, but she would be at work.

Meaning this was going to happen. This was *already* happening.

"*No!*" I screamed as loud as I could, standing there in my underwear, my hand blooming red beside me.

I don't think Darren heard me, but he did stop.

Because he wasn't completely wolfed out, he could still step back, on two legs.

I watched his skin ripple in folds. Heard his neck creak into place, his jaw pop hard like it always did.

Brittany's grandfather was trying to stand.

His throat, though—this was what Darren *did*, what he was

made for. Didn't Brittany's grandfather *know* that when he came here? Couldn't he *smell*?

"I was going to follow you today," Darren said. "I *was* following you."

"He's dying," I said.

Still, the old wolf, he was clawing forward through the mud. Trying to get to me.

"I don't think he wants you dating his granddaughter," Darren said.

I told him to shut up.

Darren looked over to me, and for once he did shut up.

"He's not going to stop," I said at last. Brittany's grandfather was getting to us inch by inch, swiping at the air with his yellow claws, trying to hold his throat together with his other hand.

"I'm not going to live this long, am I?" Darren said, silvery rainwater dripping off the sharp point of his nose.

I couldn't answer.

"I hope I don't, I mean," Darren said, wiping Brittany's grandfather's blood from his mouth, his tone so fake I couldn't even call him on it.

"Watch him," he said, and stepped over to his truck, came back with his tire beater.

"No," I said, taking his wrist.

"It's for the best."

Instead of making me let go, be a part of this, Darren ripped his hand away, was already breathing hard the way he did when he was about to have to do something he didn't want to.

"Tell my dad hey," he said, stepping in, and laid that tire-beater right into that sweet spot behind Brittany's grandfather's left ear.

A werewolf in his prime, that would be a love tap.

At Brittany's grandfather's age, it was a skull fracture. A skull *collapse*. A wet avalanche of bone in there, nine or ten decades crumbling into a pile at the bottom of his mind.

He toppled over onto his right side, his left foot twitching.

"On second thought," Darren said, kneeling to finish it, "tell my dad to go to hell," and then he raised the tire beater a second time and I looked away.

The sound, though.

You can't close your ears.

I was burrito'd in my blankets facing away from the door when Libby opened it, stared at my window to be sure she was seeing what her headlights had shown her.

It was cardboard and tape now. Not glass.

"We're moving?" she said in her clipped way, like this was just another fact, one of a thousand.

In my blankets, I nodded.

I'd been crying all night.

At fourteen years old.

About an old man with a name I didn't even know.

"Let me get one more sleep in," she said, and pulled my door closed.

Until the bus stop at the end of our road, I didn't know what Darren had done with the body.

Brittany's grandfather had been too old and frail to shift *any* of the way back, as it turned out. That made Darren's job easier. Brittany's grandfather had died wolf, and he'd stayed that way.

Instead of mucking up his cab with gore—the battery was dead anyway, would have needed the Ambassador to jump it—

Darren had carried this old white werewolf as far as he could in his arms. Not back into the trees of Georgia, to get dragged out into the light by coyotes or bears, but to the highway.

The burial he'd given the oldest werewolf of our time, the werewolf who had to have saved all of our lives fifty times over, the werewolf who had played his granddaughter's game as a way of educating her, at least until a real werewolf showed up, the burial Darren had given him, it was on the yellow stripes, about two hundred yards down from the mailboxes—the opposite way Libby came in from.

By now Brittany's grandfather was road mush.

Darren would have made sure the teeth and skull were crushed, of course, but now the body was too. Over and over.

Here a giant white dog had died.

The birds were already there, stringing his insides away, spreading him all across the South.

Maybe it was for the best.

Still, when two of the football players at the bus stop with me started tossing rocks at the body, just to watch the birds rise up, annoyed, I had to fight them, and it went the way it usually does, two on one, when the one doesn't even have his claws yet.

Brittany cleared the girls' bathroom to clean my face up.

She'd been crying already when I'd found her.

While she patted my cuts with the wet paper towels and rewrapped my bleeding hand, she told me about her grandfather. How he always made eggs with hot sauce for her and her mom. How he hadn't been there this morning, for the first time ever. How this happens with old people. They just wander off, die of starvation out in some storm drain or beside a building they think they recognize.

"Maybe he was a werewolf," I said, quietly.

"This isn't funny," she said. "He made silver bullets. Here."

She was having me hold the square-folded paper towel to my left eye.

Then—"Don't listen," she said—she stepped into one of the stalls, locked it closed, and peed.

My heart was more alive in my chest than it had ever been.

By English II she was crying at the back of the class, the hood of her black sweatshirt not quite making her as invisible as she wanted.

The whole football team was calling me Roadkill by now. As in, I ate it. As in, I'd been protecting my next meal.

The class was still reading *Romeo and Juliet*.

The second football player to have to read aloud—it was like this was meant to be. Like I should have seen it coming.

The balcony scene.

"But I'm a guy . . ." he said to Mr. Preston.

"All the roles were played by boys back then," Mr. Preston said back, hitting *boy* a touch harder than necessary, rolling his hand for the play to continue.

The football player shrugged, looked back to his teammates to be sure this was a go, and did as he was asked: He stepped up from his desk with his book, knelt right behind my shoulder, and said, his voice syrupy-sweet, "Roadkill, Roadkill, wherefore art thou?"

I stood from my desk so fast that it stood with me.

It slowed me down enough for Brittany to get expelled.

In a flash, like a true werewolf, she was on this football player, crawling up his back like an animal, biting into him hard on his thick neck, clawing his face wide open with her black finger-nails.

My girl.

We met in the old gym for lunch. She had all her books in her backpack, was supposed to be off school grounds with them. I was just going to leave my books in my locker, because screw them. Screw all of them.

Nobody else was there, for once.

"I'm just thinking about him out there," she said, her fingers laced in mine, the clump of our hands pressed between the sides of our legs.

"I love you," I said, barely out loud enough.

She lowered her forehead into the hollow of my shoulder.

"He doesn't have his juice or his toast or anything," she said into my chest. "He's—he's . . ." then couldn't finish.

The football player she'd gone after was the quarterback, I was pretty sure. He was going to miss his depth perception.

I smiled above Brittany's head, smoothed her long hair down along her back.

"I think we're leaving," I said.

Brittany nodded, sat up, said, "He told me that too. That you're always moving. Like we do. But that's because of Mom's job. He said other than that, we were like werewolves."

"I'm not going to forget you," I said.

"You will," she said. "Mom told me that."

I shook my head no, I wouldn't.

She shrugged, was looking down to the gym floor again. That single gummed-up light flickering above us.

"I could find him," she said, like speaking from a dream.

She turned up to me.

"If I—if I could use my nose like . . . like you can."

"You don't want this," I told her.

In answer, she guided the hair away from her neck, clearing the pale skin there.

"You're my only chance," she said, her other hand holding mine even tighter now. Even more forever. Then, quieter: "I've already picked out my werewolf name too."

"Your werewolf name?"

"Layla," she said like the best, most thrilling secret ever, stretching her neck out flatter for me.

"Layla" was "Juliet" for Arabia. We'd learned it in English, when English still mattered.

"Layla," I said to her.

"Not too hard," she said, still holding her hair out of the way.

I breathed in, breathed out, looked to make sure no teachers were standing in the door—this was happening, this was really happening—and I lowered my lips to her neck, opened my mouth, and set my teeth against her tangy skin. Her hair when she let it go fell like a silk curtain across my face, my arm circled her waist, my hand drawing her to me, making her take a gulp of air in, and I closed my eyes, prayed to the god of werewolves that could I please not change for just one more minute. For just one minute more. For just a little longer, please.

CHAPTER 10

Here There Be Werewolves

The mechanic needed a bowl of chocolate ice cream at the truck stop after a job like that. Most nine-year-olds don't get to work on the big trucks, his uncle told him.

It had taken all morning. First they had to remove the old grab bar from beside the driver's door of his uncle's rig—the faded red Kenworth with the white stripe sweeping back under the windshield like robot cheekbones—then they'd had to install the new one. Two bolts up top, two at bottom. His uncle had offered to hold the mechanic up but the mechanic had climbed up himself. The radio was on in the cab the whole time.

Because the grab bar's so shiny and new, his uncle requested the booth by the front window, so they could watch it. Because everybody was going to want that grab bar, he said. Nobody's ever had one that pretty, and that well installed. Not in the whole history of trucking. If either of them were strong enough, they could probably lift the whole truck with just that grab bar, those four bolts were so tight.

Instead of reminding his uncle of his age again, of the stories he will and won't buy into, the mechanic digs into his ice cream. There was only enough change in the ashtray for one scoop.

"Whoa, whoah," the uncle says, scooting forward in his seat, his hands spread wide on the table, his eyes large on the parking lot.

The mechanic plays along, looks through the window as well.

Another trucker's stepped down from his rig, is walking past the uncle's rig.

"He's looking, he's looking . . ." the uncle is saying, ready to jack-in-the-box up from that booth, explode out into the parking lot.

The other trucker ends up just beating his cap against his thigh.

"Of course," the mechanic's uncle says, leaning back into his seat, disappointed with himself.

"Of course what?" the mechanic says, in spite of himself.

"He wants to steal it on the way *out*," the uncle says, whispering it true. "*After* he's got his coffee."

The trucker peels his sunglasses off once he's stepped all the way inside. Then he ducks down the hall leading back to the pay showers.

"Just wait," the uncle says, his eyes twin slits.

The shirt he's wearing is a defect. It's supposed to say BAR-WOLF. What it says, what the mechanic's aunt just shakes her head about, is BRAWOLF. There are either wolf or shark teeth circling the words.

Probably wolf.

The mechanic's shirt is the ones they were handing out at school. His school is the Lobos. At the pep rallies everybody howls at the moon.

This is Alabama. It smells like old water, so everybody smokes cigarettes all the time.

"She watching?" the uncle asks the mechanic, about the waitress.

The mechanic shakes his head once, no.

The uncle nods and, without quite looking down, pours the rest of his strawberry wine cooler into the water cup he drank empty in one gulp.

"Oh, oh," the uncle says then, about the parking lot again, but it's just another trucker walking past. "Close one," the uncle says.

The mechanic spoons another bite in.

He's pretty sure that, because his uncle only sees him every other week or so, that he thinks the mechanic's only growing up half as much as he really is.

"You know why we both like that new grab bar better than that old rusted one?" the uncle asks then.

The mechanic looks up with just his eyes.

Usually his uncle figures some way to steal back the ice cream he buys.

"Because we're *werewolves*," the uncle says, leaning forward to keep it quiet. "In the old days," the uncle says, his hands flat on the table under his chin, "in the old days—you know about silver, right?"

When the mechanic doesn't answer, the uncle threads his thermometer out from behind his ear. It's what he's training himself to chew on this month, instead of toothpicks. Because the wet splinters he spits out, somebody with the right nose could track him by that. And the thermometer, it reminds him not to bite too hard. To always be careful. To be—a word he stole from a karate movie—*mindful*.

It also let him discover he always had a fever. So did the aunt, after the uncle cleaned the thermometer in the sink and let it cool back down to normal.

The mechanic doesn't have a fever.

He's just supposed to wait, though. Here in a few years he'll run hot like a real werewolf. That he doesn't now, already—that's how werewolves hide themselves from school nurses, right?

It makes sense, sort of.

"Silver's kryptonite," the mechanic finally says, about the mercury in the glass of the thermometer.

The uncle nods, reaches across to dip it into the mechanic's ice cream, taking a whole big chunk. He slips it into his mouth.

"Used to," he says once he's swallowed the ice cream down, "like, back in the old days when everybody said 'ye' and 'thee' and you weren't born, you were begot, back then nobody wanted werewolves to come to dinner anymore."

The mechanic pulls his bowl a little closer to his side of the table.

"They didn't want us coming to dinner because we *ate* everything," the uncle says. "The goose, the duck, the old-timey hamburgers from when they hadn't invented ketchup yet so everybody had to make a face like this when they ate them. And then we'd just leave, our bellies full. Back then we didn't even have to hunt. We'd just go from house to house and ask what was for dinner, and the rule was, if you were hungry, they had to feed you. Villagers were all polite like that. But they were running out of food. They were starving."

"Did they have hot dogs?"

"They had woolly-mammoth hot dogs."

The mechanic can't help smiling.

His uncle nods, says, "But it was good, what finally happened. We were forgetting how to hunt. How to smell and listen and see. We didn't have to chase our food anymore. We just waited for it to come out from the kitchen."

The mechanic looks down at his ice cream. It came from the kitchen too.

"Well, what the people with the houses finally did, it was they started laying out the fine forks and knives and spoons. The *silver* ones. So every time we would reach down for the soup spoon, or for the knife to cut a slice of ham, it would burn us. And if we touched it to our mouths, it would burn our lips. Pretty soon we quit going from door to door."

"What happened?" the mechanic asks.

"A lot of werewolves starved. But the ones that didn't, well, that's where *we* come from. And that's why we like shiny things. They make us think of all-you-can-eat."

The mechanic's uncle drains his cup of strawberry wine cooler, like to prove what he'd just said. And then he steals the mechanic's bowl, slurps up the melted last bit of ice cream.

"Let's go before somebody nabs it," he says then, tipping his head out to the grab bar, and they're almost to the front door when the first trucker, the one with the dirty hat, is stepping out of the bathroom.

"Hurry," the mechanic's uncle says, looking back to that trucker, trying not to laugh, and the mechanic plays along, runs with him. It's better than getting left behind.

"Ah, still there," the uncle says, jumping up onto the running board of his rig with one boot, grabbing on to the shiny bar. Then, to show how tight those four bolts are, to show how good of a job the mechanic's done, he pulls and yanks and jerks, finally planting his feet up on the side of the cab like a cartoon, the nails in one of his boots gouging into the red paint.

The grab bar doesn't come off.

And the trucker with the dirty cap, he's standing there now, watching the mechanic's uncle. "I'd save my energy, I was you," he says, working a wad of chew into his mouth, lots of the grains and strings falling down.

The uncle, still holding on, looks down, then makes sure where the mechanic is.

"You might have to push-start this one, I mean," the trucker says, cocking his boot up onto the bumper hard enough that some of the flakes of rust come off.

"Get in the truck," the uncle says to the mechanic, coming back down to the running board with one boot, his right hand still grabbing the chrome bar, like for strength.

"*Bra* Wolf?" the other trucker says, leaning forward to spit a brown stream onto the shallow tread of the uncle's front tire.

"In, now," the uncle says again, playtime over, and the mechanic does, and the last thing he sees before his uncle lowers himself from even with the window on that side, it's that his uncle's bitten through the thermometer, so that the silver is running down his chin with the blood, and the mechanic closes his eyes, knows that the people still don't want werewolves coming to dinner.

But they are anyway, he says to himself, to help his uncle.

And they're hungrier than ever.

CHAPTER 11

Bark at the Moon

We didn't know how she kept finding us.

Libby called her Darren's secret admirer.

That was fine with Darren.

The love letters he sent her were sparkly. They were colorful.

It was all a big joke.

We were in South Carolina for the first time. Darren was driving back and forth from Tulsa, just delivering civilian goods for once—"mall runs," he called them. Pallets of sweatshirts, boxes of mixed electronics, seasonal decorations. He'd had to get a Social Security number, even. It had somebody else's name on it, but still, he was paying taxes. Because he wasn't married, didn't have kids, could work the holidays the other truckers shied away from, the company wanted him to stick around, maybe make a career of it. They leased him a shiny Peterbilt and gave him all the caps he could wear.

Darren played along. Even werewolves know a good gig when

they've got it—Libby too. She was working the register at a lube place. It was out on the interstate. Some of the bays were caverns, for the big trucks to rumble through at all hours. The pits under the bays seemed to go for miles. Because truckers are around the clock, the lube place was too.

Like Darren, Libby pulled the night shift, when the rest of the crew wanted to be home.

This left me at our trailer alone most of the time.

I was going to school some—tenth grade still—but now it was just a place to walk through, a way to keep from turning a wrench in a dingy shop. I didn't have anything against the pep rallies, and the cafeteria food was like a dream that happened on a schedule, but I knew not to let myself get too attached. I didn't want to get in another Georgia situation. Another Brittany situation. Or maybe she really was Layla now. C's were easy enough to pull in South Carolina, anyway. They didn't attract attention. They worked for metal shop, for social studies, for history.

Mr. Brennan wouldn't let me slide in English, though. He said he didn't want me to fall through. That I had something the other kids didn't.

A werewolf gene, yeah.

I didn't say it out loud.

English was fourth period.

To be safe, I would skip it and fifth together.

Sorry, Mr. Brennan.

It worked out for the best, though. Because I didn't have essays to write each night, I could walk out through the pastures and the trees, my hands open, the seed heads of the grass scraping my palms. And because I was out there, I was the first one to see her this time. Darren's secret admirer.

She was driving a different RV, but it was definitely her. Who else would be out picking through the grass with a flashlight, her belt clinking with mason jars, her fingers long and chrome?

Not forceps, quite. They were closer to tongs, but sturdier and more delicate at the same time.

She moved like a water bird in the shallows, hunting frogs, and she moved so slow you could zone out, watching her, so that soon she would be walking through a dream you were having with your eyes open.

It didn't help that her hair was always pulled back in this frizzy French braid. When she pooled her flashlight in the jars so she could better see a specimen, the light would wash back up into her face and her hair would become this halo. It made her look like an angel, or an alien.

Because she was always staring into the grass, she didn't even see the silhouette of me standing there, frozen with terror.

The last time she'd found us had been Texas.

I was about fifth grade, I guess. It had taken us one long drive to get from Arkansas to Florida after Grandpa died, but it had taken us three years to make it back even that far. "Riding the yo-yo," Darren called it, talking about how all we did was swing back and forth from the East Coast to Texas or New Mexico then back again, trying to stay ahead of the cold. Trying to hide our footprints.

Libby said it was more like riding the pendulum in a clock, one that was ticking our lives away, one that was counting us down.

Clocks and yo-yos weren't the real reason we were in Texas, though. We were in Texas because Texas touched Arkansas. Wherever we found ourselves, whatever state we were in, Arkansas was the direction Libby would always be looking when she thought nobody was watching.

Red was still there, or he might be.

Even the chance was enough for her.

Darren would just thin his lips, shake his head, even when Libby told him that someday he'd get it.

"What, *love?*" Darren would say, lowering into his boxer stance, ducking and weaving like bring it.

"Dad never planned on getting hitched either," Libby would say on her way out of whatever room this was happening in, and that was that.

The secret admirer wasn't why we left Texas that time, though. We'd left Texas because I'd burned our trailer to the ground. But according to Darren, we'd been going to split out of there anyway. It was because, a couple of weeks before the fire, a clerk at a grocery store had asked Darren if he wanted any strawberry wine coolers to go with that can of store-brand chili. Instead of looking up to this clerk, Darren had looked out the front window to me, waiting in our rusted-up GTO that didn't have any get-up-and-go. My forearms were scraped red from forcing my hands between the seats, for the money for that can of chili.

What Darren was doing at that register, he told me afterward, was measuring paces. Timing things out, just like Libby had been saying all along.

That the grocery-store clerk knew about his taste for strawberry wine coolers could only mean that clerk was a former liquor-store clerk—one of those liquor stores that back up to a creek or a bluff or a pasture, some terrain no stickup artist could possibly escape into. Not on two legs. Darren had probably robbed him at some point. And now he'd migrated down to Texas.

"Wine coolers?" Darren said across the register. "You calling me a woman?"

The clerk didn't even blink, didn't look away.

"Not a woman, no," the clerk said at last, and dropped the change into the drawer, pushed it shut. "Anything else, sir?"

Which was when Darren said he decided we'd outstayed our welcome in Texas.

One thing we didn't need was our GTO's description on the radio, or smokeys in the air, bubble lights in the rearview. I mean, we're werewolves, being hunted's part of it. But no need to stand up and wave to the hunters.

But this secret admirer, the way she hunted us, it was different.

She didn't carry a gun, for one, just a canister of what Darren said was pepper spray. It made him curl his lip away from his teeth when he said it. I didn't ask.

For two, she was off in a way that didn't track. Like, she didn't fit the mold we all had in our heads, of somebody with an assortment of boot knives, somebody who chews on blue-tipped matches in a very methodical way, and threads them from their lips every little bit, like to study the square wood shaft, see if this match is going to be different than every other match in the box. In Georgia, where Libby had been sweeping and mopping an office building in the daytime for once, the secret admirer had come in to the records department. In the lobby she'd eaten three pieces of butterscotch candy and drank half a cup of coffee. Instead of just leaving the wrappers where the doors had blown them, behind her padded bench, she got down on her knees to fish them out, deposit them in the trash.

Werewolves notice this type of behavior.

It made the secret admirer a mystery.

To solve it, and because he had time then, had still been healing from a dustup with Red, Darren drifted out into the night to spy, under strict orders from Libby to leave the woman be. To be sure of it, she came home with a side of clearanced brisket, left it raw on the propane tank behind the trailer. Wolfed out, Darren couldn't resist a feast like this, right in his path. It kept the edge off his hunger like Libby wanted, let him remember what he'd promised.

One thing about werewolves that none of the movies ever get into, it's that their intestinal tract is more canine than human. Humans' intestines go back and forth like a sack of snakes, so they can wring every last bit of nutrition from their precious grains and vegetables. Meat doesn't take nearly as long to process. With a wolf or a dog, a meal can pass through them in eight or nine hours.

Werewolves, we burn faster. That trick about the bladder shrinking when you wolf out? It's to make room for the stomach, I think. Darren said he ate a whole just-born lamb once—though Libby told me later he'd had to dig that lamb from the momma sheep's belly. So it might not have been quite full size. She never would tell me the most she'd ate at once, said it wasn't ladylike, but she would say she'd seen Grandpa splash out into a pond after a swan once, a big white bull swan like swoop through once in a decade, and there hadn't been anything left afterward but feathers, floating above the pond like a pillow fight.

If you *don't* push a meal that size through quick, then you might get caught in the morning with a ruptured gut.

Which is to say, Darren's brisket, it cooked out of him in about four hours that night, while he was ghosting around upwind of the woman with the French braid, to see if she could catch his scent or not.

When Darren came back, he told us he figured she was pushing forty with a pretty big stick, had been blond at one point, didn't grow her nails long—nails were always the first thing Darren noticed—and, for the first couple of hours watching her, he was pretty sure she was the worst firefly hunter ever. Instead of going where the fireflies *were*, she was looking down in all the tall grass. Like maybe that's where firefly nits hang out? Is a baby firefly a glowworm?

Neither Libby nor me had any kind of clue.

Just because you're *in* nature doesn't mean you know the encyclopedia of it.

"She married?" Libby asked, and Darren had to turn his head to the side, to track up from the memory of the secret admirer's fingernails.

She did have a ring on, yes. On her wedding finger. Darren rubbed his own to show.

"But she's alone," I said, because I was the one who'd seen the RV first, through the trees, when I was running away.

That was the time Libby'd ghosted me, I think. Probably because the RV was lurking around.

All we wanted was for her to make sense.

We'd have been more comfortable with some scarred-up soldier of fortune on a rattletrap Harley, probably. You know to run, then. You know not to just keep watching through the trees.

Werewolves aren't related to raccoons, I don't think, but when I saw the RV that first time, my light blue backpack hooked over my shoulder, there'd been a raccoon out there with me, watching the RV as well. Casing it like they do.

I hissed at it to split, and it hissed back.

Just wait, I'd told it in my head.

Darren's story a few nights later didn't have any raccoons in it. In typical werewolf fashion, his real discovery was last, and kind of loud-whispered, for dramatic effect, his eyes bugging out as much as he could. And he only leaned forward to deliver it after we'd gone around and around the house with him, looking over his shoulder while she inspected this tree, while she drank from that thermos. With him, we watched her look at the sky, even. Like for the mothership. For giant bats blotting out the moon.

"And?" Libby prompted, because her shift was about to start.

Darren smiled.

"Then I had to, you know," he said, "off-load some of that brisket."

Libby sat back into the couch shaking her head, disgusted with herself for having trusted him again.

He wasn't done, though.

In two hours, the secret admirer's careful grid delivered her to that pile.

Usually, werewolf scat will be roped with grey hair, from whatever we've run down. The stomach acid bleaches *all* the hair grey, doesn't matter if it was brown or black or red going in. Tonight the prey had been hairless, though. Cut meat from the grocery store, the fat even trimmed off.

The woman fell to her knees. When she lifted her hand, her chrome tongs, they were shaking.

"No," Libby said.

Yes, Darren nodded. Yes all the way.

She was a scat collector, like the people who hoard owl pellets, just to dissect them later.

Just, she was after bigger game, as it were.

It was why, when Darren came back from his next Tulsa run and had a night off for once, instead of the two of us watching monster movies Libby wouldn't approve of, he fired up his Peterbilt and took us to the dollar store.

Back by party supplies, we found the glitter and the tinsel and the confetti.

Because he was flush from a run, we bought it all.

It was the best joke ever.

That night while *Jeopardy!* was playing and Darren was yelling true answers—no, yelling his answers true—I stood at the counter in the kitchen and massaged all the shiny bits into whatever random meat we'd had in the refrigerator. Other families, I've heard they keep their steaks in the freezer.

Not werewolves.

We might buy more than we can eat if it's on the day-old rack and we've got the cash, but when we want it, we want it now, not after stupid defrosting.

"I don't want to see it," Darren said when I was done, had the sparkly meat all laid out on the counter like a constellation. He blocked the side of his face so none of the light would twinkle his direction.

I'd seen him bite the heads off squealing prairie dogs, I'd seen him lower his face into day-old roadkill on a dare, but the idea of eating glitter made him cough and gag.

At least when he was standing on two feet.

I took the steaks and ground beef outside, sat it all on top of the barbecue grill concreted into an old tire. The grill was too rusted to cook on, but the big dome of a top was the perfect height for Darren to reach—in about an hour.

"You'll be good?" he said after the second *Jeopardy!*, arcing a loud line of pee out the back door. "Do your homework, all that?"

"Already done," I told him.

"Not going to go out to the highway, hitchhike into town?"

I shook my head no, obviously.

It was a play we were both acting in. He was being the responsible adult, I was being the diligent student. It let us feel less like we were lying to Libby, when she'd ask later.

"Well then," Darren said, hauling his shirt over his head, leaving his hair a mess. "Time to leave a sweet nothing for my lady, I guess." He wowed his eyes out and it would have been a classic moment, except his nose started bleeding. It happens some of the time, with transformations you flex like a muscle, that you have to think about it. It's like something in the nasal cavity jumps the gun, goes out of order. When you're shifting from instinct, there's never a nosebleed. The wolf comes like clockwork, then.

I was keeping track of every bit of this.

"*Any* the hell way," Darren said, looking at the nose blood he'd just rubbed onto his forearm, and, just to gross me out, he licked the flat of his tongue along all of it, keeping me in his stare the whole time, daring me not to watch. And then he stepped down from the trailer, into another body.

When I looked out the window like I still couldn't keep from doing, he'd already slurped the shiny meat from the grill, was running off into the night with it flapping from either side of his muzzle.

Early next week, our biology teacher, the one who made us call her "Daisy" instead of *Ms.* or *Mrs.*, she brought in another special guest.

So far we'd had the director of the wild bird refuge, we'd had a forensic specialist because Daisy's brother was a state trooper— he'd talked about decay and insects—and we'd had a chemist from the local seed company who never once looked up from her prepared paper.

This time, it was a scat collector. This time, it was the secret admirer.

As it turned out, she was a wildlife biologist.

I looked over to the door, waiting for her to fill it. At one time, that's what I'd thought I could be, a wildlife biologist. That it would be perfect, that I'd always have an excuse for running around in the woods. That I could take better and closer pictures than all the other wildlife biologists. That I could secretly use my nose to find the animals.

I was going to be a star.

It never involved using a probe to dissect my uncle's glitter-flecked crap.

My uncle's secret admirer made us all take a turn.

"Is the tinsel for—for instructional purposes?" Daisy asked, holding her hand up like the most polite periscope.

If she didn't always wear a lab coat, I'd have thought she was just a senior.

I didn't look up for the answer, but listened with every part of my body. It's a special ability known only to werewolves and fourteen-year-olds.

"I think the creator of this specimen has learned to pick through human litter," the secret admirer said. "Like a bear at a national park. Like the monkeys in Costa Rica or Bangladesh. Like—"

"—like somebody had a party," Daisy said, hopefully. Cheerfully.

"Somebody's always having a party," the secret admirer said. "This isn't the first time I've encountered this particular animal's scat."

"What is it?" a student asked.

"Good question," the secret admirer said, and cued up the slide show she'd had locked and loaded, just to answer this specific question. It was a version of the children's book I'd seen in a hundred truck stops: *Who Pooped in the Park?*

Going by size, the secret admirer estimated this particular animal weighed about a hundred and seventy pounds.

The correct answer: "Who is Darren?"

The movies always make werewolves so much bigger than their human versions. It's all bullshit. Conservation of mass. If anything, after shifting you're a few ounces lighter, taking into account all the calories you just had to burn through. All the saliva you're now stringing down to the ground.

"A bear, right?" that same student said, a measure of disgust working its way into his voice.

"The diameter is about right, yes," the secret admirer said. "But"—*click*: next slide—"I've encountered this scat across three states, now. Bears are much more territorial. They find a place they like, they stay there."

"Panther?" Daisy said then, her smile becoming less sincere somehow, probably because she wanted her students to be *right*, not stupid. At least not for special guests.

"Again, right *size*," the secret admirer said, tapping her pencil against her chin. "But, and I've been doing this for quite some time now, cougar or mountain lion scat is notoriously difficult to find."

"Because they're a cat," a different student said.

"Exactly," the secret admirer said, pointing her pencil at that student like a magic wand. One that made her right. "They bury it, and it's gone before I can dig it up. But . . . how many of you have dogs?"

"It never goes away," one of the football players said in the most dejected tone possible, and everybody laughed like they were supposed to.

"Correct," the secret admirer said. "Dogs are, shall we say, more proud of their scat?"

"So this is a *dog*?" the football player asked.

It made the part of the class bunched around the specimen give it more room.

This wasn't exotic, this was just like all of their backyards. *Eww.*

"Dogs *are* travelers," the secret admirer said. "And they do sometimes attain this size. But I'm looking for a different answer, from . . ."

Me.

Her pencil had singled me out. Not because of my blood, I didn't think, and not because she knew my silhouette, but because I was the quiet one. I was the one she could save, the one she could transform into a hero, right here in front of everybody.

I looked up, caught in the headlights.

"Mr. Tolbert?" Daisy said.

We called her by her first name, she called us by our last. I never understood.

I swallowed, was sure it was a tidal wave everyone heard.

"What's bigger than a dog, and might range across three—is it three?—states?" Daisy said, waiting for me to finally speak my first word aloud in her class.

"Wolf?" I had to say.

"Exactly what I would have said," the secret admirer said, and I somehow even heard it above the pounding of my heart. "Except that, when I do the hematrace on it—have you done ABA cards with them yet?" she said to Daisy.

"Umm . . . not *yet*," Daisy said.

"But you did have a forensic tech in to speak to them?"

"*Was* it a wolf?" a football player asked.

"According to visual identification," the secret admirer said, "yes, a very, very large canid. But the hematrace disagrees, and ABA cards aren't fooled by visual similarities. They will occasionally get false positives, but only in the case of higher apes. And ferrets."

"Was it a ferret, then?" Daisy asked hopefully.

"Or a hyena?" the football player asked.

"False positives with *what?*" one of the science stars said, just thinking out loud, it seemed.

"Exactly," the secret admirer said. Then, to all: "Any guesses?"

Daisy smiled around to all of us, waiting for one of us to be smart, to prove she was a good teacher.

She's still waiting.

"Human," the secret admirer said, a thrill in her eyes.

The cheerleader currently operating the probe let it clatter to the specimen tray in what felt like slow motion, like this probe was teasing apart the life she'd been living from the life she would now have to endure, and then she turned around and calmly threw up into her hands, tried to carry her thin vomit to one of the sinks stationed between the lab tables.

Through the laughing, coughing, gagging mob of sophomore and juniors that swelled out from her efforts, Daisy squealing above the din, what I remember best is the secret admirer sitting prim and proper on her stool, her hands crossed over one another in her lap. She was looking calmly through all the student bodies. She was looking right at me.

I should have smiled, or made myself gag. I should have pretended to be what I wasn't. It's Basic Werewolf 101.

Instead, I couldn't look away from that silver tinsel, woven through the specimen. Tinsel I'd put there. Tinsel the secret admirer could find on the shelf at the dollar store if she wanted. It was four packs for a buck.

It was just a joke.

One I couldn't smile about anymore.

———

That night I broke into the secret admirer's RV. It was parked right there in the high school parking lot.

Werewolves are good with locks, good with windows.

I pulled the flimsy door shut behind me and stood there, waiting for my eyes to adjust.

If the windows on one side suddenly glowed with headlights, I was sure I would finally shift. That I would claw my way up through a panel in the ceiling and launch off the top of the RV, fly over the car, land perfect on all fours, look back to her just long enough that she could know she was right, that the wildlife biology she'd learned at college had been incomplete, that she could have learned more in folklore.

If I didn't shift, I'd be expelled. Simple as that. No more cafeteria lunches. No more pep rallies. No more surprise guests.

But that would be okay too.

We'd already been in one place for eight months. It was the new record. Darren was paying his truck down, Libby'd got two raises and earned some vacation time she had no idea how to use—you don't go on vacation from being a werewolf—and I had three report cards stuck to the refrigerator.

In werewolf families, report cards aren't on the refrigerator because of the good grade you got. The report card *is* the A.

When my eyes wouldn't adjust enough, I risked it all, flipped the light on.

It was a kitchen and a bedroom and a laboratory and a shrine and a cab and a living room all at once.

I studied the lab first.

One whole cabinet was just mason jars, bungee-corded to the back of the cabinet that was a pegboard.

One row of jars was all love letters from Darren. Six of them, maybe. This was the shrine.

The RV's stiff leaf springs had shaken the glitter from some of the drier ones, so that it had settled at the bottom of the jar like fairy dust.

Darren's idea was always that she would think it was unicorn shit.

I'd seen her find it once or twice, even. The glitter pulled her light toward it.

I didn't know if this was funny or sad, now.

I knew what I was supposed to do, what Libby had always told me to do: Destroy all evidence. Shatter the jars, or carry them out armful by armful, drop them in a ditch.

I had a shoe box of important stuff too, though. Of secrets and dreams. Of unicorn shit.

Libby would have done it herself, I knew—burned this place down, or had Darren do it—except we thought the secret admirer was burying everything she found, that she was hiding the evidence *for* us.

It was what made her a freak, what made it all so funny.

In Texas that time, we'd followed her in the car once, at night. Her RV was a carnival of lights.

Where she was taking it was cemeteries. She'd walk in with a jar and a trowel, and walk out with just the trowel.

"I never knew I was that special," Darren had said.

That was when he started eating the glitter, the tinsel, the confetti. You realize you're onstage, you dress things up.

But now I knew what she was doing. What she thought she was doing.

She was burying the dead.

She knew what wolf scat looked like, and she knew how to read "human" from lab results. She knew what had been digested. What *could* have been digested.

A time or two, she might have even been right.

I reached out for a jar, to do what I was supposed to, but stopped, lifted my nose to the air like was natural now. Not that I could smell any better, really. But . . . the bedroom.

It felt wrong, like a violation, like real and meaningful breaking and entering, but I stepped in all the same.

It smelled like eye crust, like a thousand nights of sleep.

Once I was all the way through the short door, I looked behind me, at the wall. At what she had on the wall to go to sleep to.

It was all newspaper clippings.

There was an angel out there on the interstates of the South. Someone, a trucker probably, secretly taking care of the dead animals on the roads. Not the deer and alligators or the bears and armadillos and rabbits, but the dogs, the coyotes.

A real Wolf Man in the Sky.

It made me remember Darren from years ago, acting the toreador in the living room one night. In his story, the trucks were his bulls. And it was his job to stand out there with the smushed animals, balance sideways on the white stripes so the big trucks could sweep past, inches from the tip of his nose.

Between headlights he would drag the dead over to the ditch.

Used to, apparently, that had been part of the state troopers' duties, to scoop dogs and coyotes into the ditch.

Now the Angel of I-20 was doing that for them.

I wanted this Angel to be the secret admirer, taking samples, doing whatever an "ABA card" was to them, jigsawing skeletons back together, doing what she considered science, but then I saw it as she had to be seeing it—as she had to be *associating* it.

Was there usually less roadkill on the interstate right around wherever she was finding the unicorn shit again?

That was how she kept finding us, state after state. Because Darren always climbed down from the cab, to see if this was anybody he knew, splatted across the road. All she had to do was drive and drive until the roadkill thinned out, and then start walking through the tall grass, wait for her flashlight to sparkle something up.

Shit.

I turned away from the wall, to the bed. To her nightstand.

Screwed down by the lamp was a metal-framed photograph from years ago, the glare from the RV's weak overhead light washing it into a negative of itself: somebody in a driveway, like a thousand family snapshots I'd seen in RVs all across the South. Because it's never the department-store portraits that really capture who someone was. It's that time you caught him smiling just right over by the fence. That perfect slice of an afternoon that now has to stand in for a whole life.

Meaning whoever this was in the photograph the secret admirer had been carrying across so many states, he was dead.

I looked closer, made to pull the frame up to me but, when it wouldn't budge, when it was screwed down against all the bumps and potholes the RV would hit, I had to reorient myself to it.

At first I thought it was Daisy's brother, the one who'd come in to talk to us, who'd never taken his chrome sunglasses off, like it was important we all think he was a robot, that he had no feelings.

Except this state trooper, he was from the decade before Daisy's brother. His cruiser gave it away. It was a black-and-white Matador, the front wheels cocked over to show the right amount of attitude. No hubcaps because a high-speed chase could happen at any moment.

This photograph was day one on the job, then. It had to be. Look, Ma, I made it. Shined shoes and a burr cut, a mouth a little too cool to grin but about to anyway. Eyes like mirrors.

I had to reach down for the bed to balance against when it

hit me that I knew him, that I knew this trooper, that I'd always known him.

Not by the sunglasses, not by the build, and not by the Matador.

It was the thick black belt. It was the pearl-handled pistol cocked up out of that belt. There was a silver star set in that white handle. A *Texas* star.

He was the reason we'd driven halfway across the country in a single push, until we hit the ocean, couldn't get any farther away.

I tried to swallow, couldn't.

A week later Darren was home again, his boots kicked up onto the real coffee table.

We had a black-and-white werewolf movie turned up so loud it was shaking the walls of the trailer.

It was the funniest thing ever, like they all are, but we'd each get deadly quiet whenever the camera was running somebody down through the trees. When we were looking through the wolf's eyes.

Darren was convinced that the director had to be a werewolf, to get this much right. To have cut *this* way around a tree, not *that* way.

By the end of the movie he'd drawn a thick blue pentagram onto his palm.

Because I knew how this went, I fell sideways from my end of the couch the instant he flicked an eye my way. I was already scrabbling for the kitchen but he caught me like always, licked his palm long and gross, and pressed that ink hard into my forehead, marking me.

"Now you're like me," he said in his movie werewolf voice.

"That's not how it goes," I told him, already trying to rub the star off. "They won't let me in school if I have a tattoo . . ."

It was a lie, I was pretty sure, but he believed it, helped me wash it off, looking over his shoulder for Libby at each moment, even though she never came home only an hour after going in.

"You're so brave," I told him.

"Blow *your* scrawny ass down," he said, and scrubbed harder.

An hour later, because the RV was still parked at the high school, we were back at the dollar store, prowling the aisles for hilarious stuff Darren could swallow.

I hated it.

"Bathroom," I said, and peeled off.

Darren hardly noticed, was already carrying a string of Mardi Gras beads he planned on taking apart, swallowing one by one like an overdose.

Because I didn't really need the bathroom, I just drifted through the toy aisles on the other side of the store, and watched Darren in the curved mirror. He was trying to read the safety warnings on a pack of watercolors, it looked like.

To look like I was shopping, I pulled a couple of O.K. Corral play sets from their long pegs, to better see the pegboard behind them. It was the same pattern and hole size as the pegboard behind the jars in the RV.

I traded the O.K. Corral for a pirate kit, and stopped at the plastic werewolf mask staring up at me, left the pirate stuff there.

Darren was waiting for me at the register.

"Anything?" he asked, looking at my hands for hilarious finds, and I shook my head no.

He had a rubber severed finger, was holding it in place of the finger he was missing.

"That'll stop you up if you eat it," I told him.

In the parking lot he bit it in half. It didn't look as real anymore, with the grey foam showing instead of the finger bone, but not dying from the joke was an important part of the joke.

It was almost midnight when we got back to the trailer.

"You'll tell me if she throws a fit?" he said, unbuttoning his shirt.

He'd already peed out front, standing on the chrome gas tank of his Peterbilt.

"It'll be great," I said, kneading the ground meat on the counter, making it mushier. "I think *Wheel*'s on," I added, hooking my head to the living room.

He looked at me like I was crazy—on *this* late?—but still, he had to stand there, run through all the channels, pressing the button harder and harder like he could make *Wheel* roll up from the bottom of the screen.

It gave me just enough time to slide the second O.K. Corral kit from the front of my pants.

Werewolves can steal anything.

If a camera had been watching me at the dollar store, if someone in back had me on their little black-and-white screen—and you always have to assume they do—then what they would have seen was a tall fourteen-year-old delinquent peeling a costume kit or two up from a peg.

What their *mind* would correct that to, though, was just one kit. Because who needs two of the same, right? You have one face, you need one mask.

Then when I traded the kit they knew I had for the pirate one, the other was already slipping down the front of my pants, where, for a one-dollar item, it might not even be worth it to perform an inspection.

What I wanted was that silver star.

It was real tin, it looked like. Nearly foil it was so thin, sure, but not plastic anyway. Plastic would catch in Darren's gut.

A badge, though.

It was for that Arkansas trooper's widow, as I was now calling her. Darren's secret admirer. Our wildlife biologist.

This time I just sat on the couch when Darren left.

He could have caught me, called me out on what I'd slipped into his next meal.

But not the wolf.

I flipped the channels, going deeper and deeper into the night, and finally stopped on one of the sequels of the movie we'd been watching earlier. It was what the station was calling a Full Moon Marathon. A long mournful howl led into each commercial, and then, after we'd been sold beer and tampons, words would spin up onto the screen in scary yellow, telling us to "bark at the moon," all together now . . .

Libby would hate it.

I kicked my feet up onto the coffee table.

Soon, four or five days from now, a woman was going to follow her flashlight into a cemetery.

I could see her now, like through a camera.

She's holding her mason jar tight to her chest, she's on her knees now, she's digging a hole, she's patting the dirt over the jar and she's telling her husband what happened to him, that she figured it out after all these years, that it's all real. That there's more out there in the night than his training ever could have prepared him for. And now she's smoothing the dirt so the groundskeeper won't notice, so he won't dig this crumpled badge up. And now her hand, it's still there, on her husband's chest.

I settled in, turned the volume up.

CHAPTER 12

Year of the Wolf

Is *that* wolfsbane?" the hitchhiker says, pointing out the side window of his uncle's tall truck.

"Buttercups again," the hitchhiker's aunt says, tired of this game.

She's hitchhiking too, if it can count as hitchhiking when your car's broke down, so you have to ride with your brother.

"It probably *would* make you sick, though," the hitchhiker's uncle says, shifting into a lower gear. "If there's really butter in them, I mean."

A few miles ago, because the hitchhiker's almost ten, his uncle let him sit in his lap, steer the big wheel, even honk the horn three times. The hitchhiker's fourth-grade teacher would never have let him do that. But Miss Carlin was still back in Alabama.

The hitchhiker's aunt had written a note to her, explaining that the hitchhiker wasn't absent so please don't worry about him or report his absence, but then they hadn't stopped by the school to deliver the note.

Because of *trails*, the hitchhiker's aunt said. Because of bread crumbs. Because their rent being double-late had happened on the exact same day as their Monte Carlo died. It was a sign. It meant they were moving again. Werewolves can read nature like that, the hitchhiker's uncle explained. It's because of their heightened senses. Because of their big ears, their big eyes.

Three hours ago they'd crossed into Mississippi.

"It safe here?" the hitchhiker's aunt says, pulling the hitchhiker closer to her. It's all billboards and pastures so far.

The hitchhiker's uncle leans over the steering wheel with his whole body. "Wolfsbane only grows in movies," he says instead of a real answer. Then, special to the hitchhiker, "Want to know the real poison for werewolves?"

The hitchhiker's aunt looks over too.

"*Mustard,*" the uncle says, having to whisper it because it's so deadly.

The hitchhiker tries to imagine it, having to eat mustard. It makes him laugh and gross out at the same time.

"Don't listen to him," the aunt says, close to the hitchhiker's ear. "Mustard's *good.*"

He doesn't believe her. He'll always hate mustard, he promises himself.

"So where is this place?" the hitchhiker's aunt says.

"Right up here," the hitchhiker's uncle says.

Soon enough they're downshifting, taking the ramp.

The last meal was ten hours ago.

Where the hitchhiker's uncle is taking them is a grown-over peach orchard he heard about. Not for the peaches, but for the fat deer that come to eat the peaches.

This is a hunt.

"It's going to be perfect," the uncle says, leaning even more over the wheel, to see the turnoff. "Private property, nobody knows about it, way out in nowhere. It's a good start. It's going to be a good year. The best year."

His big truck rattles slow over one cattleguard then another. There's five sets of rattles because that's how many axles the truck has. The hitchhiker keeps count, making sure the whole trailer is still with them. By the time the road goes to dirt, the uncle has to turn the headlights on, downshift even lower, breathe only through his nose.

"How are you going to turn back around?" the hitchhiker's aunt says.

"I haven't had deer for, for—" the uncle says, and a line of on-purpose drool goes from the corner of his mouth.

"What if it has mustard on it?" the hitchhiker says, halfway hiding in his aunt's lap, because he knows what his uncle will do, here. It's part of the game he knows he's too old for but can't resist: the uncle whipping his head over, his eyes hot, his hand pulling long on the horn, his mouth moving like he's screaming about this mustard on his deer.

The horn is really three horns, all tied into one. Illegal in ninety-nine countries, the hitchhiker's uncle keeps saying. The only horn hearable from the moon.

"There?" the hitchhiker's aunt says, pointing out the left side of the truck.

"Ahh," the hitchhiker's uncle says.

Rows of evenly spaced trees going off into the distance. Like soldiers standing guard.

"X marks the spot," the hitchhiker's uncle says, and when the hitchhiker leans up to see what his uncle's talking about, the uncle pulls his wet finger from his mouth and draws an X of spit on the hitchhiker's forehead. .

"You're gross," the hitchhiker's aunt says.

"I'm not the one with spit on my head, am I?" the uncle says, rolling out his side of the truck before the hitchhiker can get him back.

They leave the truck idling, the running lights on.

The hitchhiker runs across between the cab and the trailer, high-stepping over the air hoses. The aunt ducks under the trailer, holding her hair up so it won't get fluff in it from the weeds.

It's nearly full dark.

The hitchhiker's uncle is smelling the wind.

"Where are they?" he says, opening and closing his hand like some ancient werewolf trick to bring the deer in.

"Maybe this is the wrong one," the hitchhiker's aunt says. "Aren't peach trees all curvy?"

"How many orchards can there be on one road?" the hitchhiker's uncle says.

The hitchhiker steps into the tall grass and weeds then jumps back when something gold and scaly scampers away, making the worst snuffling noise in the world.

"Think we can eat those?" the hitchhiker's uncle says. "A world of buzzards can't be wrong, can they?"

"We're not scavengers," the hitchhiker's aunt says, stepping out there too. For the trees. "This isn't peaches. It's that—it's that *nut*," she says, when she gets to the first one. "Pecan, right?"

The hitchhiker's uncle reaches up to a branch, shakes it. Black husks rain down all around them. Clusters of the pecans.

The hitchhiker's aunt and uncle look at each other about this.

"They *are* food," the uncle says, squatting to pick a pecan husk up, look at it from every side. "Sort of." He pulls the pecan out. Its looks like a giant wooden seed.

"We had them at school once," the hitchhiker says.

"That was walnuts," his aunt says.

"They're not the same thing?" the uncle says.

When he cracks the pecan open in his fist it's like a gunshot.

Inside, the meat is wood-colored too. He holds it across to the hitchhiker's aunt.

She brushes imaginary dirt from it, pops one of the halves into her mouth.

After chewing for a few seconds, she nods.

The hitchhiker's uncle eats one, eats two, then smiles. Now it's a pecan massacre. The hitchhiker and his aunt hold the uncle's shirt between them like a blanket and his uncle shakes the big limbs of the trees until the shirt's almost too heavy to hold. When there's enough for a meal—for ten meals—the aunt and uncle dive in. Because the hitchhiker only likes to eat perfect halves, not the ones that break, he only gets to eat one out of every five or so that he manages to open. And because his hands aren't grown-up yet, he can't open them nearly as fast as his aunt and uncle. And then, when his uncle finds a wasp nest, it doesn't matter because the uncle's chasing them through the trees, finally getting bit on the neck and shoulder.

The hitchhiker is eating the sixth pecan of his life, the wasps all gone back to sleep, when he hears a sound not like eating.

It's his uncle, the dry crumbs of his thirtieth or fortieth pecan oozing from his mouth like chunky sawdust.

"What?" the hitchhiker's aunt says to him, and then the hitchhiker's uncle is falling to his knees, and then he's holding his stomach. Then he's lying on his side groaning, his shoulders shaking.

The hitchhiker's aunt feels her way over to him, holding her hand out for the hitchhiker to stay where he is.

Before she can say anything, it hits her too.

The pecans.

They ate too many, too fast.

The hitchhiker drops the one he was trying to open and stands into the dusk, both his aunt and his uncle lying on the ground pedaling their legs slow, their faces twisted up, eyes muddy with crying.

Already, because it's the natural thing to do, the uncle is shifting. To protect himself.

"*Run,*" the hitchhiker's aunt says, shooshing him away, and by the time she says it her mouth is thick with her new teeth, her eyes are cloudy, between colors.

The hitchhiker falls back into the grass and then falls all the way to the truck, climbs in and pulls the door shut, cranks the window up fast.

Sitting on the middle now, on what his uncle calls the doghouse, there's the CB.

The hitchhiker takes it down, looping the spirally cable around his wrist like his uncle does. Then, still doing like he's been taught, he opens his mouth a second before he's pulled the mic all the way to his lips. It makes it feel like he's got the words ready—his uncle's words, his uncle's trucker handle.

"Breaker, breaker," the hitchhiker says again. "This is Wolf Man in the Sky, howling down at you from—from . . ."

His uncle always told him that part.

"What's your twenty again, Wolfie?" a voice comes back.

"They're dying," the hitchhiker says, and hates the way his voice is crying.

"Where are you, son?" a different voice asks, and the hitchhiker looks all around, at the rows of trees, the broken fence, the windmill.

"It's not—not mustard," he says, and then tries to turn their voices up, loses them all.

When a dark, long-legged shape steps into the glow of the running lights in front of the truck, the hitchhiker reaches up for the horn-string.

It's a deer and her baby.

They've gotten used to the rumbling truck, are just doing what they do. Maybe this *is* the right road, the right orchard.

Now the momma deer's looking up at the windshield.

Finally she twitches her tail twice like whisking away her concern. She steps past the bumper, isn't even all the way out of the road when she's jerked into the darkness like it's a giant mouth.

The hitchhiker crawls up the back of the driver's seat, and, because he wants to get higher, get away, he pulls himself up by his hands as well, not paying attention to what he's grabbing on to for purchase.

The horn-string, as it turns out. The horn blasts out loud and long, because if the hitchhiker lets go, he'll fall before he's situated.

The sound, just like his uncle says, slams up to the moon and back, and somewhere in that long loud loop, it heart-attacks the baby deer, who's never heard the world crack open like this. The hitchhiker's uncle is always saying how deer and rabbits are really the same animal, that what goes for one goes for the other. They're sensitive to the heat. They like to run and watch, run and watch. Their hearts will stop on a dime, from the slightest thing.

It must all be true.

The baby deer folds down onto its front legs, then lays the rest of itself down.

At which point a dark, lanky shape steps out into the dull orange glow of the running lights.

The hitchhiker's aunt looks up to the windshield as well. She lowers her nose to the baby deer's nose, to be sure. And then she lowers herself down to eat, starting with the thin white skin at the belly.

The hitchhiker locks one door, then the other.

For the rest of the night, then, the truck trembling below him, he sits on the doghouse with his knees under his chin and sucks ketchup packets. In the morning there will be two naked people curled up out there in the tall yellow grass, sleeping.

He hopes.

CHAPTER 13

Sad Eyes

If Arkansas is heaven for werewolves, then North Carolina, that's our hell.

It was for us, anyway.

Every quarter mile or so, Libby would slam the heel of her hand into the top of the steering wheel and try to push the gas pedal of our Impala even deeper.

Her hair was everywhere.

If we went any faster, we were going to outrun our headlights.

If we went any slower, Darren was going to be dead.

I rolled my window up so the Impala could be more of a bullet. In the new quiet, Libby looked over to the dingy mirror on my side, her hair floating but still now, like she was falling, and in that moment, the way she was holding her face, her eyebrows, the way her eyes were set, I could see her at ten years old, looking across Grandpa's kitchen, watching her brother's muzzle push out through his mouth, and feeling her tongue swelling against her teeth in response.

Until that moment, had she thought she might slip through? Be like her sister, get to have a normal life in town? Never mind that Grandpa had told her what she was.

When you're a kid, facts don't matter. It's how hard you believe. How much you wish.

For Darren, shifting that first time, it was the dream coming true.

For Libby it was the nightmare, starting.

And she had to see it happen to her brother first.

Had my mom really held them back with a broom all night, before Grandpa got home, or——or had Libby shifted to protect her, to at least let one of them get the dream?

I didn't have to ask. I knew each time she looked at me.

She'd stepped into the nightmare to keep her sister out of it.

For fifteen years now I'd been pretending Libby was my mom, because they were mirror images. I think she'd been pretending too, though. She'd been planning on watching my mom grow up normal. She'd been counting on it.

And, if not her, me.

And all I wanted was to betray her. To be like Darren, miles behind us already. In jail. Not for the strawberry wine coolers he was always pinging mile markers with either.

For graverobbing.

For cannibalism. According to Grandpa, Darren and Libby and the rest of the werewolves of their generation, they'd all been born too late.

They'd missed what he called the grave-y days.

Later Darren told me the old man was just trying to gross me out, to scare me, to make me into some boy version of a Red Riding Hood, nervous about stepping from the safety of the path.

He was probably right.

But still.

Grandpa was a hunter, definitely, could run down anything bold enough to stand up out there in the woods, run it down and hamstring it, tear its throat out, bathe in its blood.

That was the Grandpa I believed in.

There was another version, though.

There was the Grandpa who had every farmer for five counties lobbing buckshot at shapes in the night. There was the Grandpa driven farther and farther back from the world of people. There was the Grandpa who knew what proper revenge tasted like.

When he'd been a young wolf, burial practices were different.

People in Darren and Libby's generation, and mine, they get all their blood drained after they're dead, then get filled back up with the medical version of antifreeze, their lips and eyes glued shut, their fingernails painted, makeup brushed onto their faces, their new perm hairsprayed so hard it's like a helmet against the worms.

Not that the worms can even get that close anymore.

After the airtight casket's bolted shut, it's lowered into a concrete box.

Dig one of these corpses up ten or twenty years later, and it'll look just the same. Unless you touch it, need to see the jelly your mom or your brother's become.

It wasn't always like this, though.

Used to, when people were just buried in pine boxes or bags, or just their clothes, used to when they were delivered into the ground as soon as possible, well.

Werewolves aren't proud.

If we were, we'd have died out centuries ago.

Grandpa's story—he never could have told me if Libby hadn't been at work that day, sewing bags of seed shut—it was that he went to church on a particular Sunday, like a good little worshiper, and he even touched the silver of the offering plate when it came around, like that was a test the congregation was waiting for him to fail.

When everybody else filed out for Sunday picnics, though, he took a different hall, then a narrow stairway up to what he called the sinner's roost. For two days he hid in the attic with all the hymnals that had been decommissioned, from some talented individual drawing naked people in the margins.

Grandpa read the words, hummed the songs to himself, and shaded the pictures in where he could, giving the naked people pointy ears and sharp teeth.

In the living room in the glow of his old man's fire he'd crooked his fingers on top of his head to show what he meant, and raised his lips away from his yellowy teeth.

Darren was leaned against the doorway to the kitchen, listening.

He'd heard it before, he had to have, so maybe now he was just seeing how many times Grandpa was going to take me around the house.

Finally we got to the funeral that had to happen in this story. Grandpa watched it through a round window up in the attic, so that everybody through the glass was stained red and blue and pale yellow, and, when they moved from ripple to ripple of the glass, it was like they were melting ahead.

That night, the church empty, a wolf padded down the stairs, its lips drawn back from its teeth.

Grandpa stalked down the main aisle to the altar, a steady growl in his chest.

No Bibles caught fire, no statues bled from the eyes.

The only reason he didn't lift his leg at the pulpit, he said, it was that he'd just gone two days and two nights without a drink of water.

Not that he didn't try.

And then—and this was the part Darren leaned forward out of the kitchen doorway to hear—Grandpa couldn't get out of the church. Because of doorknobs.

"Always wait until you're outside," he said to me, but it was Darren who nodded once, lodging this.

Because Grandpa didn't want to attract the kind of attention a window breaking at night would, he finally shifted back, even though it hurt five times worse to do it again so quick, before all the bones were even set. To make it worth it, he pretended the whole congregation was sitting there in the pews, watching. And then he stood, walked naked to the door, and let himself out into the cemetery, the full moon making the pale headstones glow.

What he wanted me to remember was that it had been two days since he'd had a single bite.

And that this was still the grave-y days. That meat's meat.

That, instead of standing vigil with shotguns around their chicken coops and feedlots, now the men of the county would be watching their dead.

Darren took in every word.

———

Neither of us had that story on repeat when we'd coasted over the border on fumes, though. At least I didn't. I don't even know for sure that Libby knew it.

What we were thinking was had we come too far at last.

North Carolina was a foreign country for us. It was the farthest north I'd ever been.

I expected snow, and moose, maybe a white owl watching us with huge yellow eyes.

What I got was sticky air and clouds of lovebugs, rusted-out trucks and run-down tourist traps at every third exit.

"It's all one Carolina, isn't it?" Libby said.

At the first truck stop Darren stood from the Impala and looked across the gas-pump islands. He drummed his hands on the roof slow, like he was thinking. Like he was considering. Like he was trying to get a feel for this state.

The plan was to wait for a camper to pull in, for the perfect family to pile out for the bathroom, then for the dad to gas up, park the camper out in the long slots, with the big trucks.

It meant they were there for the restaurant. That they were ordering from the menu. That the kitchen was going to take twenty minutes or so to get their food to them, and then there'd be another half hour of eating, of settling into a room they didn't have to set their feet for, balance against.

Plenty of time.

And campers, they're the big white eggs of the interstate—so easy to crack into. Parking them back with the big rigs might feel manly, a job well done, but all those forty-eight-foot trailers, they're just a series of walls between the front windows of the truck stop and a certain fifteen-year-old werewolf, who maybe needs a moment or two alone with this door, with that window. And all the truckers, they're either inside at the showers or crashed out in their sleepers, and they don't like this camper parking in their slots anyway, are inclined to let what happens to it happen to it.

We stepped up into that family's life, took food, clothes, and cash. What we'd been hoping for was enough to fill the Impala with gas. We got enough for that *and* a motel room. And the cans of chili Darren had the belly of his shirt filled with now, it was his favorite brand.

He dumped them casually into the floorboard behind his seat, was easing the Impala out to the pumps, skating the sole of his left boot on the slick concrete, when we all keyed on a certain Grand Marquis coming in off the road, all four heads in there turned toward a kid a few steps too many behind his mom.

Darren identified them as werewolf before they even parked.

It was from the heavy way that Grand Marquis sat on its springs.

It was how sun-faded the cardboard box on the back dash was.

It was the hungry look in their eyes.

They didn't see us, we were pretty sure.

We waited to fuel up until all four of them had unfolded from the Grand Marquis, sloped inside. All women, but one of them older. Maybe a mom and her three daughters?

Libby had her window down, to catch their scent.

"We know them?" Darren said down to her.

Libby shook her head no, once.

They were the first ones like us I'd ever seen.

That night in the motel room we knew all the answers for *Wheel of Fortune*. Not because we were smart. It was a rerun of a rerun of a rerun, the commercials not even at the usual places but cutting in halfway through a phrase.

Was this punishment for pushing this far north?

The cash left over after gas was on the dresser. Fourteen dollars, three of those dollars in change. Libby was reading the classifieds, for a job.

"We need something faster," Darren said. "Keep us in hot dogs and ketchup, yeah?"

He was bouncing on the soles of his boots, was ready to explode out into the night.

"No liquor stores," Libby said, not looking up.

Darren smiled, rubbed it in with the web of his left hand.

His jawline was stubbly and grey-flecked. He hadn't shifted for nearly a week. It was from seeing how white Brittany's granddad had been, I was pretty sure. It had been enough months ago that he should have already forgot. But he hadn't.

A week's a long time to balance up on two feet, though. And it was turning out expensive too.

Part of the reason our gas money had barely got us here, it was that we were having to eat from drive-throughs and gas-station freezers. Because Darren wasn't running dinner down out in the trees.

Everything's a trade-off when you're a werewolf.

It's like the world wants us to be monsters. Like it won't let us live the way normal citizens do.

Darren sat down with the phone book, flipped through fast, stood with a page.

"Laundromat," he said, like asking Libby for permission.

It wasn't to run a load through—we had new clothes from that perfect camper family—it was for the bulletin boards laundromats always have. It's where people post for somebody to move boxes, or dig a ditch. A hundred things, some of them in code, all of which Darren could say sure about, that that was his specialty, he grew up doing that, his last job, he'd been *fired* for doing that too well, as a matter of fact.

He had to go tonight, though, because we'd only have the motel phone until eleven in the morning, and it would probably be a thing where he'd call, leave a message, then they'd call him back. We could do that all from a pay phone, but staking out a booth at a gas station is a good way to have conversations with police officers.

"Go," Libby said, shooshing Darren out.

He didn't need to be told twice.

"Be good," he said, tipping the brim of his cap in farewell, and the only reason Libby and me were free two hours later to jam the Impala back south at a rattly-loose hundred twenty miles per hour, it was that, in remembering to write the motel phone's number on the inside of his wrist, he'd forgot to pocket the motel key.

As far as the police knew, he was just drifting through, was alone.

It was all we had to save him.

That and a bear.

We wouldn't know the rest of the story until morning, but here's how Darren got picked up.

Like he'd practically promised Libby, like he knew was best, he was just walking down to where the phone book in the motel had said the first of the two all-night laundromats was. His pockets were even jingling with our quarters, in case he needed a sudden reason to be in that laundromat.

You've got to think of everything when you're a werewolf.

At that first laundromat there was an old index card tacked

up, about somebody needing their rain gutters cleaned out for a reasonable rate.

Darren took the card.

He was reasonable, sure. Especially if there was a ham sandwich in there somewhere.

The second laundromat was all lawn mowers for sale and tax courses he could take and haircuts he could get. He walked his fingers from phone number to phone number, being sure, and it took long enough that a taste on the air cut through the detergent and fabric softener.

Those other werewolves.

They'd been here.

Darren followed their scent to the washing machine one of them had stood at. He had his nose to the coin slot when he noticed a woman watching from her industrial dryer.

"What soap is that?" he asked, acting like that's what he was sniffing in.

She turned back around, kept stuffing her bedspread into the dryer like it was a dead body she was trying to hide.

Darren breathed in again, making sure he had this scent.

It didn't make sense, right?

If you're scamming for food, for gas—and they *were* werewolves—then wouldn't bothering with a load of laundry be pretty low on the to-do list? And, if there was blood on the shirt, then washing it wasn't going to do any good anyway.

Darren finally stood, rattled the quarters in his pocket, then nodded to himself that it was none of his business. On the way back to the motel, though, that rain-gutter index card held in both his hands so he could be sure not to lose it, he cut across that same scent again, like a line drawn in the air.

They'd come this way too.

And not on two feet.

The tang on the back of his throat, it was from them just shifting.

They'd run right down Main Street, all four of them.

Darren looked the way they'd gone, licked his top lip to cement the taste of their smell in his head.

Because he didn't want to lose it, he folded the rain-gutter index card between two bricks of the wall, and then he turned to the right, instead of following the brick road back to the motel.

Because he was focused so hard on the scent, he didn't see the police cruiser parked a block down, its engine off, a cigarette glowing red over the steering wheel.

He didn't hear its parking lights roll on, either.

What turned out to be at the end of the road he was following was a Jewish church. No, *temple*. It said it right there on the sign. Maybe the only Jewish temple in North Carolina. The first one Darren had ever been this close to, anyway.

He tipped his cap to it and kept walking.

Fifty paces past it, the scent faded.

He cut back, picked it up again. Right in front of the temple.

Jewish werewolves?

Could they not come here to pray in the daytime, so had to sneak in at night?

Darren smiled where nobody could see, shrugged his shoulders like settling an argument, and leaned forward, over the holy line of the temple's grounds.

Maybe this was why they'd stopped to wash their clothes. They were going to church.

It was something Darren had to see, he was pretty sure.

Werewolves, we aren't that religious. Religion doesn't have a very good history with us. It tends to burn us at stakes, really.

When it can catch us.

Darren looked both ways like for permission, and all he saw from the direction he'd come was a pair of headlights, turning on like two eyes opening in the darkness.

They made the decision for him.

Rather than get caught casing a holy building at two in the morning, he slipped forward, into that temple's bushes, and felt around the side of the building for where the other werewolves had broke in.

As it turned out, the temple wasn't what they were after.

It was the fresh burial out back.

Grandpa had been wrong. The grave-y days weren't gone, they were just Jewish now. While everybody was prettying up their dead, making time capsules of their caskets, Jewish practice was the same as it had always been. A pine box, and don't mess with the body, and get it in the ground *fast*.

Jewish cemeteries are a werewolf buffet.

And these other werewolves, they'd figured that out, probably watched the newsletters. It was why they'd rolled into town on this of all days.

Of course they did laundry every chance they got, Darren figured. They smelled like the graveyard. Even after shifting and showering, that grave dust would still make its way into their denim, their flannel.

Right now, with Darren watching, they were making a meal of a dead woman, probably died in labor from the looks of the baby blanket buried with her. All the dirt from her grave was sprayed out across the rest of the cemetery.

Darren nodded to himself about this.

This was nature. This was the natural order. This was medieval, man.

He had to talk to these cats.

He stepped out from the darkness so they could see him, and as one they looked up, their muzzles bloody to the eyes.

To show what he was, Darren kept walking, his hands raised, palms open, seven fingers and two thumbs spread wide. He walked out among the older graves—the food past its date. The three daughters caught his scent, backed off snarling, but the mother, she stood her ground over the dead woman, nosed into Darren's crotch when he was close enough.

This is nature as well.

Darren rotated his hips away a bit to keep from getting racked. But he kept his hands up, his smile burning bright. This would be four-on-one, after all. And they had the jump on him, already had their teeth out.

"Not a bad idea," Darren said, and squatted down, lifted the dead woman's arm, already pulled away from the shoulder. "Nice to *meet* you," he went on, shaking the dead woman's hand in his version of play, "thanks for the meal, ma'am," and that was when the three werewolves who'd backed off hunkered down, started growling, their hackles coming up like manes.

Darren looked over to them, held the arm out to show he wasn't stealing their meal, no worries, and then, like smoke, they all three melted into the night.

Darren looked over to the fourth, the mother, the aunt, whatever she was, and she'd backed off now as well, was standing in her own patch of darkness, lips raised like she was trying to say something.

"What?" Darren said, catching the scent an instant too late to duck the flat of a shovel coming at the back of his skull like a baseball bat.

The last thing Darren saw was the cherry of that cop's cigarette.

It had burst from the impact of this home-run swing, was floating its delicate orange sparks over the open grave. Over the dead woman. Over this half-eaten young mother.

And then nothing.

The sirens from the line of cop cars speeding by pulled us out into the motel parking lot. We were already on alert, since Darren had been gone too long.

"No, no," Libby was saying.

But yes.

In the second police cruiser, there was Darren. He was propped up, dead to the world.

"Go to the room," Libby said, and when I started to protest—I was *fifteen*, I was like *them*—she turned to me with a growl in her chest.

I locked the door behind me.

She was back inside twenty minutes, knocking at the bathroom window because her clothes were rags, were blowing down Main Street.

She dressed and explained to me that Darren had been caught at the cemetery. That his smell was everywhere, there. And that the others had been there as well, feeding.

"On what?" I said.

"More like who," Libby said, throwing clothes into a trash bag, flashing her eyes around for anything we might be leaving. Anything that might get put into an evidence bag later.

Grandpa's story cued up in my head.

"He'll be sick," I said. "From the preservatives."

"It's not that kind of graveyard," Libby said. "And it's called embalming. We don't have time for this."

The room was empty now. Paid for and not slept in.

It was one crime we'd never committed, not in all the years since Arkansas.

"So we're breaking him out?" I said, pulling my second boot on, no time to work my jeans over it.

Libby collected our crumpled cash from the dresser, said, "Sort of."

Two minutes later the Impala was a blur, a streak, a flash. The most desperate bullet.

We were going back south. Three exits south, specifically.

There'd been a tourist trap there, one Darren had wanted to stop at.

It was a bar where you could wrestle a bear for a chance to win three hundred dollars.

"Easy money," Darren had said, easing over for the off-ramp, to launch us into history. But he knew better, was just funning us.

Now that bear, it was his best chance.

Libby was tight-lipped, had the steering wheel in both hands because a tire had to blow pretty soon at this speed, but my guess was that the bear was going to be proof of some sort. Darren had heard a noise behind the temple, and, being a good citizen, had gone to check it out, discourage any looters.

What he'd found instead was a bear.

A *bear* had dug that body up, gone to town on it.

It was a plan that assumed a lot, of course. That Darren hadn't been chewing on a leg. That he hadn't tried to shift.

That he was unconscious in the back of the cruiser, though, not shot full of holes in a coroner's wagon, that suggested the cops didn't know what they had. Didn't know what they'd locked up.

But Darren was going to wake soon. We were racing that as much as anything.

"I never should have let him go out alone like that," Libby said, about to cry it sounded like.

I wanted to say the right thing, but couldn't think of it.

We slid to a stop in the bar's dirt parking lot, stood from the Impala before the dust we'd pulled in had even settled.

"Get that," Libby said, reaching down to touch the thick cable strung between concrete-filled stubby metal poles. It was a fence, but for truck bumpers, not people. To show that this was the parking lot, that wasn't.

I backed the Impala up, hooked the once-chrome trailer ball under the low sway of the cable, and gave it the gas. The cable whipped out ring after metal ring, and they came at me like shot, taking out the rear window of the Impala, filling the car with shattered glass.

I looped the cable over my shoulder as best as it would loop, then stepped around the side of the bar, where Libby's nose had already led her. She was stepping down from the make-do porch of a travel trailer the bartender or bouncer usually slept in. The front door of it was swinging behind her.

"Empty," she said.

Sometimes they do smile on you, the werewolf gods.

The bear was in a boxcar up on concrete pylons. Even I could smell it in there.

"He's big," Libby said. "That's good."

"What do you—?" I said about the cable, and Libby took it, dropped it right at the front of the ramp leading up to the sliding door.

Inside, the bear huffed out air, letting us know it had heard us.

"This isn't going to be pretty," Libby said.

"What'll they do to Darren?" I said.

Libby pursed her lips, swallowed, and shook her head no.

"I need that lock gone," she said, tying her hair back now, and I found a piece of rebar, popped the big padlock, dragged the chain out. Libby picked it up. It was maybe four feet long, had been a tow chain at some point, if not logging. It left her hands dusty red like dried blood.

"Shit," she said about all this, standing on the ramp before that massive door.

It was the first time I'd ever heard her cuss in years.

"We can just——" I said, about to detail some jail breakout I'd seen documented on a western from forty years ago, but Libby pointed with her chin up to the door's tall pull-handle for me, said, "This is an old trick of your grandpa's."

"What?" I asked, taking the handle in both hands.

"Letting someone else take the fall," she said, and with that I pulled the door back all at once.

The bear didn't crash out like we'd been expecting.

Libby rattled the chain once, in invitation.

Nothing.

But it was moving in there. It was breathing. It was waiting.

"I'm sorry," Libby said to it, to the idea of it, and then, on two feet instead of four like I'd figured, like *I'd* be if I could, she stepped up that ramp, into that darkness.

The bear came at her all at once, launched both of them back, clearing the ramp and the cable both, driving her down into the dirt, the dust pluming up all around.

This wasn't a black bear like we knew, from the South.

This bear was twice again as big, and more golden brown. A graham-cracker bear from a nature show.

It weighed as much a young horse, probably. As much as a motorcycle.

And I couldn't even see Libby under it anymore.

I screamed, saying I don't even know what—this was a night I could lose my whole family, something that wasn't supposed to happen for a year yet—and, maybe six seconds later, the bear arched its back like a cat and stood up, roaring from insult.

On the ground where a woman had been, there was something else now.

Libby stood on all fours, not all the way wolf yet but closer to that than anything else. Her back-hair when it came in was stiff, and the chain was still draped across her. Just the tips of her toes were touching the ground, and she circled, growling hard, clear saliva dripping down like it was all she had in her.

The way the bear looked at her too, I could tell this wasn't just a her-and-it thing. This was a *species* thing. The bear didn't have to have ever seen or smelled a real live werewolf to remember one. From centuries of fighting us over livestock. From bears moving in from one side of a war-massacred village, to sniff out a meal, and werewolves creeping in from the other side, their eyes laid back, paws reaching far ahead and delicately, because this is a landscape that explodes.

A long time ago Darren had said that bears and wolves weren't meant to get along. I thought he'd been talking about state troopers, though.

This bear, it knew better.

It came at Libby with everything it had.

Instead of meeting it head-on like I knew she wanted, like her instincts were telling her to, instead of spearing in for its throat somewhere under all that shag meant for another altitude, Libby sidestepped but hooked on, whipped around the bear's back like to ride it, only she was already shifting back, now.

Because she needed hands.

Because werewolves, they can't hold a chain.

Libby had it pulled around the bear's thick neck, her knees buried in the back of its head, and she was pulling it tight, her arms corded with effort, every vein in her neck standing out, blood seeping down from her nose and her mouth and her eyes, from shifting back so fast before she'd even been all the way there.

The bear didn't understand, but it knew to drive her back, into the side of the car, hard enough to rock it on its pylons. Once, twice, like a wrestler on television.

Bears have shorter arms than wrestlers, though. A wrestler can peel a body up from their back, sling it into the ropes.

A bear can just scratch. And this bear, it didn't even have claws anymore.

Going against drunks in a pen in a bar, you don't need claws. Or teeth, as it turned out.

That was why Libby'd had time to start shifting. That was why she still had a face.

At four minutes, then five, the bear finally started to slow, and stagger. Its lungs must have been furnace bellows.

By seven minutes, one of its eyes burst red capillary by capillary. The great bear fell forward like the giant it was.

Libby rolled to the side, worked her hand around to the bear's nose.

It was still breathing.

She did too, finally.

She used my shirt to clean the blood from her face, but it was still coming. Her hands were shaking.

"Sit down," I told her, trying to think what Darren would have done to make this mad enterprise work out.

The least likely thing, I figured. The least likely, most magical thing.

The least likely, most magical thing was a junked-out old Beetle back in the weeds. If it'd been a Corvair like you usually see people holding on to past all reason, my idea wouldn't have had a chance. Beetles are like ramps on wheels, though. You can walk right up the back of one, walk right down the front, never have to high-step it.

Of the hood and the trunk, I judged the hood to be the gentler ramp.

I looped one end of the cable under the bear's front legs and the other to the Impala, and dragged the bear to the front of the Beetle, at which point I had to unhook from the Impala and reposition, then hook on to the ball again, with the cable pressing down over the Beetle like to cut it in half. But the bear didn't weigh that much. A couple of jerks clumped it up onto the Beetle's hood, and one more pulled it up onto the roof, the Beetle's remaining two windows going white the instant before they shattered out. Then it was just a matter of unhooking the cable from the Impala and backing it up against the Beetle's passenger door, dumping the bear into the endless trunk.

We wrapped the cable around and around the bear and the trunk both, tied it in every way we could come up with.

"They usually drug them in places like this, right?" I said, looking around like for the bar's stash of tranquilizers.

"No time," Libby said, not even able to make complete sentences yet. "You, drive."

I took us three exits north, our headlights pointing at the sky from the bear's weight, and followed Libby's direction to the Jewish temple.

I backed the car right across the cut grass and through the squared-off hedges, all the way to the dead woman behind the yellow tape and the floodlights. I don't know where the police were. Unless Darren had already shifted, and reinforcements had been called in.

Not yet, I said inside, like a prayer.

Just give us a few more minutes.

We dragged as much of the bear over the lip of the trunk as we could, then climbed in behind it, pushed it the rest of the way out with our legs.

It just lay there, sleeping another one off.

Libby took the dead woman's arm, rubbed the blood on the bear's nose.

The bear's face twitched, recognizing this.

"Call them," Libby said, nodding me into the temple.

I didn't have time to be quiet, just elbowed a window in, found a phone, 911'd, said it had come back for seconds, it was eating the rest of her, get here, get here now!

By the time I got back to the cemetery, Libby had her face down to the bear's. Her words were thick because her teeth were coming in, but I could still hear her. She was apologizing as best she could. And she was calling the bear a name. *Sad Eyes.*

I cocked my head, dredged that term up. It was what Grandpa had called the moondog baby he'd brought back in a cardboard box, as a lesson for his three pups.

I'd thought the name was a corruption from some other language.

I was wrong.

It's how werewolves say they're sorry.

It's how you acknowledged the person inside the animal. How you tell them that you see them in there, yes. And you're sorry it has to be like this. Grandpa had said it to that baby before he pinched its head shut, and now Libby was smoothing this great bear's hair back, kissing it once on the nose, her eyes wet.

And then, her mouth full of teeth again, her nose bleeding freely, she hugged her left arm around the great bear's head.

It was so she could pull her mouth over to its shoulder.

She bit hard and deep, and tore a big hunk away, spit it into the grass.

The bear jerked back, its own roar seeming to wake it up.

Libby stood, walked over, planted her hand on my shoulder to guide me away. To keep herself between this bear and me.

The thing about our bite, it's that it only passes the wolf on to people.

What animals get, it's the hunger, the rage, the madness.

It's like instant rabies. *End*-stage rabies, on speed.

Even a deer you bite before it runs off, inside of a minute or two it'll come back for you. Not slashing with its hooves or sweeping with its rack, but biting with its flat teeth.

An infected animal doesn't live more than an hour. Not even long enough to get a proper name. But it's a bad hour.

This bear, it was just waking up to that.

And that's when I saw Libby's real plan.

She wasn't going to have to talk to anybody.

This bear, it was going to say it all, just by being here. It had rocked its boxcar back and forth enough that it could break out, and it had lumbered up the ditch along the interstate, snuffling for food, and here was some practically on a dinner plate.

What my 911 call had done, it was give all these good old boys a chance to put lead in an honest-to-god *grizzly* bear.

They were going to be falling over each other to get through the door.

The jail by the time we eased up, it was a ghost town.

Libby left the Impala running, walked in through the front door, walked out a minute later with Darren.

That easy.

Darren was gulping air like the claustrophobe he was, his skin jumping, his hands twitchy.

It had been close. The only thing that had kept him from shifting, as it turned out, it was Grandpa's story about the doorknobs.

He didn't want to force his way through the bars of his cell only to be trapped in a bigger cell.

It had saved his life. It had kept the guns on the rack, and in their holsters.

Because he couldn't yet, Libby drove us away. The other side of town was pulsing with police lights. The gunfire boomed across, passed us, kept going, windows glowing on up and down the street.

In slow motion in front of us, a tall man ran past in a robe and one slipper. He was carrying a shotgun in one hand, a two- or three-day infant in the other, his fingers on the back of that new baby's head the same careful way you hold a football. Or, in the same way you hold on to something that's the last bit of your wife, who's supposed to be buried down at the temple.

Supposed to be.

I tracked him as far as I could.

"What say we blow this chicken joint?" Libby said, looking over to her little brother, his hair full grey now, his chin stubbly.

Darren dabbed at a touch of blood by her mouth, rubbed it on the dashboard in what was going to be a scabby X by morning, and grubbed another cap up from the floorboard, worked it low onto his head.

At the big red light on Main Street, he pointed with his eyes to a spot of fluttering white tucked up in the brick.

"Think I about had a job," he said, then: "Why does it smell like bear in here?"

"Smells like prisoner now," I said, instead of that I loved him.

He cocked his vanity mirror down, a move he'd practiced to perfection in dozens of cars over thousands of miles, and held my eyes with his a moment telling me I was the prisoner.

"That doesn't even—" Libby said, and was cut off by the lane beside us suddenly rumbling with a low and heavy Grand Marquis.

Four faces turned slow over to our Impala, their eyes hot.

We'd ruined their dinner. Maybe there were hardly enough dead Jews in both Carolinas to keep them in meat. Maybe they were going to get caught stealing live ones, now.

The three girls in the backseat had their hands grabbed on to the front seat, like they were set to explode out the driver's-side door as soon as their mom opened it. And Darren and Libby were each too wasted to fight.

"Can we outrun them?" I said from the backseat, my skin alive in a way it never had been.

"We're werewolves," Darren said, pulling the brim of his cap even lower, and Libby smoked the mismatched tires of that perfect impossible Impala and we surged forward into the night, diving for the interstate, no lid on our trunk, the temperature gauge climbing into the red like always, no seat belts across our laps, the rearview mirror crowded with certain death.

Someday when I'm telling my grandkids about the one time we went to North Carolina, I'm going to end right there, I told myself. I'm going to end with three werewolves running hard for their homeland.

As if there had ever been such a thing.

CHAPTER 14

The Werewolf of Alcatraz

One eight-hour shift isn't going to get her *fired*, the prisoner's aunt says in the kitchen over and over. Bosses expect workers to get sick, don't they?

The prisoner's uncle says this isn't about clerking at the gas station, *sister*.

They're both walking back and forth on the crackly linoleum.

The aunt's plan is to drive the four hours straight east to Mississippi, to go to visiting hours in the morning, and then to drive back. And *not* to get fired.

"If you even make it back," the uncle says.

"I can't be this close without trying," the aunt says.

"You don't owe him anything," the uncle says. "He got what he deserved. Do you not see a pattern here? You know how moths fly into a light bulb over and over, until they die?"

"He wasn't like Red," the aunt says. "He was just in the wrong place, wrong time of my life."

"If that's what you call breaking your jaw."

"I didn't say he was perfect," the aunt says, and before she leaves, she kneels down and straightens the prisoner's shirt for him.

"Do what your uncle says," she tells the prisoner even though he's been eleven for two weeks, and adds, loud enough for the prisoner's uncle to hear, "unless it's stupid."

Then she kisses the prisoner on the forehead and leaves without looking back.

"I'll show her *stupid*," the prisoner's uncle says, lifting his pink wine cooler to toast her good-bye even though she's already gone.

Ten minutes later the prisoner and his uncle are walking down the road to the gas station, for what the uncle says is probably going to be the least stupid hot dog in the history of the world.

On the way there the prisoner's uncle smells something that makes him guide the prisoner behind him.

They find the smell in the tall grass past the rusted fence.

A pig.

The uncle lowers his face to the black hole chewed in its side, blows the flies away.

"I goddamn *knew* it," the uncle says.

"What?" the prisoner says.

"He still wants that stupid El Camino back."

The prisoner doesn't say his aunt's ex-husband's name aloud. But he doesn't have to. They're both already hearing it in every rustle of the grass, every sigh of the wind.

"He doesn't even need it," the uncle says. "You don't need El Caminos out in the trees, do you? What he really wants is her. They're *both* moths." He looks down to the prisoner, says, "You're not a moth, are you?"

"Werewolf," the prisoner says.

It's what they always say back and forth.

The prisoner looks to the tall grass behind him. How did his aunt's ex know they were even in Louisiana? Is it because it touches Arkansas?

The prisoner tries not to think of the hole chewed in the side of the pig. When he does anyway, he finds his teeth grinding together, so he can imagine what it must have been like, doing that.

At the gas station, instead of buying a hot dog like usual, the prisoner's uncle buys all the honey buns eight dollars can buy, not including the three in his pocket or the two down the front of his pants. Then, because the prisoner isn't fast enough, he slings him over his shoulder, carries him back to the trailer. It makes the prisoner feel like a little kid.

"I'm not supposed to do anything stupid," he says.

"*She's* the one being stupid," the uncle says, looking around for the sunglasses he wears when he drives his truck. "I told her he was here somewhere. He's following her right now, probably, just like he followed us to Florida."

Then the uncle looks hard at the prisoner, spins away, walks to the other wall but's back just as quick, looking at the prisoner again.

"Listen," he says. "I need you to stay here. This is too—I can't take you. But you'll be fine. You've got enough honey buns to live for a year."

Before he leaves he uses the screwdriver to turn the television on. He's the only one with the right touch.

"Cool?" he says to the prisoner, and when the prisoner nods—he *is* eleven—the uncle locks him in, drives away before the turbo of his truck is even ready. He's always talking about the turbo.

The prisoner opens the refrigerator door. Inside is the glass

Gatorade bottle his uncle keeps his cold water in. The prisoner doesn't want the bottle, he wants the metal cap. He sits on the couch with it, popping it in and out, in and out.

He eats two of the honey buns for dinner.

The television is still talking the whole time. The trailer came with it because the knobs were all twisted off. But then the uncle had a skinny pair of pliers made for snap rings that would reach all the way inside, turn to the one channel the antenna could pull in.

So far all the uncle watches is commercials, because they're great, and all the aunt watches is news about actors.

This is different. It's a game show, the one the prisoner's uncle always says is too hard.

The prisoner parks on the carpet and calls out prices anyway, just saying what everybody in the audience is already saying, and then he eats half of another honey bun, looking at the price tag first, to memorize it, and then he falls asleep watching the stripes the television goes to at night, that his uncle used to say was the flag for the land of sleep.

It's dark when he wakes from the door knocking. Or the door shaking. It was doing one of the two, he's pretty sure.

The porch creaks a few breaths later but the door doesn't move again.

The prisoner puts his fingers to the lock to twist it open, see the sound, but then he sits down on the couch instead. Because he's not doing anything stupid.

On the side of the trailer a minute or two later, metal tears like a can of ham opening.

"The skirt," the prisoner says, in his aunt's voice.

It's always blowing in from a storm.

There's no storm tonight.

Then the prisoner feels it under his feet. Something is walking under the trailer, its back brushing against the bottom of the floor like it's trying to map the floor plan.

No, like it's looking for a weak point. Like it's looking for a way in.

The prisoner has to gulp his heartbeat down.

The pig. The pig knows they were smelling of it. Now it's coming to smell of *them*. In the daytime, the prisoner knows this would be a stupid thought.

It's like he's a first grader again. It's his uncle's fault, for leaving him alone. It's his aunt's fault, for going back to Mississippi.

To show how wrong whatever's down there is, something it does makes the television go off for a few seconds. When it comes back on, it's not the stripes anymore, but one of the game shows.

Does this mean it's morning already?

The prisoner pulls his feet up beside him then steps across from the couch to the wooden apple box his uncle says is a good enough table. The prisoner stands on it.

Now there's another metal-tearing sound, this one right under the living room. The prisoner flinches, almost balances off the apple box.

"Go away," he says out loud.

Next, the heater vent in the floor under the big window behind the television goes up then down, like a test. Then it tumps up all at once, tips sideways onto the carpet.

There's just a hole in the carpet now. A black rectangle.

A pig eye is watching him from that under-the-trailer darkness, the prisoner knows.

"Two ninety-nine," he calls out to the game show. Just to hear a voice.

The price is $4.50. A woman from Minneapolis jumps up and down.

The prisoner can smell the pig now. He can hear its hard breathing.

On the couch with fuzz on its glaze is half the honey bun he started after dinner.

The prisoner peels the plastic off, throws it to the hole.

It doesn't make it.

The prisoner lays down, reaches ahead to push the honey bun, keeping his face as far away as possible.

Right when it gets to the edge of the hole, a mouth racked with teeth slashes up, takes it.

Sharp teeth. *Wolf* teeth. Long red hair for a moment. Beautiful red hair.

The prisoner scuttles back to the box, stands on it with his heart beating all over his body, with his right pants leg warm from new pee, with his breath catching in his throat.

In his head, he's counting the days until someone unlocks the door, scoops him up.

It's what all prisoners do.

CHAPTER 15

The Sheep Look Up

The reason we don't know where we come from, it's that werewolves aren't big on writing things down. On leaving bread crumbs.

It kind of makes all the movies true.

Maybe that *is* how it is, right? Or how it was.

Darren never bought it, of course.

His theory of werewolf genesis was from Grandpa. If you could believe him, he'd lied about being eighteen years old in order to get to World War II. Meaning, at sixteen, late in the war, he'd slipped across enemy lines one night in France. Slipped across on all fours.

According to him, America doesn't win the war without him back there, tearing out every throat he could, making the Axis look behind themselves instead of over their rifles, to aim. The Nazis hated him, would bomb towns they already held just on the rumor that the dreaded Black Wolf was there.

I don't know.

What I suspect is that Darren gave the story some color, in the telling. And that it probably wasn't exactly told in black-and-white in the first place.

Maybe Grandpa did go to war, and he *did* make it back, of course—otherwise there's no Darren, no Libby, no me—but those years in between, those years between shipping out and straggling back home, those are story years. Years without any photographs or paperwork or newspaper articles to prove them. Years in which a werewolf could have ridden rockets all across Europe, and probably climbed the Eiffel Tower and ate the *Mona Lisa* between kills, then got blessed by the pope.

Growing up hearing that kind of historical record, it makes me understand Darren a little better, I guess. He had that to live up to. Only, he was never quite Army material. And Army's the only military werewolves are any good for. Put us in the Air Force and we parachute down a man, can't pull the rip cord with wolf paws. Put us on a Navy or Marine boat, and when that boat pulls into port, there's blood on the gunwales. Whatever a gunwale is.

Army's the only place that could take our particular kind of stir-crazy. We're ground troops. We're meat to feed into the big grinder.

Only, with our teeth and our claws, we might make it out the other side. We might even stick around, make a meal of some of that ground-up meat.

But: the Amazing Adventures of the Black Wolf, Secret Weapon of World War II.

That it involved a fortune-teller in an actual horse-drawn cart made it even more amazing.

Darren would usually pick the story up with the Black Wolf gravely wounded, limping on two feet through Italy, or backwater Poland, or some bombed-up landscape or another. The Black

Wolf's limping along after a few days of heroics when he hears hoofbeats behind him, so crawls over to a bush to hide. The horse sniffs him out at the last instant, starts screaming and slashing at the air.

The little old woman at the reins cuts the horse loose because she doesn't want him to run the wheels off her cart.

"He'll come back in the morning," she tells the Black Wolf, who, at the moment, is just a naked, bleeding soldier who hasn't eaten in four days.

She invites him into her wagon and gives him a blanket to wear around his shoulders, offers him tea and some dried meat she claims is an aurochs, which she says his kind used to feast on.

"That a kind of yak?" the Black Wolf asks.

"What's a yak?" the woman asks back.

Darren has various jokes and sound effects to get the story through this part. At the end of it all, the old woman's telling the Black Wolf the secret of where a certain cave is. That it's near. She says that his kind used to use it in times past. It's a place men never go.

The Black Wolf keeps chewing, looks out the back of the wagon.

"Then I shouldn't go either," he says.

She has to laugh about this.

"You think because I'm old I don't see," she says.

"I'm a soldier," the Black Wolf says.

"Never said you weren't," the old woman says. "But your blood is from a long line."

At this the Black Wolf gives her his full attention.

"Wolves," she says, lighting her pipe. "Wolves used to pester the villages, the city walls. Run off with a child once or twice a year."

"That's wolves," the Black Wolf says, his patriotism rising in his voice.

"That's all there was then," the old woman says, breathing smoke out, watching it leave the wagon. "There were wolves, and there were men, and they each tried to keep to themselves, except in times of hunger. But there was also an old woman not unlike me, a woman who knew herbs and potions, a woman who knew where the corner of the curtain of the world was, so she could pull it up, look behind, into the mysteries."

"A witch," the Black Wolf says, suddenly aware of the strange meat in his stomach.

"A healer," the old woman corrects. "But there are many names, and none of them matter. What does is that a madness was sweeping through the wolves around the woman's village."

"We call it rabies."

"As I said, many names. There were different strains of the madness back then too. There was one from the rats, one from the dogs. This one was from the bats, is the kind they show up with when their numbers get low enough that they need to, in your soldier terms, conscript. But then a wolf caught it, which had never happened before. He gave it to his whole pack. And, as there usually is, there was one wolf among them bolder than the rest, who tried to run off with a child from the village, but was too weak from what the madness was trying to do to him from the inside. The arrows sprouting from his side didn't help either." To show she does her fingers from her own side. "But the child was grievous wounded. And that child's mother, she offered her life in service to the old woman, this healer, if she would but heal the child."

"Nobody cures rabies," the Black Wolf says. It's the one thing he's afraid of.

"And neither could she," the old woman says. "But never before had rabies been allowed to run its complete course. She couldn't fight the madness, this healer, but she was skilled enough to keep the child alive, though each day his teeth grew more pointed. Though each day the hair sprouted on his body. That was what the madness had always been trying to do. That's what it did for the bats, to help them make other bats. It changed the bitten into the biter, as close as it could, only it usually killed the bitten in the process, since their body couldn't hold the new shape. But it didn't kill this one. Because this healer was old, and needed help with her pots, she mustered all her arts, all her songs and chants, all the hard-fought potions she'd been saving for herself."

"You're not saying—"

"On the day this boy could *walk*," the old woman goes on, brooking no interruption, "it was on all fours. And he ran into the forest quick as that, never to return, but, to keep her deal, his mother served the rest of her days at the healer's house, always watching at the doorway for her lost son. And the healer didn't hold it against her that she would some days leave choice cuts of meat on a cast-off footstool beside the road. Such are mothers for their sons. They want the best for them, whatever life they choose. And this is where the old custom of—"

"So what happened to him, this kid?" the Black Wolf asks, pulling the rough blanket tighter around him.

"Nothing, it would seem," the old woman says, indicating the Black Wolf, born all these generations later. "But I fear my horse won't return until you've left. Have you had enough to eat?"

The Black Wolf looks to his hands, surprised the meat's all gone.

"Always feed a wolf his fill," the old woman quotes out loud, "lest you wake with your throat in his jaws."

And so the Black Wolf takes her directions up the side of the mountain and sleeps in the cave of his ancestors that night, and traces his fingertips over faint charcoal drawings that seem to confirm the old woman's story, and though he returns to that cave many times throughout his many amazing adventures during the war, he never does see that old woman's brightly colored cart again, but he does hear her horse's hoofbeats some nights, and taste her pipe smoke on the air.

"He never sees her again because it's probably all bullshit," Darren liked to say at the end of the story, then he'd lean back, finally pull his left hand up to his mouth, take the curved-up stem of a fancy wood pipe between his lips, and breathe in deep and thoughtful through it, like that showed a line of continuity from the Black Wolf to him, one he was too cool to actually say out loud.

When I was a kid, it had kind of worked. It was like an out-loud comic book, the way Darren had told it, doing the sound effects, acting out the more amazing parts in slow motion. I even imagined the Black Wolf with a shield strapped to his back. And I never questioned why that pipe was never lit—otherwise he wouldn't have been able to hide it down between the couch cushions.

Libby's theory of werewolves was more direct, called for fewer sound effects, less theater. In her version, a wolf got hungry one day, so dressed up in the clothes of a man he'd just eaten and walked on two feet into town but got lost in the tangle of streets, had to keep walking and walking like that, until he forgot who he was. And now here we were.

"Why a man?" Darren would say. "Why not a lady wolf?"

"Because women don't get that hungry," she would say back, not even the hint of a grin at her mouth.

Since I couldn't pick between either of their stories, I made up my own: the unholy union. Those two star-crossed lovers the world always needs. That werewolves needed them too, that kept us part of the world. The story was simple like Libby's but sweeping and grand like Darren's. A wolf and a logger's daughter meet out in the moonlight night after night, trying to figure out the precise mechanics of their relationship. And the tragedy of it comes when the woman gives birth to the first of us, has to die from it.

Except I guess that makes love the actual infection in our blood.

I don't know.

One thing we all agree on anyway, it's sheep. Our traditional enemy, our intended prey.

Just when you think they're all gone, another'll peek around the corner at you, catch you in its dead eyes.

This one Libby found at a car wash in Augusta. We were living on the Georgia side of the state line, but this car wash was in South Carolina. The plan after the Night of the Bear had been to book it west, start the grand tour all over, do it right this time, but then 95 South had been more downhill, and the Impala's temperature gauge had needed some downhill.

It was for the best, probably. Darren said Tennessee had too many horses anyway, and snow in winter, fog for miles.

Still, even Augusta was more north than we usually kept, this late in the fall.

But there we were.

As for that sheep at the car wash—maybe the north is full of sheep, I don't know.

I guess it's where I would go.

———

The way Libby told it, she was drying cars and then whipping her rag over her head like victory.

It was a daytime job. For the first time in years, she had real color in her skin.

Her cars were always like mirrors on wheels after she was done. Like flying saucers with license plates. And she didn't have to wear a stupid hairnet either. Just the uniform shirt. The theme of the car wash was bowling. The waiting room was black and white checkered, and, because the geometry of it gave Libby a headache, she'd asked to work the line instead of the register.

Either way she'd have made the sheep, but, out there with the soap and chemicals, his scent nearly slipped past her, she said. She didn't cue into it until the exact moment she was handing the car's green ticket over. Green means go, leave, you're clean, you're done.

The gentleman she was handing the ticket to was carrying a toolbox with a pawn ticket tied to the handle. He was carrying it because people never trust the car-dry crew not to go shopping in the backseat.

His beard was full-on bird nest, his sunglasses black and thick.

"Thank you," he said, tipping a single dollar bill her way.

Libby took it without looking right at him and walked the dollar over to the big metal tip-jar-on-a-pole like she was supposed to. Because sometimes the tip will be a test.

But not this time.

This time, it was a werewolf.

His hair was perfect.

Darren was all for what he called going BJ McKay on this werewolf's town home.

That meant driving his Freightliner through the living room wall, into the werewolf's lap.

Libby said we'd have to *find* his town home first.

They had to explain to me what a "town home" was, here. I thought it meant a house in town. Like, if our trailer was in town, it would be a town trailer.

This werewolf was a town *wolf*. Just, one who never *went* wolf.

It happens.

When we're up on two legs, and not around our own kind, then who's to know we're not regular citizens, right?

Especially if you let your beard grow.

Especially if you let your breath get rank.

Especially if you don't start in eating all the dogs in the neighborhood.

I'd heard of these nonwolves before, from Darren. Real horror stories. They were usually ones who'd been living out in the trees for five or ten years, like Red. After that long, you can't shift back on your own anymore. Not even when sleeping. Usually what it takes is some massive injury, some real near-death event to bring you back to your human form. Because, when we die, if we're shifted, then we relax back mostly, if given a day or two to lay there dead. Being born, the shifting back and forth and sticking in the middle is like a seizure. Dying, it's a lot calmer. Instead of tunneling back in, the hair all over you just breaks off, drifts away.

With Grandpa, when we'd come back from burying him, the grey hair in the doorway of the kitchen had been floating away like a last breath. It had made Libby blink her eyes fast. Darren had made a face, spitting the hair out.

These wolves who have been wolf too long, though, who have forgotten how to come back to the man-side, if they get slapped by a truck hard enough, or shot through like half their vital organs, that shock like they're dying, it kick-starts whatever survival thing it is in us that hides the wolf, that tells the hair to start letting go. And once the hair starts to let go, the wolf does as well, slithering back inside, prepping the corpse for discovery.

Only, if you take a hit like that, hard enough to shift you back, *and* you manage not to die from it, then you can wake with a wolf's mind and a man's body.

It can be ugly. Most won't survive this, or, they only survive it in a padded room for the rest of their lives—"Real *lycan*thropes," Darren would spit. "Real sad sacks."

A few luck through, though. Except they've been so burned by the whole experience that they can't shift anymore. It's not a muscle they've needed to keep in shape, living out in the trees, so now they don't know to flex it. The wolf's still inside them, but it's sleeping.

You don't go vegetarian or anything, but you might take a job changing tires, and then keep that job for the rest of your life, never strip your clothes in the moonlight, race a train just because there's a real chance you can win, and maybe freak some people out while doing it.

That's all understandable. Sad, but there's nothing to be done, really. And, at least they had a taste of the real life, right? At least they know what the night really smells like. How beautiful it is. How deep.

And it's not like working at a tire place is punishment or anything.

I was a tire expert, by Augusta.

This was my first sheep, though.

Darren's estimation of him, going off Libby's description, was that he probably couldn't shift. That, for him, his life as a werewolf was something he was already remembering like a dream, one getting farther and farther behind him.

Libby wasn't so sure.

He'd been at the car wash, for one. It didn't mean he had extra money to burn, but it did mean he cared if his car was clean or not. It didn't fit.

Taking pride in your *car*?

Cars are disposable to werewolves, cars are nothing, a necessary evil.

Darren wanted to argue, I could tell, but his Freightliner was out front, coated in the grime of six weeks, the bumper already pitting with rust.

So, this sheep having an actually *clean* car, what this told Libby was that he had bought into town life, and all the standards of town folk. Which meant he was selling all of us out.

"Why do you care so much?" I'd asked, and Darren had rolled from his chair, ducked into the kitchen for a wine cooler. The kitchen was out of Libby's line of fire.

She reeled it in, though, whatever bad history she had with sheep. Though she tracked Darren's retreat, every cowardly step of it.

An old boyfriend, maybe? But not Red. Not Morris Wexler.

One I'd never know about, I guessed.

Her second argument not in favor of this sheep was that he hadn't clocked her, she didn't think.

Even those werewolves who couldn't change anymore, they usually kept their nose, more or less. It was part of what drove a lot of them into the state hospitals: They were being overloaded with scent, and it was kicking up associations and impulses that the wolf knows to act on, no matter the current company,

"Maybe he did and he's just cool cat enough not to show it," Darren said, sitting back down in his folding chair.

"I guess," Libby said.

"Maybe it's for his old lady," Darren said. "Or maybe he just wanted to grow a beard for once in his life."

"Or maybe he's—what if he's still hunting?" Libby said.

Darren took another long pull on his wine cooler.

"You mean, like, he can still change?" I said.

"Just never does," Libby said.

"Why?" I asked.

"Not everybody's loud and proud," Darren said, slapping his bare chest.

"Because he's a sheep," Libby said.

"As long as he's not hunting, though . . ." Darren said, and then Libby had to explain that to me as well: Tamp it down as much as you want, pretend you're not werewolf, it doesn't matter. The wolf always surfaces.

That's okay if you're in the country, if all you're going to run down in your sleep are deer and possums. Nobody cares about deer and possums.

Town is full of people, though.

You can be a mad dog, never know it. Just like the movies.

And the thing about mad dogs, it's that they get put down. They get shot, documented, put on the news.

"If he is sleepwalking, then it's time to leave," Darren said, deadly serious.

"We're the ones who found him, though," Libby said, flashing her eyes up to Darren. Like calling him out.

"If he even is one," Darren said.

"Check under his bed," Libby said. "See if there's bones, right?"

"*Find* his bed first," Darren said, accepting her challenge, and that was where they left it, because werewolves aren't detectives. The way they find their prey, it's by smell, not clues.

I already had one, though: the pawn tag on his toolbox.

If you ever want to find a werewolf, stake out a pawnshop for two or three weeks. Soon enough you'll see a low heavy car with mismatched wheels roll up, then have to watch some shirtless dude in sunglasses maneuver a big-screen television from the backseat, try to balance it through the front door.

Pawnshop owners love to see us pull up. They know we're never coming back.

That's us, though.

Sheep—sheep are a completely different breed.

They stay in one place, drink from the same still waters day after day.

But still, no werewolf in the history of werewolves has ever been so rich he didn't want to see what he could get for this set of golf clubs he just happens to have. For this rifle he found in his dead uncle's closet. For this spare tire he has to roll two miles to pawn, and air up in secret at the gas station two lots down.

Without asking permission, I quit going to tenth grade again. It was my second run at it anyway. I'd already made it farther than Darren or Libby, so it wasn't like they could say anything. In two or three months I would be sixteen, I mean. For werewolves, that's adult, that's grown the hell up, that's don't let the doorknob hit you on the way out.

My clock, it was ticking down. It was getting down to do-or-don't for me. To wolf or not to wolf, that was the question.

Maybe catching a whiff of this sheep, though, maybe that would raise my hackles. And maybe my teeth and claws would follow.

Because that pawn ticket was my one, only, and best clue, I staked out the pawnshop down from Libby's car wash. My blind was the stoop of the book and record store across the street. It was called By Crook or by Hook. I wasn't sure what that was supposed to mean.

The pawnshop, though.

The pawnshop was Gru's.

As in, French for werewolf, if you listened just right.

I figured an American sheep probably would.

Nearly two weeks later, he finally drifted in again.

What he drove, the car Libby hadn't been able to tease up from the hundreds she saw each week, was a pretty pristine old Mercury Monterey. What else she'd forgot to mention was the black fenders, the white doors.

It was a retired cop car, stripped down and pushed through auction.

It still had that police package stance, though, like it wanted to move. When the sheep had come through Libby's car wash, it was probably on some half-off certificate her work had stuck under the wipers of all the cars with lot numbers on them.

It made me hate him a little less, that he'd paid half price, and that the car wash wasn't part of his usual rounds.

His beard was mountain man like she'd said, was really something to see.

On his back dashboard were two hard hats.

What he was pawning was a clutch of VHS tapes in colorful sleeves, each with red Xs over their backs, meaning they'd been clearanced once already. He wasn't flashing them to me or anything, but before he went in, he reshuffled them. Probably trying to get the best ones on the outside.

I'd guess he got maybe a dollar and a half. And that wasn't necessarily for the tapes, but for the business—for the next thing he might bring in, if this was a place that would make deals.

It was lunchtime for him, I was pretty sure. It should have been for me.

I made my way across, eased past the front of his cop car.

Just like I'd been hoping, there was a parking sticker on the front glass. Mayfair Village. Because I didn't want to blow this—I might have been old enough he could smell me over his beard, I don't know—I kept walking, "Mayfair Village" lodged in my head.

All I had to do then was plug it into the phone book.

Our rental, it was out past the outskirts, where you started seeing cars put out to pasture.

Werewolf country.

Not the safe green meadows of town. Not Mayfair Village.

I saved my pennies for three days, then saw Libby off to work, and got on the bus.

The thing to do—Darren's complicated idea—was to stalk the sheep. To make his life hell. To leave raw bites of meat throughout his day, to bring his senses back alive. To slip him a raw ingot of silver and tell him to make a fist around it, see how cold it was. See if he flinched from the smoke seeping up through his fingers.

Then it was going to be dog whistles, blood in his coffee, and Darren was even thinking he could record himself howling one night and play it through the car speakers, just drive back and forth while the sheep slept.

Libby's idea was to step into a closed room with him, and step out five minutes later alone.

One less sheep in the world.

I just wanted to watch him.

He didn't make sense to me.

At first I'd wanted him to help me, to spur me into shifting because maybe I'd hate him with the same rawness Libby did, but waiting for him so long, building him up in my head, I'd realized what I was holding my breath for—my transformation—it was exactly what he was pretending he didn't have. What he was probably having to medicate down with rum and black tea. That was Darren's special formula for keeping the wolf down.

Libby's trick was the breath mints that came in foil tubes with green pull-strings. The string had to be green.

I didn't know what mine was going to be. I wasn't ever going to want *not* to shift.

The sheep's apartment was ground floor, number 110 on the corner.

He went in, had long enough to warm a can of lunch, maybe, then walked out policing his Brillo pad of a beard for drips.

It must feel weird to him, I figured, having that after so many years without.

I shoved my hands in my pockets, rounded my shoulders, and kept walking, not looking behind me.

He was anywhere, now. At whatever his job was, that he needed a yellow hard hat for. And I didn't have bus fare back, had forgot to even get a transfer.

Libby was going to ask, this time. Usually I could beat her home, my backpack strategically slung up onto the counter.

Coming in after dark, there would be questions.

It had been stupid, following him here. So I knew where he lived. Great. Now, tell Darren and Libby, or protect him, let him go on ruining it for us all?

Was I a traitor or was I a killer?

I walked on, kicking a rock that was supposed to roll into a storm drain.

Instead it jumped at the last instant, ricocheted off the curb, up into the undercarriage of a cop-white door.

The Monterey.

The sheep had gone around the block, was parked in my path, waiting for me.

I turned hard right, to veer across the empty lot.

My plan was to jump the fence. To go all the places a car couldn't. To go places even a cop car with performance suspension couldn't.

"You," he said, and I kept walking. "Think I can't catch a scent anymore?" he said, quieter, more secret.

This made me stop.

He'd smelled me. Or who I was living with.

But maybe me.

I cut my eyes up to him, not a hint of a smile on my face.

"Get in," he said. "I'll drop you back at your bookstore."

One thing werewolves can't say is that they're not supposed to take rides with strangers. Werewolves *are* the strangers.

"I don't bite," the sheep said, stepping back to the rear door on his side. To open it for me. "Not anymore," he added.

"How do you know I was at the bookstore?" I said.

"You look like a reader," he said, and sat back in his driver's seat, his hands on the wheel, the back door open in invitation.

I looked right, and left, and over the top of the car.

It was just us in the world.

A werewolf, a sheep.

I bared my teeth, crossed the sidewalk, stepped in.

———

The first thing I realized, before he'd ever turned back onto the main road, was that the door handles in the backseat, they were dead, they were props.

This was a cop car.

He angled the rearview mirror onto me, through the cage wall that was still his headrest.

"How old are you?" he said.

"Where are you really taking me?" I said back, sliding to the center of the bench seat.

The sheep settled the mirror on me again.

"You want to know why," he said.

"Why you're *hiding*," I corrected.

He nodded, accepted this.

"People with—with tuberculosis, they used to go to these asylums, like," he said. "This is all back when. Do you know why?"

"Is that like leprosy?" I asked.

He chuckled, his generous frame shaking with it. "You don't know TB, but you know leprosy?"

I stared at his reflection.

"Same principle," he said. "Lepers and coughers, they knew what they had, so they went to where their own kind were. To keep from killing their families."

"I don't smell any of our kind around here," I said.

It was a bluff—that I *could* smell. He didn't call me on it.

"It's the 'killing their families' part you should maybe pay attention to, here."

"I don't need a lesson, thanks."

"That's good," he said. "Because I'm the last dude to have one to give. But I do know what happened to me."

"You let the world tame you," I said. It was straight from Darren's mouth.

"If that's what you want to call it," he said. "Imagine you fall for someone . . . outside the pack, as it were."

"A human."

"A woman. A wife. And you try to make a go of it. No more barking at the moon. But it builds up inside you, doesn't it?"

I nodded the grimmest nod I had.

It meant yes, I knew this, because I'd had to hold back the change too.

I could understand where he was coming from. Completely.

"It builds up until you wake in the bedroom one night, only it's a slaughterhouse, it's a killing floor. It's a feeding trough."

I looked away.

This was what Libby and Darren had been saying, down to the letter. The wolf, it always claws its way to the surface.

But this was different too.

"Say, then, after a night like that, after a *morning* like that, you maybe get a strong inclination to let your beard grow. Like, all the way to your boots, if that's what it takes."

"If that's what what takes?" I said.

We were almost to the pawnshop parking lot.

"To get the taste out of your mouth," he said. "You think it's this great thing right now." He eased over, keeping me in the mirror the whole time. "It's the best thing ever, isn't it?" he said.

I nodded, still living that lie.

"And it is," he said. "But there's a price. It's not a gift, the blood. It's a curse, the way I hear it. The way I've lived it."

He was ready to go now, but I asked it: "The way you hear it?"

"We're all bastards," he said. "Mutts, mongrels. Here's how it started—how we all started. A woman who was dying anyway, she decided to make her death count. This is back when, peasants and scythes. So she drank a bellyful of some poison plant, then walked naked out to the wolves who had been snatching the village's children. To kill them. But, because she *offered* herself to them, the wolves didn't want her, wouldn't eat her. Instead, they invited her into the pack, and when she died from the poison, they licked her eyeballs hard enough to roll them back around from the whites. She came back to life, and she bore litter after litter for them, and she never put clothes on again."

He stepped up from his seat, pulled my door open.

It was the first time anybody'd ever done that for me.

"That's us," he said. "That's what we are, kid. Animals that never should have existed. Accidents. Reminders about who should mount who, and who shouldn't."

"It's the same thing you were doing, then," I said.

Standing up, I was as tall as him.

"You went cross-species just like she did," I said, and before I could even get my arm up, before I could even think it, he'd punched me so hard in the stomach that I lifted up off my feet.

And he kept me there, lifted on his fist, his knuckles probably outlined in the skin of my back.

"Stay away from me, kid," he said right into my face. "I'm not as soft as you think. We won't meet again."

When he drove away, I was still face-to-the-asphalt, trying to breathe. His second punch had been across my face. It had sounded just like the movies.

I felt better after puking, and then worse again.

Across the street, the By Hook or by Crook owner was out on the stoop watching me, like waiting for a Polaroid to develop.

I waved her back inside, closed my eyes.

———

That night it was Darren's favorite brand of chili. He'd hauled a case of it back from Georgia.

We ate in silence. Nobody said anything about my face. This is how it is with werewolves. So I'd caught a black eye at school again. Hearing about it, that would make them feel like they had to do something permanent about it. And then we'd have to move again. Anyway, this was my thing. I was old enough for that.

Over the six o'clock game shows, Darren went into this long, made-up story about a chicken Grandpa had tried to raise one time. It ended with Grandpa finally coming in one night hungry, and reaching down, taking that chicken between his jaws. The punch line was that chicken squeezing out an egg that wasn't all the way ready yet, so it had a clear shell.

Darren had wanted to play with that egg, to grease it up, try to put it in some other bird to let it cook, but Grandpa had slurped it up before he could, see-through shell and all.

Libby wasn't listening, was just reading her paperback.

At the car-wash break room, there was a whole shelf of books people would leave. She was burning through them all. This one was a western.

"Your hair's going to be white," she said when she finally stood, stretching for bed.

Darren ran his hands through his stubble, shrugged. "Think I'll finally get some respect around here?" he said.

"Bring something back that's not that," she said, about the plundered case of chili, and Darren tossed a couch pillow at her as she was leaving for her bedroom. She caught the pillow, flung it across at me. I let it bounce off.

The black eye had earned me the right not to play tonight. Not to talk.

"Me too," I said, and eased off to my bedroom.

"What, do I smell?" Darren said, but he kept the volume down, and didn't say too many answers out loud.

I lay in the bed that had come with the trailer and pulled my blanket up over my mouth, trying to imagine what a mountain-man beard would feel like. And then I wondered how long your beard would have to get before it made you forget about killing your wife. And eating her.

Sheep was the wrong word, I was pretty sure.

More like *Sleeping. Sleeping Wolf.*

"I won't tell," I told him out loud, because that would make it real. Even though he'd cracked some bone around my eye, I was pretty sure.

And then I tried to imagine that dying woman, that wolf mother, the first of us, walking out into the woods, her insides swirling with poison, her eyes set on certain death.

If they'd just eaten her like they were supposed to, like she'd wanted them to.

Darren's howl shook me awake in the morning.

He was hanging sideways in my doorway, the worst alarm clock ever.

"Going to miss the bus," he said.

You still go to school, I told myself, and rolled out, into that charade, and halfway through brushing my teeth, instead of checking my tongue like I always did, for if it was flattening out, if it was getting that blurry black stripe down the middle, this time I rubbed my jaw in the mirror.

I was just like the sheep, walking through the steps of a life where I was just pretending.

I wasn't a sheep, though. I bared my teeth to prove it.

In the kitchen ten minutes later, five minutes after I should have caught the bus, I looked up to Libby, told her I was quitting school. That it wasn't doing me any good.

She kept mixing her coffee, finally nodded.

"I can't make you go," she said.

"You mean you're never going to be smart like me?" Darren said. He wasn't in this discussion.

"I can get a job, help out," I said.

She didn't disagree, just raised her cup to her face, the steam washing over her.

"I'll ask Hector at the car wash," she said, and that was that.

I wasn't in danger of being a sheep. I was living my real life, not a pretend one.

"But you could have told me two weeks ago," Libby said, and left me with that.

Half an hour later, Darren's game shows blasting through the house, I eased out onto the plywood and cinderblock porch for my shoes.

They were black with ants.

I flinched back but they were my only pair.

"What you been walking through?" Darren said, suddenly in the doorway again, his first wine cooler of the morning hanging from his door-hand.

"Town," I said.

He looked down to the ants, raised one slow motion foot above the, fixing them in his shadow.

"It's like I'm a giant," he said, then started in quoting: "'The villagers ran left and they ran right, but there was nowhere they could—'"

"Tokyo doesn't have villagers," I told him, disgusted.

"If you're not a beautiful monster, then you're a villager," he said matter-of-fact, his real attention on bringing his foot down, flattening a city block in slow, crunchy motion.

"Thanks," I said, bringing his eyes up to my tone.

"Said the monster-in-waiting," he added, and began the complicated process of guiding his mouth up to his wine cooler but stopped right at the last moment, his head cocked over for the game-show host's question. "Kenworth," he said, in pure wonder, his eyes to me like a question, like to be sure this could really be happening. Then he smiled, let his bottle drop. "Kenworth. Kenworth Kenworth!" he said, louder each time, holding me by the shoulders, shaking me with each syllable.

He'd finally got an answer right. Good for him.

I used a stick to pick up my right shoe, and shook it. The ants calved off in sheets. I brushed the clingers away with the side of my hand.

On a nature show, I'd seen somebody in South America use ant-mouth pincers as stitches. Just hold them to the cut, let them clamp down, then pinch the head off.

These ants, it would have to be like a paper cut.

I shook the shoe some more, and a black negative of the tread fell out. I *had* stepped in something.

The ants I'd shaken off were already massing toward it.

I stood up to let Libby pass, on her way to work.

"Another car, another dollar," she said, then, about my shoe: "Oh, that's where that ground meat went."

I looked down to it, didn't even say bye to her.

The beef from the refrigerator?

When could I have *stepped* on it?

I picked my other shoe up, its tread just as packed with ground meat, and eased inside with it, held it up for Darren, on the couch, waiting for the next question. Two in a row would be the new world record for his age division.

"Why would somebody pack hamburger into my shoe?" I said, holding it up.

"Old werewolf trick," he said, still in game-show mode. "You can follow somebody anywhere like that. But you've got to mix some of your own blood in too, so the dogs know to stay off the trail. Only thing at the end of a trail of werewolf blood's a hurt, pissed-off—"

The next answer in this "kategory"—words that start with *K*—was Kamchatka. Darren hissed, fell back into the couch, wronged again.

"Why?" he asked, about the shoe.

Why.

I looked to the idea of the road Libby was walking now, to work. Her big purse looped over her shoulder.

"She went out last night," I said.

"Oh, yeah, almost forgot, man," Darren said, biting his lower lip with excitement. "She found him, I think. That one sheep."

I nodded. Of course she had. She'd tracked him down. She'd tracked *me* to him. I'd as good as led her right there.

"Hey, hey," Darren said then, pinching me closer with his voice. "That reminds me. What do you get when you cross Lib with one of them? You know, with a sheep?"

I just stared at him.

"You need to get a new *sheep*," he said, slapping his thigh, and, because I was locked into a pattern, I went down to the bookstore again, taking the long way around the car wash this time.

I couldn't see Libby yet.

She'd used me. She'd *been* using me. Worse, she'd known I wouldn't smell the meat on my shoe.

I wanted to run away, but I come from werewolves. Our life is already running away.

Give it a week, or two, and we'd be gone again. And maybe it was for the best.

I didn't know everything. She probably had her reasons.

It didn't make it any better.

I ran my fingers over my black eye. Soon it would be gone as well.

I walked down to the bus stop, just drifting, and got off at my usual stop, stood there like seeing what was different.

Everything.

For the first time, then, I stepped into the air-conditioned pawnshop, the bell clanging over my head from the door.

"Help you with anything?" the big man behind the counter said.

"Just looking," I said, no eye contact, standard procedure.

Touching all the same things the sheep might have touched would have to do, I figured. It would have to serve as apology, as good-bye.

Mostly apology.

The big man behind the watches and handguns moved along his counter with me, so he had a clear view down whatever aisle I was on. Today wasn't a stealing day, though. This was a funeral.

Still, to keep him on his toes, I picked up this spark-plug socket, that spray-painted chisel, and inspected them on each side, like seriously considering. I made sure they made noise when they went back into their trays, and I kept my hands far from my pants.

"See anything you like?" the big man said, when I'd shopped the place dry.

I looked to the wall of guitars behind him, then scanned the glass counter. For binoculars I couldn't afford, watches I'd lose inside of a day, knives with wolves scrimshawed into the blade.

And movies.

The sheep's six VHS tapes were right there on the glass, red clearance tape and all. They were a complete set. The big man had even propped it up on both sides with bookends.

"Got a little girl already?" he said, seeing where I was looking.

I shook my head no, but was smiling too, smiling too much, my eyes heating up about it.

She was out there somewhere, this girl, this daughter. She was out there and she was close. Living with his dead wife's parents, probably.

Maybe wolf, maybe not.

No, I told her, in what I knew was my Black Wolf voice, *no, your dad's not coming home.*

But remember him. Remember him hard.

CHAPTER 16

Never Say Werewolf

But that makes me one too, doesn't it?" the villager says, about to cry even though he's eleven and a half.

"Nope," the villager's uncle tells him, parting the curtains just enough to sneak a peek outside, at the mob. "You're like us. You know that. Give it another year or two, bub."

"That's what you said last year," the villager says.

"This isn't happening," the villager's aunt says.

"You're not going to believe this," the villager's uncle says back to the villager's aunt, his smile as wide as the villager's ever seen. "One of them's got a *pitchfork*."

This is Texas. It's right under Arkansas.

"If they knock——" the villager's aunt says, right exactly when the knock comes.

The villager steps back, his lips thinned out.

The reason he's a villager is that you're either a villager, like the mob outside, or you're a werewolf.

"Don't answer that," the villager's aunt says, reaching her arm across the living room like her arm's long enough to stop the villager's uncle.

He's still smiling from the pitchfork, though.

It's easy to smile when you're already a werewolf.

"I'll just ask if they need a torch," he says, and licks his lips to normal his mouth down, opens the door the way he always does, with one arm hooked high above.

"Gentlemen," he says, his head moving because he's going from face to face.

The villager watches through the window.

"You heard anything strange around here?" the leader of the mob asks. "Maybe at night?"

"Hunh . . ." the uncle says, taking his hand off the wall to rub his smooth chin. "Like, what do you mean, *strange?*"

"I've lost two calves," a face in the mob says.

"Crisp's wife saw it the other night," another says.

The villager leans sideways to look down the tunnel the mob is making. One guy is at the end of it.

"Crispin?" the villager's uncle asks.

"Just Crisp," the man says. He's the one with the pitchfork. The rest of the mob is carrying shotguns. Two of them in back have dogs. The dogs are already screaming.

"What did she see?" the villager's uncle asks.

"Doesn't matter," Crisp says, looking around at the mob. "It was late."

They're all ready to laugh.

"Bigfoot," one of them says.

"*Big*foot?" the villager's uncle says, stepping out onto the plank that's the last step before getting into the trailer.

"Whatever it was," the leader says, "it's eating the livestock, scaring the women."

"You need some light, don't you?" the villager's uncle asks, having to bite his lip to keep from smiling all the way.

The villager looks back to his aunt, who's shaking her head about this. Who's trying to wish herself back in time, it looks like. Into a different family.

"I got a light right here," the uncle says, stepping over for the big flashlight in the windowsill. On the way back to the door he drops the two batteries from the back of the flashlight.

"Man, I don't know why this won't . . ." the villager's uncle is saying now at the door, slapping the head of the flashlight into his palm.

Next he's running back to the stove to turn a burner on, light the dishrag he's wrapping around the rubber part of the brand-new plunger.

"This is perfect, perfect," he's saying, bouncing to make the flame catch. He looks up to the villager's aunt, who isn't looking at him, so he looks down to the villager instead. "I'm going to find *Bigfoot*," he says. "With a *mob*."

When the torch is lit he holds it over the sink, is captivated by it.

In the refrigerator is what's left of the second calf.

In the mud behind the house are clear wolf prints, deep enough that the water's seeped back in to fill them. They're part wolf prints, anyway. There's the heel of a person connected to them too. Because the villager's uncle was still shifting when he left those tracks.

As the uncle's passing back through the living room, the villager's aunt reaches up, has his wrist in her hand.

The villager's uncle is almost too excited to stop.

"What?" he says, pulling. "What what what?"

"Just Bigfoot," she says, making sure he hears. "Don't get them started looking for anything else, got it?"

"*Wolfenstein . . .*" the villager's uncle says, loving the way it sounds. He's still pawing, trying to get past.

The villager's aunt opens her hand and holds it high, fingers spread, letting the villager's uncle go.

"You're not going to be stupid when you grow up, are you?" the villager's aunt asks after the noise of the mob has gone.

The villager doesn't answer.

He picks up the two batteries, stands them up beside each other in the windowsill where the flashlight was.

Half an hour later, lying on his back in front of a game show, he looks up to the ceiling during a commercial. Where the uncle passed with the torch is a smudgy black line, like the smoke stuck there. In the middle of it is dim red line.

Instead of saying anything, he just stares at it.

"You know that one," his aunt says about the question on the game show.

"This is a rerun," the villager says.

"Then why are you watching it?" the aunt says, closing her celebrity magazine because she's got to get to work.

At first the villager thinks she's talking about him watching the red line in the ceiling. But it's already gone anyway.

At least until his aunt's gone to her job.

Just to see if it's really dead, the villager balls a clump of toilet paper to a coat hanger, pushes it into the black smudge in the ceiling.

There's a wisp of smoke, then nothing.

"Figures," the villager says, and sets the coat hanger down, goes to get a *wet* clump of toilet paper. By the time he walks back into the living room, the toilet paper he left on the floor has caught fire. He drops his clump of wet toilet paper, picks up the coat hanger, and holds the torch away from the carpet.

It doesn't matter. The carpet smokes for a moment, then licks a fast flame up.

The villager steps on it with his shoes but it's already too wide. And his uncle is still out in the pasture playing Wolfenstein, sure he's seeing Bigfoot there, and there, the mob following him deeper and deeper.

The villager watches the flames jump across the carpet. He shakes his head no, please, he'll take it back, he didn't mean to, but it doesn't matter, it's already too late.

He runs to his bedroom for his light blue backpack with the shoe box in it, and is standing outside watching the trailer burn when the uncle gets back, minutes ahead of the mob.

Because he's running so fast, his footprints half and half again, he doesn't stop for the villager, sitting between the burn barrels because that seems like the one part of the pasture that might not burn tonight.

Instead of stopping there, the villager's uncle dives straight through the burning door, already screaming the villager's name.

His throat is wrong for words, so it's just a tangled howl.

For the first time ever, and mostly because he's hidden between the burn barrels, the villager lifts his own mouth, howls back.

The rest of the mob finally crashes out of the bushes breathing hard, their shotguns and pitchforks useless against the fire.

"Is he—" the one called Crisp says to the villager, shaking him from his daze.

Inside, in the fire, things are cracking, things are exploding. Everything's sparks that keep puffing up into the black sky.

"Did you find him?" the villager says, his voice like in a dream.

Crisp shields his face from part of the trailer falling down into itself and says, "Who?"

"*Bigfoot,*" the villager whispers, instead of the real word.

CHAPTER 17

The Mark of the Beast

I.

For a lot of years we'd been pallbearers, carrying my mom from state to state.

What we had, what I never looked at because I was scared that it wouldn't be enough, was a lock of hair in a black velvet ring box.

Things go away, though.

That's how it is with werewolves. You have something, then you just have the story of it.

We were in Florida again. Ten years ago it had been the farthest place we'd been able to get from that creek bank Grandpa was buried in, from that trooper dead in a parking lot. From Red.

Parts of us had been peeling off already, even, that first night out of Arkansas. Driving fast across a forever bridge, the wind had curled up from the surface of the lake passing beneath us and all our cardboard boxes in the bed had opened to that pull, lifting our lives up into the rearview, spreading it out across the moon-dark water.

Darren had been driving then, and he'd nodded about what was happening behind us and finally just punched the El Camino faster, sucking the headlights back in with a distinct click.

"This isn't your best trick, you know," Libby had told him, about driving blind. "Someday it's going to get you killed."

"Some *night*," Darren had corrected, looking over just long enough to flash his devil-can-go-to-hell smile.

That's the picture of him I wanted to put on a flyer, staple to a utility pole, to every utility pole Jacksonville had.

Darren was missing.

When you live with a trucker, you get used to him being gone for days at a time. It means that, when he really is gone, you can have pieces of your day that are just normal. But then you remember.

After the first few days of him being gone, Libby quit her job stocking the grocery store. That's how I knew this time was different. Over the years she'd had exactly one grocery-store job, and she'd dug her claws deep into that one. All the damaged boxes of cereal, all the meat past its date, all the bread with the wrong-color twist tie, somebody had to take it home.

We didn't even know where to start looking for Darren, either.

We walked the pound, we called the jail, we watched the ditches for roadkill.

If it wasn't town, Libby might have been able to track his scent.

If I were a detective, it would have been easy, finding him. *The detective stepped into the room and knew immediately which door the perp had taken.*

I wasn't a detective, though. I was almost sixteen. I was tall and lanky, hair in my eyes, scruff on my jaw that rasped in my ear when I pushed the pad of my thumb along it. It was a sound I couldn't stop making, a sound just for me, a constant reminder of what I wasn't becoming. What I was probably never going to become.

I wanted to bare my fangs to the world, wanted to show Darren and Libby and everybody what I had coiled up inside me. No matter how hard I scratched, though, the wolf wouldn't surface.

"If I knew my dad," I said to Libby one no-Darren afternoon, both our eyes tracking each blade of grass in the ditch, traffic stacking up behind us. "Maybe he was a late bloomer too. For a villager, I mean."

Because Libby didn't think I was watching, I caught her face in the mirror. The way her lips thinned and tightened at the same time. It wasn't because I was using Darren's terminology. It was because my dad was strictly off-limits. Anybody is who gets a fourteen-year-old pregnant.

"Wish in one hand," Libby said, her voice just usual.

"Wish in one hand," I agreed.

Sort of.

We heard about the hot-dog competition on the radio. Kind of in early memoriam, we had the Catalina's dial set to what had become Darren's favorite station. Classic rock, corny DJs.

The radio station was holding a hot-dog-eating contest.

I looked up to Libby about this.

"He's always saying," I told her.

She knew.

Darren's big plan if trucking ever fell through was to get rich and famous being a competitive eater. The advantage he'd have is that he could shift before and after. It would make him ravenous enough to win, then would burn all the calories away he'd just swallowed.

He even had his signature trick planned: Twelve or fifteen hot dogs in, he would hold up his right hand and fall back in pain about his missing finger. About the finger he'd just ate.

He would win on style and ability both. The crowd favorite *and* the best athlete at the table.

All his life he'd been waiting for a radio ad like we'd just heard.

The contest was two days away.

We checked the pound again, and then the clipboard on the wall, listing roadkill that had already been scooped out into the marsh, for the alligators.

"We shouldn't have come back to Florida," I said. "Florida and Texas are always bad news."

"We're running out of places," Libby said back.

While she was walking back and forth in the living room reading the same page of her book over and over, I called the two alligator farms in the area. To ask if they had any new wrestlers, any new wranglers. Any who didn't even want money, were just doing it to show off.

There was the zoo, of course, but just that I could hear them on the phone when I called meant Darren wasn't there.

I couldn't even dream where he might be.

"Think he found somebody?" I said at last to Libby, because she had to be considering it too. He'd shacked up with women on the road before, for days at a time, even, and this year he was the same age as Grandpa had been when he'd seen Grandma in that parade. But still. "Do werewolves do that, just leave?" I added, when Libby wasn't answering.

Her eyes when she looked up to me, they were ancient and tired and sad and mad all at once.

"*Men* do that," she said.

"But he's your brother," I said.

"He's your uncle," she said back.

I shouldn't have asked. Just—when Darren had announced that, about him being Grandpa's age when he met Grandma, the way he'd lilted his voice up, it had been like he was testing out how this sounded. Like there was going to be more.

Maybe this was it.

One morning, he's in training for NMV Exterminators— "No More Vermin"—and that afternoon he doesn't come back from work.

Had he just kept walking? Had he even looked back, like to catch one last scent?

When Libby'd gone into NMV's front office, asked after him, one of the exterminators had come in from back, his goggles on his forehead, the pesticide rolling off him in waves thick enough that her eyes watered.

The story he finally admitted to was that Darren had started drinking at lunch, and had been asked to take it home by mid-afternoon. End of training, end of story, he was sorry.

"He'll show up," the exterminator told her. "But we can't let him—he won't be working here. If anything, you know, happened, we'd be liable."

Libby understood. Darren belonged on the interstate, not in a shop, not on a crew.

The night before the hot-dog contest, she walked out the back door. To read one of her paperbacks under the floodlight, I thought, but when I looked, her clothes were folded on the rusty lawn chair the way she always did, for when she came back.

Ten minutes later, and for the rest of the night, her howling filled every nook and cranny of the city, seeped into every pore.

It's not something werewolves do just all the time, like in the movies. And it's not at the stupid moon either.

You howl like that when your brother's gone.

You howl like that when you want him to hear you. When you need him to.

I don't know if she was saying *good-bye* or *where are you?*

The next morning all the DJs were talking about the wolf. They were even playing clips, piping in specialists, mixing Libby in with songs.

"Good," Libby said.

She was still on the exact same page of her book.

The contest was down at the water, with the cruise ships like giant walls out against all that scary blue.

The hot-dog contest went the way they usually do, except this time one of the contestants had a white canvas sack over his head, with eyeholes cut into it. It made him look like a scarecrow. The DJ hosting the event made a big production of pinching the cloth away from his mouth, using scissors to snip a mouth out.

When the bell rang to start the eating, I tried counting how many hot dogs the mystery contestant was dunking and downing, but I also wanted to see his fingers at the same time. It made me lose count, and it didn't matter anyway. The mystery guest didn't win, and Darren would have. Even before the DJ pulled the hood off, showed it was the *morning* DJ, I knew we'd made the trip all the way out here for nothing.

"They never look like they sound," I said to Libby.

She was pulling her hair beside her face, trying not to cry.

I led her to the car.

"What does 'Catalina' even *mean*?" she said, slamming the heel of hand into the dash. Darren had pried the car's name off the side, screwed it to the glove compartment because, he said, this was Florida, and we needed a real boat to get around, right?

"Catamaran" is the boat, though. Not "Catalina."

And werewolves don't go on boats anyway.

Because it was town, Libby was having to drive. Because she couldn't, we just sat there.

"Sometimes you can forget," she said, finally.

I looked over to her, waited.

"Dad told me about it. That—that if you get hurt bad enough as a wolf, that when you come back in the morning, back to a person, that you can come back not knowing anything."

"Amnesia," I filled in.

"Sort of," Libby said. "But he said he'd even seen it happen once that a guy's face . . . like, *forgot*. When he came back, his jaw was different. Like, since he couldn't remember who he was, the wolf was just putting him back together however. It didn't have directions to follow, didn't have memories to go on, so one face was as good as the next."

"Did he still know he could change?"

Libby didn't answer.

I tried to imagine Darren with a different face. I remembered touching his face with my fingertips in the darkness once, to be sure it was him. I could still see him crashing through the wall of my bedroom to save me. I remembered every swimming pool his favorite used-car salesman had fallen back into, and the look in that salesman's eyes each time.

I stood up from the car, took off walking.

Libby let me.

It was all falling apart, I could tell. It was just going to be me and her. It was enough, but it wasn't.

I hated Darren, and I would have chewed my hand off just to see him one more time.

Where I spent the night was under the stoop of an abandoned strip mall across from NMV Exterminators. All their vans were parked out front like giant white beetles. They even had comical feelers sprung up from above their windshields. It was how you knew you were getting NMV.

I was the first one through the door at nine.

"I'm looking for my uncle," I told the woman at the desk.

She was maybe ten years older than Libby, I thought, kind of a honky-tonk reject, too many cigarettes, not enough sunlight, fingernails curved over like talons, fake red hair, her left ear pinched through with probably twenty silver earrings all in a row. This wasn't the annoying high schooler who had helped Libby. I hadn't been hoping for the high schooler, though. I was hoping for answers.

"Does he work here?" she asked, holding my face with her eyes in a way I had to look away from, because she would read everything.

"He used to," I said. "For a day or two."

"Oh," she said. "The new—Daryl."

"Darren," I corrected.

Soon enough the exterminator came in from the back to tell me the story again. He didn't smell like pesticide this time, but his goggles were still cocked up on his forehead. Maybe it was how he kept his hair out of his eyes.

After making sure I was with that other lady who'd come by, the exterminator shrugged, looked through their plate glass at the road, and said the same thing: Darren had started drinking at lunch, at that taco place, and then he must have had a bottle or a flask in his pocket, because by three he could hardly stand.

"He just walked out?" I said.

"He said he knew the way."

It sounded like Darren, all right. Of the two things he wouldn't take from anybody, one was directions. The other was advice.

"Could he have got, like, sprayed with the spray?" I asked, doing my finger on the trigger of an imaginary spray-rig, one aimed up into my face.

"Got to be licensed to handle that," the exterminator said. "He was strictly a gofer."

No, I said in my head. *He was a wolf.*

"Thanks," I said, not sure what else I could even ask.

The exterminator clapped me on the shoulder and shook my hand at the same time, pulling us close enough I *should* have been able to smell the pesticide on him.

Maybe Libby just *could,* though.

Maybe it was because I hadn't shifted, didn't have the right nose.

Maybe it was because, in every way that mattered, I wasn't wolf.

I had my hand to the push bar on the door when I stopped, looked over to the woman at the desk. She was trying to get a pen to work. How she was even able to hold on to it with her nails, I had no idea.

"Hey," I said, back to the exterminator, who was halfway out of the room as well. "What was he drinking, do you remember? I can tell how long until he shows up again, you know?"

The exterminator nodded, understood.

"Coronas," he said like he was sorry to have to be the one to tell me.

Beer.

And either more beer in his overalls, clinking with every step, or a flask.

For a guy who lived on strawberry wine coolers. For a werewolf whose only and main religion was strawberry wine coolers.

"Anything else?" the exterminator asked.

The woman behind the desk was watching me too.

The exterminator's name was Rayford, sewed right there on his chest in cursive.

The woman was Grace-Ellen, by her nameplate.

I shook my head no, nothing.

Because I didn't trust my voice.

That night when Grace-Ellen came in from wherever she'd gone after getting home from work—I'd ground hamburger and Libby's blood into the tread of one of her tires—I was waiting in the living room. Just standing there in the dark.

Werewolves don't care about breaking and entering.

Werewolves care about their uncles.

We were trying her first because Rayford had his lies all ready. Grace-Ellen might have to make it up as she went. She might leave cracks we could see through. She might leave cracks we could see *Darren* through.

When the light from the porch hit me she startled, dropped her keys into the deadspace behind her console television.

"Guess you could say I'm still looking for my uncle," I said.

Grace-Ellen turned to run, to shriek out into the night, but there was a gigantic wolf-thing standing in the doorway behind her.

Or, that's probably what she would have called Libby.

It would have been close enough.

Libby growled deep in her chest, her lips snarled back, a single line of clear drool drawing a line to the floor. When we want to, when we're really trying, we can look eviler than sin. We can kick-start thirty centuries of legends.

Even when we're not trying, I guess.

Libby took her weight off her forepaws, was going to stand, I knew, really put the fear into Grace-Ellen, but I didn't want pee on the ground.

I stepped around, eased the door shut on Libby.

"Now that we know what's out *there* . . ." I said, and turned back just as Grace-Ellen slashed at me with her claw.

No, I saw in slow motion: not *her* claw, not one of her curvy fingernails.

This was—I almost had to laugh.

It was a cockfighting spur. Because this was Florida. The spur was just two or three inches long, perfect for a purse, and it had a little loop for her finger, even, where the rooster's leg would have gone.

My blood sprayed up in front of me in a slow-motion fan of deep red before I could even get my hand to the slash she'd made down from my shoulder to the ribs on the other side. It didn't feel like a cut so much as like she'd found the pull tab for a wire buried in my chest, and was pulling it out all at once, fast to keep it from hurting.

But it did.

Without having to think about it, I knew this was going to be a stitches-and-staples fix. You see enough bodies torn up, you get to know. Not because Grace-Ellen's spur had cut deep, but because it had cut ragged. And it would likely heal that way, if it got the chance.

I was getting my own stories.

I think I might have smiled, the two of us caught there in that flashbulb of an instant.

But then the silver hit me.

It was like nothing I'd ever felt. I'd had spider venom in me before, sending out red tendrils each way from the bite, and that was the closest thing. Except, for this, the spider would have to be the size of a motorcycle, and have electricity in its jaws.

I locked eyes with Grace-Ellen, could see that she knew, she knew about *us*, she knew what to *do*, and then there were splinters blooming in the air all around the two of us.

Libby had heard my intake of breath, had smelled my blood.

Grace-Ellen came around with her silver spur, but, like Darren says, it's going to take more than that. It would take a thousand roosters with a thousand spurs, and even then they'd all have to get past Libby's snapping teeth.

After a flurry of motion between Libby and Grace-Ellen, it was me on the kitchen floor, Libby naked and so human, so my mom at last, holding her face close to mine and screaming at me to look at her, to look *right fucking directly at her,* that she wasn't losing both of us, not tonight.

It was the third time I'd ever heard her cuss.

I closed my eyes.

2.

We never should have come back to Florida. But we had to.

Libby was right: We were running out of places. Coming back to Florida—none of us would have said it, but it was like if we hit it just right, we could back up time, start all over again. Do it right. Do it better. Do it where we didn't end up where we'd started again.

I didn't shift to save myself from dying, like werewolves are supposed to.

Maybe I never would, I figured.

Maybe some never do. Maybe I was doomed to just be a werewolf in my head. Or maybe I was trading in being a werewolf for getting Darren back.

It was a deal I would have made, I think.

Damn the future, right? It's right now that matters. When you don't *have* a future, it's always right now that means everything.

Especially when right now hurts like that spur did.

After the silver hit my blood I was in and out, thrashing against arms I thought were Libby's, arms I was pretending were my mom's, until I opened my eyes.

Grace-Ellen was standing over me, Libby right beside her gripping a kitchen knife in her hand, the blade to Grace-Ellen's throat, hard.

Libby never told me, but what I figure is that I never even hit the ground. Grace-Ellen catching me on the way down, holding me like you hold a child, it was the only reason Libby hadn't ripped her throat out in that first second.

But she was right there ready to, teeth or no.

As it was turning out, though, Grace-Ellen, she knew how to kill us, but she knew how to bring us back too.

The secret was boiling a broth with werewolf blood as the water, dog bones as the stock. Libby supplied both. Really, she'd supplied every dog from the street, it looked like, in case breed or volume of blood made the difference. The kitchen floor was slick with dead dogs, like she could stack them up, weigh them against my life.

It worked.

The broth wasn't for me to drink. It was to pour directly into the cut, with Libby pulling the skin apart so that the cut could be an open mouth, one breathing out a steam that smelled like gravy.

I thought she was screaming, or that some dog owner outside was screaming, or that the villagers had finally mobbed up, found us, but I'm pretty sure it was my own voice I was hearing.

Grace-Ellen cooled my forehead with a damp washcloth.

Libby paced back and forth by the front window. Because of

whatever had happened to all the dogs, there was a police car trolling up and down the street, angling its dummy light into all the cracks and crevices of the night.

We couldn't stay here long, I knew, not with the front door just balanced in its frame. Not with Libby's voice on the radio, her bloody paw prints on the sidewalk. Not with that look in her eyes, like her back was against the wall and she was about to have to come out slashing and snapping, take down as many as she could when she went out.

When the dummy light glowed the front window hot white, Libby bared her teeth.

Like the light knew, it kept moving. For now.

"She'll fight them all, don't you worry," Grace-Ellen said, re-folding the washcloth so the coolness it had left could be on the outside.

"She shouldn't have to," I said, closing my eyes. The tears came anyway. And my stupid chin was doing its stupid thing, bunching up like a stupid-ass prune. "I should be able to—to . . ."

"Shh, shh," Grace-Ellen said, and did me maybe the best kindness I'd ever had done for me in fifteen years: She pushed the washcloth down over my eyes, to hide my crying. "Do you think that silver would have hurt you if you weren't like her?" she whispered.

"But—"

"Being a werewolf isn't just teeth and claws," she said, her lips brushing my ear she was so close, so quiet, "it's inside. It's how you look at the world. It's how the world looks back at you."

My hand found her wrist to keep that washcloth there.

By sunrise I could stand. Grace-Ellen squeezed superglue onto the end of a Popsicle stick and smeared it up and down my cut then held the ragged, boiled edges of the skin together, blew on the glue, her breath cold in comparison to the searing heat of the glue's drying.

It held me together. It held me together enough.

Libby was wearing Grace-Ellen's clothes—jeans that fit, a shirt that didn't, flip-flops that left her heels still touching the carpet. She didn't care about any of that. She was opening and closing her left hand by her leg. Her mouth was pinched tight.

"Thank you," she said, guiding me over from Grace-Ellen. No: taking me *back* from Grace-Ellen. "I'll pay for your door."

"It's just a door," Grace-Ellen said.

"And your car," Libby said, her eyes darting away.

"My *car*?" Grace-Ellen said.

I didn't need to look to know the state of Grace-Ellen's tires. Libby had been out there alone with them for probably twenty seconds. Any longer and her little Honda probably wouldn't have a windshield, or a hood, or a roof.

"I don't know where he is," Grace-Ellen said, the challenge rising in her voice.

"You just happen to know about *us*," Libby said, rising to that challenge. "And he happens to *be* one of us. Working at the place *you* work."

Grace-Ellen breathed in, breathed out, and flicked her eyes away from Libby's hand by her thigh—flicked her eyes in a way I could tell she knew what Libby spreading her fingers like that meant: It's what you do when you're about to shift. If your hand's a fist, the claws will embed into your palm when they push out.

No, not "embed." *Impact.*

I nodded, was ready for whatever this was going to be, wherever this next part of the day was going to take us, but then Grace-Ellen was wading in: "I know because of my *husband*," she said, hijacking Libby's tone. "You're the first other ones I've met since . . . it's been two years."

"Then I need to talk to your husband," Libby said, closing her hand into a fist that was hardly less threatening.

"Me too," Grace-Ellen said, then settled back on me. "Y'all've really just been living out there on the road, not knowing any of the old ways?"

"We're from Arkansas," I said.

Grace-Ellen smiled a polite smile. "My husband, Trigo, he was from Texas."

"We don't all know each other," Libby said.

I asked the obvious question: *"Was?"*

"He's smart for a wolf," Grace-Ellen said to Libby, about me.

"He's smart in any room," Libby said, her voice gearing down for a climb.

Grace-Ellen grinned a thin grin, liked that.

"He wouldn't just leave us," I said before I could stop myself.

"Your uncle," Grace-Ellen said.

"My brother," Libby said.

"I'm sorry," Grace-Ellen said.

"And he's not dead," I added.

Grace-Ellen didn't look at me about this. Maybe because it was better to let me believe.

"He's not!" I said, baring my teeth, wolf in everything but body.

Libby took me by the upper arm, held me in place.

"Your boss was lying about the beer," Libby said. "Why would he lie if he wasn't hiding something?"

"Rayford," Grace-Ellen said. "He probably just forgot what everybody was drinking."

"And if it wasn't just forgetting?" Libby said.

Grace-Ellen did finally look up about this. Something passed between her and Libby. Grace-Ellen nodded, pushed up from the back of the couch she'd been leaning against.

"Here," she said, lobbing something across.

Because I was closer, I snagged it out of the air, my chest screaming from the effort. It was the silver cockspur.

"Truce," Grace-Ellen said.

Without asking for permission from the two werewolves in the room—the *one* werewolf—Grace-Ellen pulled the phone up to her ear. The plastic rattled against all her earrings.

"Rayford," she explained to us once it was ringing.

Libby stepped in, her eyes hot, but Grace-Ellen held her hand up, like that could ever be enough.

Rayford's wife was Marcie.

Twenty seconds of polite nothings later, Grace-Ellen hung up, held the phone on its cradle, looked over to us.

"What?" Libby said.

"Rayford's not there," Grace-Ellen said, speaking like from a trance. As if she was just waking up.

"Where is he?" I said, because somebody had to.

"Hunting," Grace-Ellen said, defeat in her voice.

"Where?" Libby said.

"He's back tonight," Grace-Ellen said.

"Not good enough," Libby told her.

"It's Sunday," Grace-Ellen said then, like the answer to a question we hadn't thought to ask. "The office is *closed* on Sundays."

"We've already been to the *office*," Libby said.

"You've been to the waiting room. I can go—I can check their schedule against business expenses, receipts, see where they were that day, show you that they're not involved. How long ago can you still track someone from a place?"

"He's my brother," Libby said.

"It's not Rayford," Grace-Ellen said then, standing from the phone, taking a key ring from a peg on the wall.

"He is an exterminator," Libby said. "How did you get that job? Think it was random?"

"I being interrogated now?" Grace-Ellen said, setting her feet and her eyes both.

"You do work there."

"They gave me the front desk when they were trying to get Trigo to come work for them. Then when he disappeared—I already knew how to run the place."

"Trigo?" I said, when it was suddenly too quiet.

"My husband," Grace-Ellen said, for the second time.

After a glare-off—more of a dare, really, for me or Libby to ask any more questions—Grace-Ellen hooked her head for us to follow her down the hall she was already walking down.

"Where are we going?" Libby asked, being sure she was ahead of me. For all we knew there was a pistol-grip shotgun behind every door, on top of every shelf.

"We can't take my car, right?" Grace-Ellen said, hauling open the scratched-up door to the garage.

"You've got *two* cars?" I said.

"Trigo had the county Ford," Grace-Ellen said, slapping the wall for the electric door to hitch and grind up. "But this was where he kept his heart."

It was a project car, under a splotchy canvas tarp.

"Your brother," she said to Libby. "He older or younger?"

"The same," Libby said, stepping in, casing the whole garage at once, to be sure it was safe for me. "We're twins."

"And both wolf?" Grace-Ellen said, impressed. "You know that's not how it works, right? There's usually a feeder."

"A *what*?" I said.

"How have you stayed *alive* this long?" Grace-Ellen said to me and Libby both, and in one grand gesture then, she swept the tarp off her dead husband's project car, dust and dead moths fluttering behind, settling down onto faded black paint. Onto the chipped-white racing stripes. Into the unlikely bed, the uncracked rear window, onto the base of the whip-antenna that had been mounted on the roof one bad-idea afternoon.

My heart hammered once in my throat, and my hand pulled into a fist, my head turning half away, like to avoid a blow coming in fast.

"No," I said.

But yes.

It was the El Camino. It was *our* El Camino. Because it was parked backward I could zero in on the cigarette burn on the dashboard above the radio. The whole drive out from Arkansas that first time, I'd stared at that burn, pretending that it had got hot enough one day to melt the glass from the rearview, drip it down onto the dash, sizzle that crater into the vinyl.

Libby opened her mouth like to say something but it was just that yawn kind of feeling you get behind the jaws when you want to breathe but can't.

It's a feeling particular to werewolves, I think.

If we really are what we are because we caught something from the bats, then that hollow feeling under our bottom row of teeth, it's probably an old sonar instinct. It's what you use when you want to send a quiet little sound out, find somebody with it.

It's what you do when you're alone, but don't want to be.

I took Libby by the wrist, guided her into the car, and because Grace-Ellen didn't know this pedal, and because the El Camino was parked on smooth concrete, and because Red had bolted 427 heads onto this 396 block, the El Camino chirped the tires when we pulled out, the nose jerking up, Grace-Ellen clamping the brakes down, stopping us in the harsh morning light.

"This isn't happening," Libby finally said.

It was, though. It had been happening already for ten years.

3.

When the receipts Grace-Ellen needed were in Rayford's office, I elbowed in the window part of his door.

"He's going to know we've been here now," Grace-Ellen said.

"Not if I see him first, he won't," Libby said.

Grace-Ellen considered this, considered it some more, then she reached through, careful of the glass, unlocked the door.

We followed her in, sat in Rayford's client chairs while she peeled through years of receipts.

"Thought you just needed last week," Libby said.

Grace-Ellen didn't answer, had some complicated organization going on all over the floor.

"So?" Libby said, thirty minutes into it.

"Shh," Grace-Ellen said.

Libby hissed through her teeth, pushed up from the chair, walked back out to the waiting room. The watercooler in there gurgled deep, then gurgled again.

"You're supposed to drink as much water as you can before you shift," Grace-Ellen said, not looking up from the invoices and receipts. "If you don't, your skin—you can start to get old before your time, like."

I leaned back in the client chair, studied the tile ceiling, knew that I didn't even know how much there *was* to know.

"I met a werewolf who made fake silver bullets," I told her, like trying to go toe-to-toe in the lightning round, double or nothing.

"That's just a legend," she said, not remotely interested, still digging.

"But I did."

She was sorting by color, it looked like, but double-checking by shape, then stacking by date, carefully, like one wrong breath could ruin what she thought she was seeing.

"This can't be happening," she said.

Her fingers were trembling.

"What did your husband do about sheep?" I said, a touch quieter. Because Libby was still close, but more because I still wasn't sure what she'd done up in Augusta had been right.

"Sheep are for eating," Grace-Ellen said, only half listening.

"I'm talking *sheep*-sheep," I said.

"Something's wrong," she said then, laying down the last receipt like the worst tarot card then pushing back from the whole spread, for the bigger picture, the better vantage.

"Hey," I said into the other room when Grace-Ellen wasn't saying anything out loud. Just, I could tell, in her head. Like double-checking. Like trying to talk herself out of something.

Libby appeared in the doorway, wiping her mouth with the back of her forearm.

"This can't be right," Grace-Ellen said.

"Explain," Libby said.

Grace-Ellen touched a pile of pale green invoices. "They must have found a different vendor," she said, her eyes watering up. She turned her face from me to Libby, like we could tell her this wasn't true, whatever this was.

"This the restaurant they went to?" Libby said, stepping in.

Grace-Ellen scooted around, held her hand up to stop Libby from messing the papers all up again.

"Where—where they get their chemicals," Grace-Ellen said. "Their pesticides, applications, all of it."

"And if they *didn't* change suppliers?" I said, standing now too. Just from the tension in the room. From everything about to be said.

I could see it in Grace-Ellen's eyes.

She set the guilty invoice back down with the rest of its color, its shape. "If they didn't change vendors," she said, "then what have they been spraying the last two weeks?"

"What do you mean what have they—?" Libby said, but cut herself off, her eyes heating up. *"No,"* she said.

Grace-Ellen was breathing hard, about to cry. Shaking her head no. But it meant the opposite.

"They used to want Trigo to work for them . . ." she said, looking up like one of us could shake our heads no about whatever she was thinking.

"What?" I said.

"Trigo, he—he was a big show-off," she said, barking out a little laugh on accident. One that made her eyes shiny.

"We know the type," Libby said, urging her on.

"He was always—he was always, when he'd be out drinking beer at the . . . where they stuff deer heads."

"Taxidermist," I filled in.

"Trigo, he could, if he peed into a storm drain, all the alligators would crawl out."

"And snakes too," Libby added.

I was nodding, remembering rats scampering out from under all our trailers once Darren started peeing around the skirts.

"That's why they wanted him?" Grace-Ellen said, looking from Libby to me and back again. "For his pee?"

"They figured out what Darren was," I said. Somebody had to.

"He would have to be on-site, then, right?" Libby said, and when Grace-Ellen just hitched her shoulders up with a sob, Libby stepped forward, through the receipts and invoices. She hauled Grace-Ellen up, and, when Grace-Ellen was still just crying, Libby slammed the heel of her hand into the wall by Grace-Ellen's head, Rayford's business certificates and licenses and fishing photographs and carnival caricatures all dislodging, falling to the floor in awkward stages.

"Where are the keys?" Libby growled.

Grace-Ellen nodded to the waiting room, her tears flowing freely now.

Libby pushed her ahead of her, and like that they were gone.

I started to follow, but went back to the receipts and invoices first. To the pile that had convinced Grace-Ellen.

That stack went back three years.

I flipped through, learning the size the orders usually were, and compared that to the most recent order. The difference was night and day. The prices hadn't gone down even close to enough to account for the change. As near I could tell, the prices had gone *up*, really.

And then, because I could, because Grace-Ellen *had*, I went back three years, worked invoice by invoice up a year.

There it was again, for three months: orders that had been cut by eighty, ninety percent. By two then three *thousand* dollars.

Like there had been another vendor. Like there had been another source.

"Trigo," I said, and looked up to the doorway Libby had pushed her through.

I let that invoice flutter down, walked through it to the noise they were already making up front.

———

The bulk of NMV was a warehouse, as it turned out. The front, the waiting room and Rayford's office, that was just a small portion of the floor space that had been walled off for the public. The real NMV was huge, a skating rink with chemical-wash stations at every pillar, posters and calendars on the walls, flytraps hanging where they could, two beetle-vans parked crooked just inside the line of tall garage doors that opened onto some different backstreet.

Libby lifted her nose to taste every particle of the air.

"Wouldn't they need him close?" she said to Grace-Ellen. "He would have to be here somewhere."

"They'll lose their license for doing this," Grace-Ellen said, wiping her nose hard, like mad at herself for crying.

"They'll lose more than that," Libby said. "Check the trucks," she said to me, lifting her chin to the two vans.

The interiors were thick with chemicals even *I* could smell, and the keys of one were in the ignition. My weight made the bug-feelers shift and spring, their shadows writhing on the concrete. But there was nothing, even when Libby ducked her head in, took a deep smell.

"Then we'll just wait until he comes home from his hunting trip," Libby said, and walked around the edges of the warehouse again, double-checking, double-*smelling*. I sat at the out-of-place picnic table with Grace-Ellen, just out in the middle of everything.

"Sorry about your husband," I said.

She touched the top of my hand with her fingertips, then looked up to the only other sound in this big empty place: Libby, falling down to her knees, her hand on the doorknob. Her shoulders were shaking. She was the last of her litter, now.

"Don't look at her," I said, and Grace-Ellen did look for a

moment more, then turned around, studied the big key ring instead.

"Hunh," she said.

I looked over to what she was talking about. The keys?

She worked one set off, held them out to me, said, "They go to that one."

The van. The one without keys in the ignition.

"So?" I said.

"So . . . so they don't *go* here," she said. "They go on the wall, over there. On that third hook. And they would have come looking for them."

I took the keys, studied them as well. They were just keys.

"Mind?" I said, holding them out to the van, and walked them across.

Libby looked up. Grace-Ellen was following me.

I climbed into the driver's seat, pushed the square key into the ignition, turned it ahead a quarter turn. Not enough to engage the starter, just enough for the bells and beeps to ding, the lights to come on.

None did.

"It's dead," Grace-Ellen said, obviously. Like that explained why she'd found the keys in such a wrong place. Hiding with all the other keys. *Hidden* with all the other keys.

"It's a stick," I said, working the four-speed. On a van, where you sat right on top of everything, that stick was bent in eighty places, about.

"Rayford says manual's better for gas," Grace-Ellen said.

I left the transmission in neutral, and, just to see, reached down, pulled the emergency brake off.

The van eased forward maybe two inches, from its own weight.

I nodded, not sure yet what I was thinking.

Libby was standing right in front of the van now.

"*What?*" she said, a giveaway line of blood seeping down from her nose.

"Was this place always a warehouse or whatever?" I said to Grace-Ellen.

Grace-Ellen narrowed her eyes, thinking, trying to figure how this mattered. Finally she said, "Used to be a lube place when I was in junior high. For semis. Then they changed the highway."

"Shit," I said, and stepped down, dropped to my stomach to look under the van.

Libby met me. The smell coming off her was all about change.

Dead center under the van was a square hole in the concrete. A pit. A shaft angling down *to* the pit.

"There used to be bays all along here," I said, my voice loud under the van. "For oil changes."

Libby peeled her lips away from her teeth.

Together we pushed the van forward, let it just keep rolling. Its front bumper tapped into a wall on the far side of the warehouse and none of us even looked over to it.

The square hole in the concrete was like pictures I'd seen in magazines, of going down into Egyptian tombs for the first time in thousands of years. The hole opened onto a metal staircase with rubbed-smooth handrails.

"I didn't know this was—" Grace-Ellen said, but Libby raised her palm, shut her up.

"They put lids on everything," I said, looking up and down at the gradations of discoloration in the concrete that were obvious now, the shades of difference that lined up with the garage doors. They'd put lids on the bays, but they'd left this one staircase, for access. So the bays could be used for storage. So they wouldn't be completely *gone*.

"If he's down there . . ." Libby said, and stepped onto the top metal step without needing to finish the threat.

I followed, and Grace-Ellen followed me, her bracelets rattling on the handrail.

It was pitch-black, except way at the other end, under what had to be the front office. Libby ran ahead, her arms crossed in front of her face in case of pipes, and we followed, and the worst was true.

The worst is always true for werewolves.

It was Darren.

"Is he alive?" I said to Libby.

He was in what had to be a shark tank, since this was Florida. And shark tanks, they're made to be lowered down into the water. Meaning there's an industrial-strength eyehole welded to the top. There was a thick chain threaded through that hole, running to hooks set in the ceiling ten feet to either side, those chains anchored to the floor.

It left Darren dangling six feet off the concrete floor.

"Crowbait," I would have said—those old medieval cages hanging at crossroads, always moldering with skeletons and scavenger birds—except no bird would ever come down into this warren, this labyrinth, this deathtrap.

That's exactly what it was.

Suspended from straps above the cage were five-gallon jugs of water, with tubes running down from them into the cage, a little stopcock valve at the end of each.

Under the cage were four kiddie pools laid out edge to edge. Because they were round, it left some concrete in the middle, right under the cage.

As far as Darren could pee in any direction, the kiddie pools, they would catch his pee.

It was the best pesticide ever.

Against the far wall, by the only plug, was a chest freezer. Either stocked with clearance beef and pork or with roadkill, probably. To keep their golden goose alive.

It had worked, so far. Barely.

Werewolf or not, there was no getting through a cage a shark couldn't.

But Darren had tried.

His mouth, it was scabbed over, his whole lower face dark with it. It was from shifting, I knew. From biting the bars.

And one of his arms was broken too. The left one. Probably from when he had man-arms, told the bars it was him or them.

It had been him.

Libby was just shaking her head no.

I stepped forward, between the pools, and reached my hand through the bars, gave Darren the back of my hand to smell, if he could.

"Darren," I said. "Please."

Behind us, all around us, Libby, always the quiet one, screamed. At herself. Because she'd been ten vertical feet away and never known. Because Darren was all that was left of her dad, all that was left of the mom she'd never known. Because they had a deal, not to die on each other. To always be there, no matter. She screamed because he was her brother.

But he was my uncle.

"Dare," I said—what I'd never called him.

The wolf in him rose to this. The wolf in him heard the challenge.

His nose woke first. Then one of his eyes.

It was yellow still. It meant he'd passed out as a wolf.

As I watched, it shot through with tendrils of brown, clouded like a tea bag in water.

He reached his good arm out to scruff my hair.

"Nephew," he said, the word taking him longer than it should have.

Not that I wouldn't have waited however long. I closed my eyes in thanks, his stub-fingered hand on my head, and I flinched when Grace-Ellen made the noise she made, not really in her throat and not really in her chest.

It came from her soul.

She was at the freezer.

There was meat in there, but it had been there a while.

Her husband, frozen between man and wolf. Stashed here after his usefulness had run out. Stashed here when he wasn't saving NMV money anymore.

Libby was already there, hugging Grace-Ellen away, keeping her from thrashing, keeping her from kicking.

They fell down together and Libby held on, her face sideways against Grace-Ellen's back.

Her eyes weren't wet like I'd have expected, though.

Crying, that's for humans.

Libby was a long way from that.

4.

The story we got from Darren that afternoon—he was in and out, and Grace-Ellen had no remedy other than to hold his head in her lap in the backseat of our boat of a Catalina—was that . . . but he would always start laughing. Because he loved it: He'd been *shanghaied*.

He'd always told us he had the makings of a real ninja, a natural-born killer, deadliest assassin in the world. It turned out he had a lot more pirate in him.

Grace-Ellen threaded his greasy bangs away from his eyes.

His chin and jaw and cheek were baby-smooth, brand-new. He'd shifted so much that he was starved down to skin and bones. His body had probably even plundered his marrow, scooped it out to rebuild him again and again, from less and less.

Grace-Ellen had his forearm splinted in two magazines she'd bought with her own cash at a gas station. The straps were her hair bands. It left her red hair trailing down over both of them.

"I knew my piss—" Darren said, then started over: "If I knew my piss was worth that much, I'd have been selling it the whole time, right? We'd be Beverly Hills werewolves. We'd be . . ." but he lost it, turned his face to cough into Grace-Ellen's hollow stomach.

Libby had one hand at the top of the steering wheel, the other grabbed on to the side mirror, like to keep the world steady with brute force.

Rayford's wife hadn't known where his blind was—he didn't trust her *that* much—but she did know he usually parked in that turnout just past the taxidermy place. That, coupled with the overalls Libby had taken from the van he drove, would be enough.

When we found his pickup, Libby stood from the car already shedding Grace-Ellen's clothes.

I followed behind, shaking the seed heads from her shirt and pants, folding them as best I could, which wasn't very.

Before stepping into the green-green trees of Florida, she brought the coveralls to her face one more time, breathed Rayford in right down to his first lemonade stand.

I sat in the car with Grace-Ellen and Darren, still in the back-seat, the Catalina shaking with each big truck that slammed past.

Because it was awkward to sit backward in the seat, leaning over like hanging on a railing at the zoo, I watched them in the rearview.

Darren was showing off.

Half dead, he was still reaching up with his good hand to dab at a mole on Grace-Ellen's cheek, see if it was real.

When he smiled, he was snaggletoothed now. It made Grace-Ellen wince.

"Not going to be winning any beauty contests," he said, shrugging, then corrected to, "Not going to be winning any *more* beauty contests, I mean . . ."

When Grace-Ellen shushed him he told her she might still win a few, though.

If she was ten years older than Libby, then she was ten years older than Darren too. Ten years older than Darren *had* been, anyway.

When we'd come to Florida, he'd already been a few years ahead of Libby. After his captivity, now, he was just about caught up with Grace-Ellen, I figured.

The way they took him, he said, it was with the bug spray, right in the face. Enough to kill all the termites in Africa, probably, plus most of the ants, and maybe a rhinoceros or two, the horny bastards. By the time he woke from it, he was already in the cage.

"Did you hear her?" I asked, adjusting the vanity mirror down as close to his face as it would get. "Libby, when she was howling?"

"Lib doesn't howl," Darren said.

"It was beautiful," Grace-Ellen said, which got her a more interested look from Darren.

"What?" she said.

"Got to go drop a few quarters," Darren said, and sat up as best he could.

Now that he knew what his pee was worth, that was going to be the new joke, I knew.

I could live with it.

Maybe I'd even use it someday.

Grace-Ellen let herself be his crutch, then, instead of leaving him out there to totter, she stood with him while he leaned back and peed.

"You shouldn't change when your bones are broke like that," she said, helping him zip up one-armed. "It starts the healing all over again, don't you know?"

"Guess you'll have to stick around, then," Darren said, "help me get better. I might keep forgetting, I mean. I might change every night, like."

Grace-Ellen looked down and smiled what I'd always read about but never understood: a little girl smile.

"Goddamnit," I said, and then all three of us startled at the dry rustling coming from the trees.

It was Rayford.

He'd been run ragged.

No, I knew: He'd been herded. When Libby'd found him in his blind, she could have taken him right then and there, painted the plywood walls with his insides. And she could have run him down at any point in between, hamstrung him then dragged him around by the back of the neck, never biting down quite deep enough to kill him.

That would be too easy, though.

He didn't deserve easy.

People say werewolves are animals, but they're wrong. We're so much worse. We're people, but with claws, with teeth, with lungs that can go for two days, legs that can eat up counties.

Rayford lurched out, his compound bow dragging the ground,

its strap still circling his wrist. His face was cut from breaking branches, his crotch was dark with pee, and his breath was only coming in rasps.

Still, he stood all the way up when he saw Darren.

"Rayford," Darren said as easy as could be.

"Gracie?" Rayford said, to Grace-Ellen, and she just glared, her open hand on Darren's chest now, like protecting him. Like she could.

And then Libby's low, steady growl rumbled out from the trees.

Rayford flinched away from it, looked up to Darren and Grace-Ellen, said, "Something—there's something goddamn *after* me! There's some sort of—"

At which point Libby snarled hard, even going so far as to shake a greasy Florida bush, which no self-respecting werewolf would ever do on the hunt.

This wasn't a hunt anymore, though.

The end of Libby's snarl, it snapped up into a full-on scream, the kind she'd have to set her front feet for, and the bone-deep instincts in Rayford, they responded like his kind had been responding for thousands and thousands of years.

He flinched back more, into the gravel at the shoulder of the road, and then he clambered up onto the blacktop, the fiberglass limbs of his bow scraping the rough asphalt, his eyes set on that sound, that terrible sound, and then what I'd been feeling in the ground for thirty minutes finally registered: the big trucks, the semis slamming past in their steady line back and forth, probably from some construction site.

Libby had been listening to their spacing for miles, I knew. Timing this all out.

I breathed in—to do what, I don't know, will never know, because the palm of Grace-Ellen's other hand, it cupped over my eyes at the last minute, so that all I heard was the air horn's long mournful call, the splat of meat against chrome.

Grace-Ellen's hand came away from my eyes when she leaned forward, to spit into the road, where Rayford had been. To lean forward and spit and scream after it, like emptying out all her grief and anger for her dead husband at once.

"I think I'm in love," Darren said, looking over to her.

There was still a red mist in the air, swirling into the wake.

I closed my lips to keep from breathing it in, and flinched from the semi's air brakes locking up. Its tires were leaving those careful black stripes the cops would need to declare this an accident.

Cops never know the truth, though.

Werewolves, we're the ones who have to carry that. We're the ones who remember the grainy wet feel of it settling on our cheeks.

A half minute later, Libby stepped out, just standing up onto two feet, grass and leaves in her hair.

She looked to Darren, her muzzle right at the end of retracting, and, because it hurt to see how broken and skinny he was, she kept walking for the car, for her clothes. For the rest of whatever was left of our lives.

It wasn't much.

5.

Six, seven weeks later, Libby was a flagger for road construction, so wasn't around our trailer to monitor what Darren told me when I said I'd never get kidnapped like he had. That my pee wouldn't scare a mouse.

He'd looked at me for about ten seconds, like deciding. Then he looked to the bedroom door, making sure it was shut, making sure Grace-Ellen was still sleeping off the night before, and then he shook his head like this was stupid. But then he lowered his eyes into the heels of his hands and told me anyway.

It was a story, of course.

It's all we've got.

Imagine you're a piece-of-shit werewolf pack, he told me. Not like us, but one of those tail-tucker crews that does the whole alpha-thing, and's always growling each other into submission, wearing flannel shirts, glaring at people through the smoky darkness of roadhouses.

You'd think that behavior would come natural to werewolves, but it's learned, really. From the movies, mostly, but from nature shows too.

We're families, not packs.

Some werewolves drink the Kool-Aid, though. Darren told me to remember that.

Anyway, so you're this piece-of-shit werewolf pack, and one day to show who's boss, to protect your territory like you think you're supposed to, you go dig up this one old wolf's just-dead wife. To teach him a lesson, show him who's boss now, tell him that what he's been smelling traces of on his nightly rounds, it's true: There's a new wolf in town. A new pack. Let the nightmare begin.

"There's cocky," Darren said, holding his still-broke arm out to one side then reaching as far as he could the other way, with his good arm, "and then there's stupid, right?"

I nodded right, didn't want to mess this story up.

It was going to be about me, I could tell. It was the answer to the question I'd asked him: What was I?

"So they dig Mom up," Darren said, wincing from just having to put those words together in that order, "and they don't eat her like real wolves, they just gnaw on her some, leave her out by the front gate."

"Did you know?" I asked.

"I was a pup," Darren said. "All three of us were."

"Not my mom," I said. "She was like me."

"She was my sister," Darren said, zero give to his voice, holding my eyes until I had to look away, and then he went on: Grandpa, finding his dead wife under a blanket of crows. Grandpa, smelling the other pack on her.

What they expected, Darren figured, was for Grandpa to start running right then, to lose his clothes in the road behind him, to come sliding into their gravel driveway on all fours, long trails of clear spit dangling back from his mouth, his eyes blind with grief and rage.

Instead, because this is Grandpa we're talking about, he knocks on the door with his hands. Real polite, Darren said, like a Bible salesman. Cocked under his arm, the two over-under barrels broke over like a goose neck, is his prize shotgun. Instead of shot or slugs, though, he's poured all the silver jewelry he could steal into it. His hands are still smoking from funneling the necklaces and rings and bracelets in.

His first shot takes out half the pack. A diamond stud in a silver setting from a ten-gauge thirty-six-inch barrel, it can pass through the bones of the face like the whole head's made of butter, and once the poison gets to your brain, Darren said, then ding-dong, you're dead.

The ones he can't kill as a man, the ones that slip and fall out the back of the house, he runs them down on four feet, takes his time with them out in the pastures, back in the trees—a night so full of screaming that the newspapers from three counties drifted into Boonesville the next morning. But they were all too late. There was nothing left.

The only reason Grandpa doesn't kill the last one, it's that dawn catches him out in the open, in a stock tank, holding the boy's head under until he passes out, then pulling him up, starting over again.

But it's always good to leave one alive, Darren told me. As warning.

This was the backside of the story I'd already known versions of for years. This was the version with teeth. But still.

"So?" I said.

So fast-forward ten, fifteen years, Darren said, then shook his head no, said what he meant: "Fast-forward fourteen years."

Two of those kids cut out of that old wolf's woman, they've got the blood. The third, she doesn't. It's a different life for her. Instead of learning to run things down in the woods, she's going into town.

She dates one boy, she dates another, and when her brother keeps fighting with her callers, she finally just starts meeting them in Boonesville, which is off-limits to Darren, for reasons.

One of those boys, he leaves her with me. Like I've always known. Dear old Dad.

"You're saying it was your fault," I said across to Darren. "It wasn't."

He just looked at me.

"You want to know why she hates sheep so much," he said at last. "Libby the Liberator. You think it's okay, that we should just let them live, let them be, that they're not hurting anybody?"

"Different generation," I said, trying to shrug it true.

"It's because of your dad," Darren said. Just that.

I looked down into the lost-cause carpet of the living room, trying to make the connection that was obvious to him, and when I did my face went cold, my breath too deep.

"No," I said.

"He'd been hiding in town for fourteen *years*," Darren said. "He knew he couldn't fight your grandpa, nobody could, but— if he planted a pup in his little girl, that'd be worse than killing him, really. Because it would kill *her*. Because it would rip his heart out. So you—why you haven't changed yet? It's probably because you're part sheep. No offense, man."

"But sheeps are wolves, inside."

"You probably are too," Darren said, holding my eyes with his so I could read that he wasn't judging against me, here. "You're old enough now to know. Your dad, that boy Grandpa let go, he hadn't shifted since that stock tank he nearly got drowned in. He'd probably even forgot how."

"And my mom wasn't wolf at all."

"But she had the blood in her somewhere. Your grandpa's blood."

"Your blood."

"Let's not get carried away, here . . ." Darren said, getting down in his boxing stance, shadowing a jab that ended in the lightest slap on the underside of my jaw.

I pulled my head away, didn't want to play.

"Is he—?" I said. "My biological dad, I mean."

It was a term I knew from television.

Darren not saying anything was answer enough.

My dad was gone, dead, buried, and probably not in that order. I couldn't conjure the specific afternoon, but Grandpa had told me a story about somebody he knew, once upon a time, who'd done just that to somebody who deserved it worse than anybody.

His hands had shook when he told it to me.

I should have known.

This is how it is with werewolves. Even when they lie, it's the truth.

And now I knew the truth about myself. I was a murder weapon. I was revenge. I was a burden my aunt and uncle had been carrying around for ten years already, out of obligation to my mom.

I was maybe a wolf, maybe not.

The silver, though. That silver spur, it *had* nearly killed me.

That had to mean something.

Where Darren couldn't see, I bit my lip, sucked the blood, whatever kind it was.

This is the year we never left Florida.

Not all of us, I mean.

The thing that finally won me over a little bit about Grace-Ellen, it was that she could smoke me at game shows. That more than any of her lore or stories or lessons told me she'd really been married to a werewolf.

Because she knew somebody who would buy Rayford's truck, no questions asked, she was able to quit going into work. Not that NMV existed anymore, except as a sign on an abandoned building. Libby had visited all of the other techs in a single night, to see who matched up with the cluster of scents she'd cataloged from Darren's dungeon.

None of them saw the next morning.

She deposited them as scat all over town, and said even that was too good for them.

"She's forgetting how to be a person," I heard Grace-Ellen say about her to Darren one day, when I was supposed to be farther down the hall than I was.

"Just rough around the edges," Darren had said back. "Like a certain brother you may or may not know . . ."

What Libby said about Grace-Ellen was that at least her hair was red, like their mom's had been.

"It's not real," Darren told her, a snicker riding the slant of his mouth.

"I don't want to know," Libby said back, holding her hand up to stop whatever he was going to say next.

"*She* should enter a hot-dog-eating contest," he said anyway.

I had been sitting on the edge of my bed for that. The walls of our trailer were cardboard.

Across from me on the backside of the shut door was a mirror. In it I could see the scab across my chest. It was deep and important. It cut my right nipple in half, made me wonder if that nipple would still be twisted if I ever went wolf. It made me wonder if werewolves even had nipples.

A week later I was standing directly in front of the television set, aiming the remote right at it. It only worked if you were practically touching it to the set, and since the numbers and pictures were worn off all the buttons, it was easier to use the dial by the screen, really.

This was the week Darren was fixing the door of Grace-Ellen's house for her, the week he was taking care of the dog carcasses in her kitchen, the week he was liberating her a set of tires for her Honda. He was working off what-all Libby had broke that night. Except, after finding the right tires, showing me how a werewolf gets them on a wheel—it involved butane from a hand torch, then a match dropping in slow motion, a blue donut of flame flaring up—he'd parked on the couch, claiming not to be a carpenter, really.

"Hey hey," I heard him say behind me, and I turned.

Grace-Ellen was in the door, in, of all things, a yellowed-at-the-edges wedding dress.

She had enough lipstick on for two of her.

What she was holding in front of her, holding by its long floppy ears, was a fat struggling rabbit, fresh from the pet store.

Darren met her halfway across the room, the rabbit pressed between them, kicking slow with its paddle feet, and said it right into her mouth: "Marry me."

She cried even as Darren was unbuttoning her dress, even though those buttons weren't made for that, I was pretty sure.

"Want I should . . . ?" I said, trying to make motions to my own bedroom.

I did anyway, and tried not to listen, even when the rabbit screamed its last scream.

I was happy for him, I think.

And maybe it could work, even.

Werewolves can't ask for anything more than that.

When Libby came home, heard the news about the impending nuptials, she just pursed her lips tighter and nodded.

"Nice job," she said. "You know it can't work. Start a family, she dies."

"What?" Grace-Ellen said.

"I've seen it happen," Libby said, not looking at me so purposefully that she might as well have just gone ahead and scratched my mom's name on the living room wall.

"What are you talking about?" Grace-Ellen said. "Maybe five hundred years ago that's how it went, yeah," she went on without waiting, not so much incredulous anymore as just disgusted. She reached back for her purse, and in three shakes of her wallet she'd worked a faded photograph up.

"She's nineteen this year," she said. "She's mine. *And* she's Trigo's."

"No," Libby said, taking the picture, studying it like there was some way she could smell the wolf in the print.

"Wait for it . . ." Darren said, to Libby.

Grace-Ellen looked from him to her, like to be sure they were doing this, then pulled her hair on the right side back, to show the line of silver hoops clamped through all around the edge of her ear.

"Keep the silver fresh," she said to Libby, "clean them every week, and the silver gets in your blood. Not enough to hurt, just enough to kick the wolf in the baby. To keep it down for the birthing process."

"This is what Dad was always *looking* for," Darren said to Libby, trying to infect her with his sense of discovery, of finishing what Grandpa had started.

Libby studied him a moment, then looked back to Grace-Ellen.

"Earlier, at the—the place," Libby said, directly to Grace-Ellen. "You said that twins were . . . rare."

"Two pups in one litter," Grace-Ellen said. "Way it usually works is that one's born without the wolf. For food. A first meal. Humans have colostrum. Werewolves have blood."

I looked over to the living room wall. For where my mom's name would have been scratched. We could all see it—Darren, Libby. Me.

My mom, she never should have even got to grow up. She never should have got old enough to have me.

"What?" Grace-Ellen said into this new and awkward silence.

"Why would she have told this to you?" Libby said, to Darren.

"You can't smell it already?" Grace-Ellen said, cradling her lower belly.

Darren wasn't saying anything, was just smiling a smile he couldn't stop.

"Real silver," Grace-Ellen said, tapping her right ear.

"Something new every day," Libby said. But not in a good way.

"So she's coming with us?" she said to Darren later that night, when Grace-Ellen was down at the gas station, after ice.

Darren shook his head no, slow, and Libby nodded, had to have known this was coming.

"You can stay *too* . . ." Darren said, reaching across to hold his sister's hand.

Libby pulled it from him and spun away, her arms tight across her chest.

"We're werewolves," she said.

That answers every question.

6.

A week later, the screaming and throwing things all done, Libby's flagger job over, we were packing the Catalina with blankets and our three cardboard boxes.

It all fit better. I hated that.

On the way gone, we stopped at the docks, and sat staring at the Atlantic Ocean for probably two minutes before standing from the car.

"Well then," Libby said, about the big ship tied to the big dock.

"Guess so," I said back to her.

Though Darren's wedding had been at the courthouse, for the

honeymoon Grace-Ellen had earned a free cruise by cutting ten thousand box tops or something. The ocean was her dream, apparently, one she'd never been able to talk Trigo into. And she *was* the mother of Darren's unborn pup.

"You're really going on a *ship?*" Libby said to Darren, holding both his hands in hers. "You know they go out on the ocean, right? And that the ocean's made of water?"

"He'll be okay," Grace-Ellen said, draped across him like a duffel bag, her shorts so short they were pretty much just a wide belt.

Darren's eyes weren't quite as certain—we were at the bottom of the gangplank, I think it's called—but he tried a smile. His broken teeth didn't help it any.

I didn't know where to stand.

I kept looking back to the Catalina, because the passenger door didn't lock. I kept thinking what if Grandpa could see us right now, right here? And then I remembered Darren's old CB handle, Wolf Man in the Sky, and then I couldn't swallow for a few breaths.

"Say bye," Libby said, passing me, headed back to the car.

She wasn't even crying. After thirty-one years of having a brother, she was just walking away. I wanted to scream to her, to tell her what was happening here.

Instead I just looked out at the water, at how it went forever.

"I don't think I can do it," Darren said, his chin suddenly right on my shoulder from behind, his voice directly in my ear, his eyes following mine.

"You can do anything," I said to him. "I've seen."

The footsteps on the gangplank were Grace-Ellen's.

It was just me and Darren, now.

"Figured you might want this," he said. "Since I'm going to my certain doom and all."

It was the little black velvet ring box. My mom's hair.

I looked away from it. From her.

I shook my head no, all I could do, and pushed her back to him. "Take her out there," I said. "She would have wanted to go."

It was a lie, I think, because I'd never really known her.

But maybe I had.

She was the girl who went to town, the girl who fell in love. She was the girl raised by wolves.

Darren checked my face to be sure.

"I'll be back, man, you'll see," he said, knocking me on the shoulder. I rolled with it, kept my hands stuffed into my pockets.

"Go," I told him.

"You'll wait right here for me?" he said, the smile there in his voice, and before I could say anything he took his middle finger from his mouth, drew a wet X right on my forehead, told me it marked the spot, and then he was walking up that gangplank, his feet single-file-directly-in-the-middle-heel-to-toe, Grace-Ellen waiting for him at the top, his eyes trying hard to watch her the whole time, to take this just step by little step.

I didn't wipe the X from my forehead until Georgia.

No, I mean, that X, it's still there, it's still marking me.

CHAPTER 18

Wolf Like Me

Burn what?" the nephew says to his aunt.

She just told him he's going to have to burn it.

He's driving the car now. An ungrand Torino with sprung springs and two too many doors. A real werewolf car. The nephew doesn't have a license, but at sixteen he's old enough not to get stopped, anyway, and still young enough to run if he needs to.

"I know you've been writing it all down in that shoe box you keep in that old blue backpack," his aunt says. "About us."

The nephew changes hands on the steering wheel.

"We never had a camera," he says. It's his only excuse.

"It's sweet," his aunt says. "And stupid."

This is Arkansas. The edge of it.

"It's all different anyway," the nephew tells her. "The way I did it, I mean. Nobody would know anything, if they found it. If they got it."

The aunt looks over to him, holds him in her eyes for a moment. "You saying you went around and around the house with it all?"

"You may have fought a bear," the nephew says.

"I may have," the aunt says back.

It's enough.

All four windows are down.

There are no buildings out this far. No people.

"Here," the aunt says, and the nephew slows the heavy car.

They're on a dirt road now.

"I'm proud of you," the aunt says.

The nephew doesn't say anything.

Three weeks ago in a motel in Texas, where they'd gone to the coast special to see the big ships pass, the nephew woke with something in his mouth he couldn't at first identify.

It was his tongue.

It was thick and wide and rough, and moving it made him roll over to dry-heave, and hunching over sideways like that, the vertebrae in his back locked together in a tighter way, like a zipper. That was just the clench before they pushed violently against each other, though. He spun over, away from the pain, but there was nowhere to hide. For a few moments, as if electricity were coursing through him, the only parts of him touching the mattress were his head and his heels.

Keep your hands open, some dim part of him remembered.

Not that he could have closed them.

The claws pushing through, it was like having the long bones of his fingers pulled slowly out. And his teeth, his jaw thrusting forward, taking bone mass from the back of his skull, his memories writhing in there, pale colors shooting across their skies. He tried to hold on to Libby, her teeth at the back of his neck so she could carry him through the woods, but kept falling back into the passenger seat of one of Darren's trucks, when he'd been hiding below the level of the window.

And then his legs.

His fingers had been nothing compared to the exquisite torture of his knees turning themselves backward one after the other, all that pressure threatening to crack his pelvis in half. He'd shaken his head no, please, that this was enough, and reached for the ceiling of the motel room only to find that the ball-points of his shoulders allowed a more canine range of motion now. It sparked a yellow flash behind his eyes that faded to a smoky grey, and then a soft black like ash falling over his face.

He passed out. He knew it was happening, Libby had told him that there's a limit past which the mind will shut off to protect itself, but knowing didn't mean it was anything he could stop.

In his first wolf dream, he was bounding through a field of chalk, and there wasn't enough air in the whole land of sleep to fill his lungs.

He woke kicking, fighting the sheets.

His claws kept catching in them.

He opened his eyes and the room was alive with scent, with the stories the scent had to tell.

It would take him years to taste each one.

He scratched at the doorknob to get out and run through the night but he couldn't make it work, so he padded around the room until he chanced on the mirror. He didn't recognize himself.

He stepped forward on his gangly legs, lurched his front half onto the counter, one paw scraping the plastic bowl of the sink, and this wasn't really happening until he touched his nose to his nose in the reflection, startled back.

Working on instinct, no thought at all, he yipped a bark out at this other wolf and spun away, his voice loud, terrifying. His big flinch back tangled him in the hangers fixed to the rod somehow, and so he spun harder, heard more than felt himself growling with frustration.

Finally he pulled what he thought was free, but then the hangers and the rod were still dragging behind him.

Now, on purpose, he snapped back with his teeth.

The rod turned to splinters so fast it was more a show of respect than having submitted to the steel-trap *snap* of his jaws.

The nephew spit the splinters out, had to use his paw to drag them from the side of his tongue.

He could taste the forest in them. He could taste the woods.

He growled again, just to hear the deep rumble.

Outside, in the motel parking lot, two men with hard hats were walking from truck to door. A woman was loudly inhaling smoke through her cigarette by the ice machine. On the second floor a baby was about to wake, but for now it was just kicking through a dream.

The world was alive in a way he'd never known.

There were tiny feet in the walls, soft wings circling the light bulbs, and above it all, the bats with their piercing cries.

The nephew felt like his throat was swelling.

Again he went to the door, but this time just to touch his wet nose to the knob. A spark crossed from it to him and he jumped back again, his haunches landing on the bed.

His skin was quivering. With joy. With speed. With hunger.

The small trash can was empty, though.

Because werewolves know better.

He stepped easily onto the bed that smelled like him, and then he felt himself circling, padding down a soft place. When he laid down it was nose to tail, his eyes still open, still watching. Watching for as long as he could.

There was no panic, no fear. This was like falling deeper into himself.

When his aunt got back from her hunt, two big white birds in her hand, held upside down by the feet they used to have, she tasted it on the air, what had happened, and dropped the birds, their wings opening on the way down.

She pulled the nephew to her, held on tighter and tighter, her breath hot against his chest.

"You know you look more like him every day," she's saying from her side of the car now, officially back in Arkansas at last.

The nephew doesn't know if she means his grandpa or his uncle or his dad.

When the road dies out, the nephew drives through the grass, because he doesn't want this to be true, what's happening. His aunt finally puts her hand on the dashboard, though. It tells him to stop.

"You'll be fine," she says.

They stand from the car together.

The wind brushes the grass of the meadow over and back.

His aunt is peeling out of her clothes one last time. Just letting them fall away from her.

When I am a werewolf, I will wear jean shorts.

It's the secret graffiti the nephew's scratched into a thousand restrooms all across the South.

Sometimes he still finds one, runs his finger over the metal.

"I'll still be here," the aunt says, reaching her hand across, taking his.

"Just like Darren," the nephew says. "Werewolf promises aren't any good, don't you know that by now?"

His aunt smiles.

"You're sounding like him too," she says, patting him once high on the chest and leaving her hand there for moment.

In all the stories and all the movies, there's human footprints walking along, becoming wolf prints at the end.

In the heaven of werewolves, there's just new grass folding back into place. There's a wolf running across one part of the meadow, her true husband waiting under the shadow of the trees, and there's a wolf standing behind as well, taking snapshots with his eyes, with his heart, with his nose. With his pen.

It's hard to remember every single thing. But not this.

I'll never burn this, Libby.

That's all.

Acknowledgments

Thanks to those who don't even know I'm involving them in this: Art Spiegelman, Leslie Silko, Rob Zombie, George R.R. Martin, Gerald Vizenor, Louise Erdrich, Barry Lopez, *Good Will Hunting*, James Welch, *Near Dark;* I stole little bits and pieces from you all. Thanks to Joshua Malkin and Zack Wentz, for always talking werewolves, and Bill Rabkin, for showing me how important a first chapter is. Thanks to Ray Cluley, for bedroom-decorating tips. Thanks to William J. Cobb, for telling me early on that you only ever get one novel like this. Thanks to a guy named Craig Wheeler I used to work with at a library; I stole from you as well. Thanks to Sabine Baring-Gould, and to Herodotus, and to Curt Siodmak. Thanks to Wally Charnoff, for sparking one of these chapters, via Tod Goldberg's *Gangsterland*. Thanks to Jeff Barnaby's *Rhymes for Young Ghouls*. Thanks to Eddy Rathke and Axel Hassen Taiari and Jesse Lawrence and Theo Van Alst and Paul Tremblay for early reads. Thanks always to Warren Zevon, and John Landis, and Gary Brandner. Without *The Howling*, I'm nowhere, I'm a different person. Thanks to Jesse Bullington, for prompting me to start this, and thanks to Neil Gaiman, for "The Hunt," which showed me how. Thanks to Laura Payne, for so much research help. Thanks to Bill Pronzini and John Skipp. Thanks to *Mud* and *The Things They Carried* and *Knockemstiff*, models all, that I can never quite match. Thanks to Matthew Hobson, for taking me to a place in Baltimore where I bought a Very Important Werewolf Figurine. Thanks to Carrie Vaughn and Benjamin Percy and Christopher Buehlman and Toby Barlow and the rest of the werewolf people—too many, not enough. Thanks to Cynthia Romanowski. Thanks to Alan Moore, for asking What if superheroes actually existed? There's a variable in that question special for me, I always thought. Thanks to Deanne Stillman, for introducing me to BJ Robbins, my new agent, who took a little short nothing of a novel and helped turn it into something Kelly O'Connor, my new editor, could turn into something else yet again. Without BJ and Kelly, *Mongrels* would have stayed a pup, never got its proper teeth, and without the team at William Morrow—Dale Rohrbaugh, Marty Karlow, Barbara Greenberg—it would never have cleaned up proper for the shelf. Thanks to Owen Corrigan, for the beautiful cover, and to Jessie Edwards and Ashley Marudas, for making sure the world saw that cover, and then peeled it back for the story inside. And thanks to my wife, Nancy, for sitting up with my kids, Rane and Kinsey, so many nights when they were young, and couldn't sleep because, when they'd come into our bedroom certain there were werewolves outside the house, I could never tell them for sure that there weren't. But I would always go look, just on the chance.

About the Author

Stephen Graham Jones is the author of fifteen novels and six story collections. He has received numerous awards including the NEA Fellowship in Fiction, the Texas Institute of Letters Jesse Jones Award for Fiction, the Independent Publishers Award for Multicultural Fiction, the This Is Horror Award, as well as making Bloody Disgusting's Top Ten Novels of the Year. Stephen was raised in West Texas. He now lives in Boulder, Colorado, with his wife and children.